HUMAN ERROR

HUMAN ERROR

PAUL PREUSS

TOR

A TOM DOHERTY ASSOCIATES BOOK

HUMAN ERROR

Copyright © 1985 by Paul Preuss

First printing: October 1985

A TOR Book

Published by Tom Doherty Associates
49 West 24 Street
New York, N.Y. 10010

ISBN: 0-312-93332-0

Library of Congress Catalog Card Number: 85-51760

Printed in the United States of America

for Karen, with love

A god can do it. But how, tell me, shall
a man follow him through the narrow lyre?
His mind is cleavage. At the crossing of two
heartways stands no temple for Apollo.

—Rainer Maria Rilke, *Sonnets to Orpheus,* I:3

PROTOPHASE

Protophase. An assembly of precursor molecular structures capable of epigenesis.
—Handbook of Bioelectronic Engineering (*revised*), Blevins and Storey, eds.

◆◆◆

THE BIG MORON AND THE LITTLE MORON WERE WALKING
ALONG THE EDGE OF A CLIFF. THE BIG MORON FELL OFF. WHY
DIDN'T THE LITTLE MORON?

The words glowed greenly into existence on Toby's screen:
simple English sentences, sufficiently ambiguous even at
their roots, enclosing the pun like an unlaid egg. He stroked a
key and leaned back to let the machine do its thing.

He knew he had a long time to wait. Through the windows
that formed one wall of the artificial-intelligence laboratory
the mustard yellow cabinets of an ancient VAX 11/780 hummed
in air-conditioned isolation, straining the hoary riddle through
the algorithms of a program Toby had dubbed, hopefully,
COMMONSENSE.

As if the rigors of his own program weren't sufficient to
stretch the VAX's mental capacity, Toby time-shared the
machine with three colleagues who were pursuing linguistic
theories of their own.

While he waited, visions of supercomputers danced in his

11

head, shiny new dedicated Crays shaped like miniature Roman temples, with nothing to do but run Toby Bridgeman's programs twenty-four hours a day. . . .

Minutes passed, and then there were new words on the screen: BECAUSE HE WAS A LITTLE MORE ON.

Toby blinked and suppressed a giggle. The damned thing had got the joke! By George, it's got it! Though he was more than a foot too short to do a convincing Rex Harrison imitation, Toby had a mad urge to leap up dancing. He backed hesitantly away instead; what if the machine were only waiting for him to turn his back before letting the proof of its perspicacity dribble into the electricity?

"I say, fellows"—casually, now—"have a look at this."

Dave Droege shambled over from his paper-strewn corner to peer at Toby's screen. "The big moron and the little moron . . . ," he mumbled, moving his lips while he read (behind his back they called him Droege Bear). After half a sentence he stopped mumbling and just moved his lips. Finally he stopped moving his lips; under his bushy brows his eyeballs twitched.

Lassiter and Murch appeared, one beside each of Droege's thickly upholstered shoulders. The three of them stood in silence a few seconds, and then Rodney Murch started absentmindedly scratching his balls; all his slacks had a furry patch in the crotch from when he was thinking. By now the tip of Droege's blunt nose had turned pale with envy. "Very suggestive, Toby," he said.

"Think it can do it again?" Tim Lassiter asked.

"Well, surely if—"

"Without coaching, I mean." Lassiter crossed his muscular forearms over an expanse of plaid Pendleton shirt and tried to stare Toby down; a decade earlier he'd been a third-string wide receiver on the Princeton football team, and he had the notion he was frightening to men like Toby who were barely five and a half feet tall.

Murch kept thinking and scratching.

"Thanks, then," said Toby, irritated now and letting it show. "I'll call when I've something more interesting." Like hell he would. He squeezed between his associates and rapped at the keyboard. The screen went blank.

Slowly the three wandered back to their corners, avoiding each other's eyes, while Toby pondered this fresh evidence that his repeated successes were beginning to upset the delicate emotional ecology of the lab. Perhaps after all it was time to stop trying to be friends and start pressing the department chairman for a larger wedge of the ARPA grant pie.

His fingers flew over the keys, restating the riddle's premise, repeating the question. This time the machine ran a mere thirty seconds before displaying the answer: BECAUSE SHE WAS A LITTLE MORE ON.

Take that, Lassiter. But what's this "she"? Is the machine exhibiting nonsexist tendencies, or is it waffling?

He returned to his daydreams. Face the truth, old fellow, a Cray is not a serious option—fifteen million dollars or so, and that's merely the hardware—but if you could just get the little VAX wholly to yourself . . .

This time his thoughts were interrupted by his name shouted from the hall: "Bridgeman!"

He stared at the apparition in the doorway, a wild-eyed, disheveled creature, far taller even than Tim Lassiter. For an instant Toby took him for some sort of violent protester come to bomb their defense-supported research—this *was* the University of California at Berkeley, after all, and old ways die hard.

Toby sat motionless as the man loped across the length of the cluttered room; his skinny body was draped in rags, his knobby head was crowned with blond hair resembling a

Brillo pad, and his face—big-nosed, big-lipped, beetle-browed—was a mass of freckles. "You get any work done on this bag-biting piece of shit?" the man yelled at him, fleering at Toby's fingerprint-smeared terminal and the decrepit VAX (was it really wheezing?) beyond the windows.

"I say, who the hell are you?" Toby sputtered. Idiotic thing to say. Don't antagonize him. Toby was conscious of his ears glowing red, of the others staring at him.

"My name's Storey. And by that silly accent, you're Bridgeman in the flesh. But seriously now, how do you get anything done on a bletcherous kluge like this?"

"Storey?" Toby suppressed a giggle. One must be cool. With professorial calm he said, "Sorry, Storey, I don't know who sent you to me, but we allow no flaming free-lance hackers in here before midnight." Was *this* the notorious Adrian Storey?

"You're the hacker, twerp." Storey grinned alarmingly, displaying crooked yellow teeth. "I was just trying to talk your demented language. But with that accent—shit."

"Quite," said Toby, nettled. He had been made to understand that after ten years in the States he had practically no accent at all, but then people persist in telling you what they think you want to hear. "What can I do for you, uh . . . Stores, was it?"

"Say"—Storey looked genuinely upset—"don't you know me? I'm Adrian Storey, man. From *Comp*ugen. I'm a big cheese—I'm bigger than Chuck E. Cheese himself. I'm the hottest germ jockey in the valley."

Toby laughed outright. "Perhaps I've heard of you after all."

"And all horribly true!" Storey shouted enthusiastically; his relief was evident. "I have a terrible temper! I'm ugly as sin." He tapped his bulging skull. "But I'm *smart*."

"Mmm." Ugly, perhaps, but not lacking in self-awareness.

Abruptly Storey thrust out his right hand. "And so are you. That's why I'm here."

After the briefest pause Toby took the huge limp hand. "Dr. Storey."

"Call me Adrian."

"Adrian, then. In that case, I suppose I'm Toby." On closer inspection he saw that Adrian Storey wasn't really dressed in rags, although his faded blue jeans and dingy white shirt looked as if they hadn't been changed in days. His running shoes were tattered remnants of their former selves, shreds of rubber and strands of nylon from which his sweat socks bloomed like gray patches of bread mold.

"Know thyself, that's my motto," Adrian said cheerfully.

Ugly, but sincere. And a mind reader. "But I see you've chosen to ignore the other piece of Delphic advice."

"Yeah? What's that?"

"Nothing in excess." A cheap shot—Americans paid little attention to the classics, they were too busy creating the future.

Adrian seemed unperturbed. "Whatever you say. Listen, I haven't got all day, why don't you show me your stuff?"

He'd taken the edge again, and Toby reflected that it would not do to let this man keep it. "I have an idea, Adrian. Why don't I show you what we're doing here? While you're in the neighborhood. If you've got a few minutes."

"Yeah, yeah." He had the grace to look uncomfortable.

"Nothing secret, I assure you," said Toby cheerfully. (So don't be shy, prick.)

"Look," said Adrian. "Like I told you, I lack the social graces."

Toby pulled a chair over for Adrian and moved his own closer to the keyboard. "Well, you were asking about hardware. Hardware's of secondary importance to us, really—a computer is a computer is a computer"—the standard spiel, and what kind of fool does he think I take him for?—"but a program . . . now *that* can be something different. . . ."

Adrian folded himself onto the chair and, as the minutes stretched, began lolling like a rag doll, while Toby painstakingly outlined his most recent attempts to shape programs that could generate diverse descriptions of linguistic objects and relate them in ways not only logical but, as Toby dearly hoped, pragmatic—and maybe creative as well.

That final goal, he was forced to admit, was still far in the future. But pragmatism was within reach.

The higher—the more "perfect"—the organism, the more slowly it developed, said Toby, and the same was true of programs capable of learning from experience. Only by acquiring knowledge about the world and expressing that knowledge in words, by experiencing success and failure in using words to influence the course of events—by talking up a storm and taking the consequences, like any two-year-old—only thus could a machine master language, beyond a few stock phrases manipulated according to structural rules of limited flexibility. Only by combining experience of language and the real world had a machine, on two occasions now—and here Toby dared hint at what was uppermost on his mind—been able to understand a pun.

But Adrian seemed bored by Toby's lecture. From time to time he interrupted with such remarks as "You really happy waiting five minutes for that subroutine to run?" meanwhile leaning precariously backward in the folding chair, his thumbs hooked in his frayed pants pockets.

Toby assumed his questions were rhetorical.

When for the third time he got no answer, Adrian started howling. Howling like an infant, or so Toby thought, until he realized Adrian was singing.

"I once knew a woman named Salleee/ Her hair was as

bright as theee sun/ But when I told Sally I luvved her/ She said I was no goddam fun. . . ."

Toby had heard the tune before, but that time the words had had something to do with "acres of clams."

Adrian really leaned into the chorus: "She *said* I was no goddam *fun*, me boys/ She *said* I was no goddam *fun*. . . ."

By the second verse Lassiter had already walked out. Droege followed not long after.

"I play the guitar, too," Adrian offered, interrupting himself. "But I can't do both at once."

"How sad it's not with you."

Adrian continued the serenade. "I once knew a woman named Suzeee/ Her thighs were like two marble slabs/ But when I told Suzie I loved her . . ."

With a grieved expression, his hands in his armpits, Murch, the last of Toby's associates, now slouched out of the room.

Verses of escalating obscenity accompanied Toby's struggles to converse by keyboard with the overburdened VAX. In a desperate attempt to impress Adrian enough to shut him up, Toby typed in the magic phrases: THE BIG MORON AND THE LITTLE MORON WERE WALKING ALONG THE EDGE OF A CLIFF. THE BIG MORON FELL OFF. WHY DIDN'T THE LITTLE MORON?

The machine hesitated barely an instant before displaying BECAUSE IT WAS NOT NEAR THE EDGE.

"Balls," said Toby.

Adrian broke off and leaned toward him intently. "Look, Bridgeman, you do know it's *me* who wants you at Compugen? You think Jack Chatterjee ever heard of you before I told him about you? I've read your stuff. I've run some of your programs, just for fun. I want you in on what I'm doing."

"That's nice," said Toby. "But I haven't an inkling of what that is."

"Then come on," said Adrian, grabbing Toby by the elbow and almost lifting him out of his chair. "I'm going to

have to sneak you in—our stuff really *is* secret." He looked
down at Toby. "But that won't be hard. I can't believe
you're this short."

Whenever Adrian was forced to stop for a traffic light,
Toby caught a whiff of oily smoke seeping through the
permanently open window on the passenger side of the ancient brown Saab. The car smelled like an outboard motor-
boat, and Adrian steered it like one, swashing from lane to
lane down jam-packed University Avenue toward the freeway.

A mile south along San Francisco Bay they came to the
Compugen Corporation's modernistic mission-style buildings:
the two-story research institute, the administrative headquar-
ters fronting Berkeley's waterfront Aquatic Park, and the
square expanse of the factory and warehouse backed up to the
Santa Fe Railroad tracks. Squeezed between the freeway and
the tracks, Compugen occupied a stretch of raw landscaping
in an area where so many bioengineering firms had located in
recent years—displacing the scavenger steel mills and chemical plants of times past—that wags had taken to calling the
neighborhood Protein Valley.

Adrian rolled the Saab through a guarded gate and into the
wide parking lot. Beside the short walkway to the door of the
research building there were two empty spaces, one of them
reserved for the handicapped, the other reserved for "Dr.
Adrian Storey, Chief Scientist."

Before they got out of the car Adrian rummaged in the
glove compartment, found a plastic clip-on badge with somebody else's picture on it, and told Toby to fasten it to the
lapel of his linen sports jacket. The security guard in the
lobby glanced at Toby's face and then at the badge, and then
up at Adrian. The guard smiled; the forms had been preserved. Toby was allowed inside to see, for the first time in
his life, a bioelectronics research facility in action.

Chief Scientist Dr. Adrian Storey presided over a virtual maze of laboratories. In some the furnishings were mundane: long benches with outlets for electricity and spigots for gas and water, sinks, shelves of glassware and reagents stacked to the ceiling, and everywhere boxes of tissues and paper towels. The aisles were narrow, and technicians worked elbow to elbow. Toby was reminded of his science classes in public school; here the facilities were shiny and new, but to his surprise, the crowding and mess and noise were intense, worse than school days.

Toby was struck by the refrigerators. The walls were fairly lined with refrigerators, some with radiation symbols on their doors, others bearing the similar but somehow more menacing crab-clawed "biological hazard" warning signs. The monotony of refrigerators was only occasionally relieved by an egg incubator, a centrifuge, or a tubby autoclave. In time Toby was to learn that when biochemists fight for territory it is more likely to be wall space than floor space they scrap over—not so much a place to stand as a place to stand their refrigerators.

The biology labs were only the beginning. The maze continued through rooms devoted to electronics and optics, equipped with gleaming instruments of glass and steel, some of which Toby recognized, some completely alien.

They passed air-locked clean rooms where electronic circuitry was transformed from drawings into engraved crystal, etched into existence. They passed closed steel doors behind which thousands of small mammals were born, lived, and occasionally died—though most died on the bench—in stacked plastic and steel cages.

Finally Adrian brought him to the center of the labyrinth, the computer graphics room. They entered and closed the door behind them.

It was a dark place, silent except for the hiss of air

conditioners. Toby imagined monumental supercomputers lurk-
ing beyond the walls, serving the giant video screens in front
of him.

"Sit down. I'm gonna show you some bugs." Adrian
began busily tapping at a console keyboard with fingers that
were remarkably nimble for their length: on the triple screens
an extraordinarily twisted shape sprang into existence, a form
that resembled nothing so much as a Henry Moore sculpture
some vandal had splashed with gaudy paint.

"Here's a classic," said Adrian. "The coat protein of
Type II polio. The proteins pack to form its shell." He
tapped the keys, and on the screens identical copies of the
protein multiplied to form a spheroid, like a radar dome.
"That's the A form—and here's the B." The diagrammatic
proteins reassembled themselves on the screen as Toby watched;
the packing was different, but the resulting spheroid was
much the same, forming a protective shell. "And inside the
shell is this little string of RNA."

"The RNA is what gives this geometric beast its killing
power, then?"

"Shit, you're a poet."

Toby recoiled. "Really, must you speak only in scatologi-
cal obscenities?"

"I was yelled at a lot when I was a kid," said Adrian
contritely.

"Spare me the self-analysis." But Toby was mad at himself for using big words to ask dumb questions.

He looked on in fascination as Adrian played a manic
game with his computer screens, conjuring up diagrams of
involute protein structures, rolling them in space, examining
their spines and undulations and cavities, flexing them, tearing them apart, making them dance. It went on a long time,
and occasionally Adrian emitted groans and murmurs of delight as he put the graphic creatures through their paces.

Suddenly Adrian slumped in his chair. "Well, a virus can do only so many tricks. You're probably wondering why I'm wasting my time with 'em."

"Actually, it hadn't occurred to me to ask," Toby said. "I'm quite enchanted with your pretty pictures."

"When it occurs to you to ask"—despite his evident determination to make a good impression, sarcasm crept into Adrian's voice—"it's because I'm looking for the simplest possible natural models for self-replicating systems. You really do know what we do here, don't you?"

"Only that you make protein-based computer parts. Or so Dr. Chatterjee has led me to believe."

"That's only the first step," said Adrian. "Cook 'em in a vat. We've already got that hacked. Now we're trying to get them to build themselves. Viruses don't really qualify, of course—they have to take over a cell's machinery to reproduce. But the artificial organism I'm trying to build needs a scaffolding as simple as the coat protein of this virus—a molecule with no more than a couple of thousand atoms in it. Something that can be built, torn apart, modified with artificial enzymes I'll provide. Following directions from a program I want *you* to write."

"You're trying to build a self-replicating computer?"

"Yeah. Maybe it'll even look like this. But this is just the box the chips come in," he said, tapping the screen. "The box-building program is only one of the things I need you for, though."

"Oh? What else?"

Adrian turned from the console, the dim-colored light from the screens illuminating the head that was too big even for his gangling body, the features that were too broad even for his outsized head. Adrian Storey was not an attractive man, but

Toby had already glimpsed in him the passionate dreaming, the capacity for excited discovery, of a bright and lonely child.

Adrian smiled. "I gotcha hooked, don't I? You twerp."

ZYMOPHASE

*Zymophase. The onset of bioelectronic activity in an
assembled epigenetic system.*
—Handbook of Bioelectronic Engineering
(*revised*), Blevins and Storey, eds.

♦♦♦

Harold Lillard distractedly tugged a wool suit out of the closet, unwrapped it from a wooden hanger, rewrapped it around a wire one, and shoved it into his worn, fake-Gucci garment bag. In nearly thirty years of travel he'd never really gotten used to packing; for a man who'd been a salesman all his life, he figured this had to be some sort of a Guinness world record.

He heard a feeble clunking from the direction of the front yard. He went to the bedroom window, pushed it open against its warped wooden sill, and peered out. He could see the wet street through bare elms. Yesterday's snowfall was turning grudgingly to slush under a hazy morning sun, with temperatures barely above freezing; winter hung on in Massachusetts, antiseptic and frigid.

Down on the front lawn his oldest boy—the oldest still living at home, the fifteen-year-old—was hacking at the ice on the flagstone walk with the corner of an aluminum snow shovel.

"Anthony, you know better. Put that down and get the sledgehammer." Harold's breath puffed visibly as he leaned from the window.

"Awww, Dad . . ." The boy's complaint sounded far away, without resonance in the still air.

"You heard me. You want to buy me a new shovel?" The boy disgustedly let the snow shovel drop and trudged off toward the garage.

He knew his chores, thought Harold, feeling like a scold; if he'd cleared the walk before the snow turned to moguls under all those galosheed Lillard family feet, he wouldn't be wasting his weekend.

Harold tugged the window shut and turned back to his packing. Better be safe; he pulled another dark wool suit out of the closet and stuffed it into the bag. He heard the television set in the downstairs family room abruptly change its rumbling tone as someone switched channels, followed by an outraged cry from a ten-year-old girl and an angry reply from her thirteen-year-old sister. He caught his breath, awaiting the customary stream of gruesome threats, but nothing happened. This time, apparently, Theresa approved of Donna's choice of programming.

Behind him the bedroom door creaked open. Marian looked tireder than usual. Harold blamed her drained appearance on the day; diffuse light from the overcast sky filled the bedroom, bleaching her faded cotton dress and threadbare apron to pastel grays, picking out her silver hairs and illuminating each wrinkle. Once prettily round-cheeked and dimpled, Marian's sweet face had settled many years ago into an expression of lumpy determination.

"Shouldn't we start for the airport soon?" she prompted.

He checked his watch. "Guess I'm running late. Hope I've got everything." He zipped up the garment bag and looked around. Nervously he jingled his pocket change. "What did I do with my briefcase?"

She smiled. "I found it by the garage door. I put it in the station wagon."

He leaned over and pecked her cheek. The textured skin was soft under his lips. He rubbed his cheek against hers and felt the catch of a patch of whiskers he'd missed shaving. "I love you." She put her hands on his bulky sides and gave them a reassuring pat.

Harold pulled the change out of his trouser pocket and separated the quarters, leaving them on the dresser. "Take care of the kids' savings, okay?"

She nodded and turned. He followed her down the stairs, his overstuffed bag slung over his shoulder. "Come on, gang, we're off," he shouted.

Theresa leaped into the hall at the foot of the stairs, all knees and elbows, her hand half-covering her face. Harold frowned. "Theresa, take your thumb out of your mouth."

She popped it with a sound like a cork coming out of a bottle. "Mommy said we couldn't go to the airport this time," she announced wetly.

"Oh?" Harold looked at his wife.

"Time for a private chat," she said.

"Oh." Harold's smile faded. What kid was it this time? Agnes, was she going to drop out, get married? Or Gary, he'd put some girl in the family way. Or Paul, he'd been making noises about refusing to register for the draft. Or . . .

"Don't worry, Harry, nobody's in trouble," said Marian with a faint smile. "I'll tell you all about it."

"Okay. 'Bye, girls." No reply. "Good-bye, Donna," he called, a bit louder, poking his head into the family room. The thirteen-year-old turned away from the TV movie long enough to wave absently.

Theresa tagged along to the double garage. Anthony had

left the garage door open, and the cold was bitter. Marian slid into the front seat of the rusted brown Ford station wagon as Harold retrieved his briefcase and slung his bag into the back. Theresa perched on the rear bumper of the black Cadillac, Harold's business car, and watched.

Oblivious to the cold, the scrawny little girl waved dutifully as her father backed the wagon down the icy drive, narrowly missing the sagging spruce.

As he turned into the street Harold saw Theresa, before she went inside the house, stick her thumb back in her mouth. In the front yard Anthony kept pounding ice, refusing to glance up.

On the turnpike trailer trucks whined past, their multiple tires hissing in the slush, bouncing on the eroded concrete. Harold kept the wipers going to push the freezing mud off the windshield. The car heater was stuck on high; the interior was stifling. "What's the big secret?" he asked.

"I'm pregnant, Harry," Marian said.

He gaped at her, then hastily looked back at the road. "Marian, you're forty-four years old."

"It's God's will, Harry," she said gently.

"God doesn't take the risk," said Harold bitterly. He glanced at her again. Her face was closed, disapproving. "Sorry. No disrespect." He had to keep such thoughts to himself, he'd learned that long ago. Marian wouldn't hear of artificial birth control, so they practiced the rhythm method. Religiously. There was no other word for it.

What was he supposed to do, pretend he was ninety years old and didn't care? Patronize floozies? Maybe he should just have himself cut and not tell her. The Church ought to join the twentieth century.

"You'll be all right while I'm gone?"

"Of course, Harry. You just do your job and come home as soon as you can."

His hands tightened on the steering wheel. The older he got, the more people depended on him, and the more complicated the world became. Thank God he made a pretty penny from the Compugen Corporation. He needed it. They all needed it.

Six years ago, on the strength of a single article in a trade magazine, he'd gone looking for the Compugen Corporation. At the time he'd been stagnating, high up in the sales department of one of Route 128's oldest firms, and he suspected that his employers were stagnating too. He'd read and reread the piece about the brash upstarts out west who claimed to have made biochips work in a commercial computer years before the analysts said it could be done. At the end of the week he'd sworn his wife to secrecy, emptied the secret cache of quarters he kept in a number-10 can in the garage, and caught a night flight to the coast.

Compugen then was located only a couple of blocks away from its present site, down by the tracks in Berkeley's industrial flatlands, but six years ago its offices, laboratories, factory, and storerooms had all been crammed into one small converted chemical warehouse. Jack Chatterjee, Compugen's chief executive officer and top scientist—concurrently on the faculty of the University of California's medical school in San Francisco—had taken a half-hour of his busy Saturday morning to show Harold around the place. He exhibited the new Python computer with sanguine pride.

Python was to be a business-oriented machine with merely adequate speed. But it was dirt cheap, and by virtue of its biologically grown memory units (crude organic devices by the standards of just a few years later), the Python, if not fast, was very capacious indeed, able to store whole libraries of data on a desk top. Chatterjee had made sure the Python was compatible with the more popular hard- and software already available; Compugen's quality control was excellent, their warranty generous, and they planned a lavish advertising campaign. Harold knew Compugen would sell a lot of computers.

The more important question was whether Compugen could keep up with its product, or whether the company would be caught in the vise of capital-versus-cash that had crushed so many of its predecessors. By the time Harold was back on the plane to Boston, Chatterjee had convinced him that the company was financially and administratively prepared for growth. For his part, Harold had talked himself into a job as Compugen's New England sales representative.

On the plane Harold had second thoughts. It was like starting over—and him with a daughter at Boston College, two boys in high school, little ones dressing in hand-me-downs. Salary? None: he'd earn a healthy commission on each Python he sold, and authorized expenses would be reimbursed upon presentation of proper receipts (Harold had no doubt that Chatterjee would personally inspect his expense reports). And there were those promised year-end bonuses. In stock.

By the time he'd gotten home to Newton he'd swallowed his fears, and through the difficult months that followed he'd kept up a cheerful front for the benefit of the wife and kids.

The Pythons sold as well as he'd expected. Harold began to breathe easier. There was a scare when the novelty of biochips wore off, because everybody started to use them and the Python lost its price advantage. When IBM decided to steamroller the marketplace, the bottom almost fell out. What Harold didn't know at the time was that Jack Chatterjee had foreseen that development, that Compugen had already hired a genius of bioelectronic engineering, a man named Adrian Storey, to design a new generation of biological computers.

The first Tygers appeared—not only their memories but their arithmetic and logic units were organic structures. The

Tygers were smaller and faster and had more memory and were less temperamental than the Pythons, and they sold even better. Harold, along with Compugen, prospered anew.

Now, only three years later, came the Tyger II. It was said that the only inorganic parts left were the screen, keyboard, and miniature life-support systems. Its innards were made of something called Epicell. The heart and brain of the Tyger II were alive.

Of course the public was not yet officially aware of the Tyger II's existence, though rumors had been swirling for months. And although he'd already begun taking orders, Harold himself didn't know all the details.

He steered through freezing slush on his way to Logan Airport. On to sunny California once more; there he would learn the truth—surely it would add up to more prosperity.

But the Lillard family seemed able to expand to absorb any amount of prosperity Harold could provide.

If he could persuade his wife to stop having children, thought Harold, he could achieve equilibrium with the world and the flow of time. It seemed only reasonable. He glanced at Marian and sighed. Life, in the three or four billion years since God had created it, had displayed only minor tolerance for reasonable behavior.

◆◆◆

Though it was not yet clear of the Berkeley Hills, the sun had already rouged the tattered clouds overhead, the remnants of last night's storm. Above the clouds and to the west the sky was fresh and blue.

Wrapped in his ragged blue bathrobe, Toby Bridgeman squinted at the sunrise from the dining room balcony of his apartment. After months of rain the brown hills had turned an electric green. Wisps of fog still clung to the ridgeline, slowly dissipating.

Toby could see the sprawling, overcrowded campus of the University of California tucked into the base of the hills. He found it difficult to believe that only two years ago he had been working there in a drafty corner of a thirty-year-old "modern" building, one of those pseudo-Bauhaus excrescences, patiently coaxing dimwitted machines to express themselves.

In those days he'd lived a few blocks away from the university in a small house on a tree-shaded cul-de-sac, where he'd contented himself with a simple existence, the kind of life appropriate to a bachelor professor with a modest independent income and relatively inexpensive tastes. Now he lived in a glass tower, oddly named the Bay Plaza (it had no plaza), set obliquely on a tongue of landfill that diminished San Francisco Bay by several acres.

Just a mile north of his new home Toby could see the red tile roofs and windowless facades of Compugen. There, to his mild surprise, he'd found that his research in artificial intelligence was valued by someone other than the military—that in fact his skills could bring heady rewards.

Yes, he'd been hooked. The science had hooked him, not to mention Compugen's unbelievably lavish resources. And something about Adrian had hooked him. There was something nakedly honest, something powerful but at the same time helpless, that drew Toby to Adrian more strongly than he'd been drawn to anyone in many years. . . .

He turned back to the kitchen and lifted the coffeepot from the range. He filled two painted porcelain mugs with coffee and sipped at one as he carried them into the dark bedroom.

A woman slept soundly in the shadows, sprawled naked under the sheet, her breath rising and falling in musical sighs. The blue down quilt was in a heap on the carpet. "This is your wake-up call," he said, standing by the bed and holding the coffee cup close to her nose. When she didn't respond, he put his own cup aside and gently rocked her shoulder.

She opened her eyes groggily. She smiled tentatively—he wondered if she recognized him—then turned away. "Too early."

"Sorry, my dear. I must get to work. I work at home, you know. And I'm much too easily distracted."

She groaned. "Toby, you're not kicking me out?"

"Well, I wouldn't put it that way myself."

"You beast! Let me have that." She took the cup and sipped. "Hmm, this is good. Why aren't you a tea drinker?"

"When in Rome," he said.

She took a bigger gulp, then sat up, letting the sheet fall away. Her form and texture suffered nothing from the filtered light of day. Toby was delighted by the sight of her, but it was an abstract delight, sidetracked somewhere along the way between thought and motive.

She eyed him a moment and saw that his intention was elsewhere. "To hell with you, Toby Bridgeman," she said cheerfully, swinging her legs off the bed. "I've got work to do too." She rose and, carrying her coffee with her, moved smoothly to the chair where she'd draped her silk dress. "Learning how to sell that thing you and that creepy Storey built."

"Umm, there're new toothbrushes in the cabinet," he offered, bemused, as he watched her make her way in bare majesty toward the bathroom.

"There would be," she said grumpily. She closed the door firmly.

Toby twisted a plastic rod to open the narrow blinds, allowing skylight to enter the bedroom. The Bay Bridge glinted with the windows of ten thousand cars, moving west into San Francisco, bumper to bumper.

Toby had already shaved and showered in the predawn blackness, in his big apartment's other bathroom. Now, while his new friend was occupied, he threw open his neatly arranged closet—suits, slacks, polished shoes lined up at attention—and quickly slid into tan gabardine slacks and a fresh white shirt.

He went back into the kitchen and put a pot of water on the stove. Boiling an egg was near the limit of his culinary expertise.

He didn't really have that much work to do today—he'd be

killing time until the noontime ceremonies. Principally he wanted to speed Ruth Slatkin on her way. Ruth was a Compugen saleswoman from Atlanta, one of the company's fast-rising stars, smart and insatiably ambitious. She wasn't insatiable only at work.

Toby went into the dining room, where bits and pieces of computer sprawled on his glass dining-room table. Some were functional and some were not, and since he rarely entertained in his apartment, over the months he'd allowed a pile of papers to spread across the surface of the table like a mat of algae. One never knew when inspiration would strike—but his real motive for working in his apartment, aside from the modest tax deduction it afforded him, was that it helped him maintain a semifictitious independence from Jack Chatterjee. When Chatterjee had first asked him to join Compugen, Toby had refused to leave the Berkeley faculty.

Finally he'd negotiated a compromise: he would take the money, do the work, but only as a consultant on leave from his university post. Thus he forewent the insurance programs and the stock options but kept a tenuous hold on academic respectability.

Toby slipped three cold raw eggs into the boiling water in the stainless steel pot and set the timer on the range.

Perhaps academic respectability mattered less to him than he'd supposed. Certainly his partnership with Adrian Storey had blossomed into the most productive association of his career.

More unusual was their friendship. Toby suspected Adrian had never found it easy to trust anyone, had never, in fact, had a friend. As for himself, these days Toby habitually avoided involvement, any form of emotional commitment; he did not see much advantage in close human relationships beyond a certain sentimental coziness, a sticky mutual dependence that smacked of the marketplace.

He turned as Ruth, perfumed, made up, fully clothed, entered the kitchen behind him.

"Ugh, what's that?" she asked, peering into the pot. "I never eat eggs."

"There may be some dry cereal."

She looked at him and pursed her red-lipsticked mouth into an amused pout. She took a step closer, pinched his shirtfront in her long-nailed fingertips, pulled him against her breasts. She kissed him.

He worried about his clean white shirt.

When she leaned back she said, "Can you get away after the announcement? For lunch? Just a quick nibble?"

"Oh, golly, Chatterjee's tied me up with a bunch of Europeans."

"Tonight, then. Here?"

"Umm, tonight. Dinner."

"It will be a long day, Toby."

"It certainly will. Let me call you a cab." He reached behind him for the kitchen wall phone and punched the familiar number. He smiled at her as he gave the dispatcher the address. "He's on the way. I'll walk you down," he suggested as he hung up.

"I know my way around, Toby," she said. "You get on with your important work now."

He watched her walk across the wide living room, with its leather furniture and Indian brass and Chinese porcelain lamps and its abstract paintings on white plaster walls. Her high heels pushed the bright Arab rug into the wall-to-wall wool carpet beneath. The way she went away tempted him to ask her to come back. He resisted the mindless urge.

She turned at the hallway arch to blow him a kiss. Something about her glittering smile made him cautious. She disappeared into the hall, and he heard the door close behind her.

He turned away and went onto the balcony. The glass walls around him reflected the heat of the sun. The freeway traffic rumbled far below; despite a sea breeze from the Golden Gate, he could smell the exhaust fumes. As he gripped the steel railing he had a sudden longing for the aromas that used to greet him when he'd bash open the sticky sash of the bay window in his little house in the hills: wisteria and dew-soaked grass. And the air vibrant with birdsong.

The egg timer chimed. He emptied the pot and ran cold tap water over the eggs, then plucked one out and peeled it. He found himself standing alone at the kitchen counter, staring at the wall, eating his boiled egg. He licked yellow crumbs of coagulated yolk from the corners of his mouth.

It was a morning like most others.

◆◆◆

Adrian Storey lay motionless on his bed, staring at the ceiling. He had not moved for as long as he could remember. Every few minutes the surface of his eyes would become dry, and he would blink. And then he would have to start putting the world back together again.

He knew that an hour ago, or two, or three, light had begun seeping into the room—he had watched it collecting like a milky precipitate high in the corners of the ceiling.

The light had grown brighter when the fog began to lift. Local winds moved with the roiling boundary of the mist, up the ridge, through the trees, rattling windowpanes and snapping the shredded plastic that had once protected the unfinished upper floors of the house in the Berkeley Hills. He could hear moisture dripping from the eaves—nothing was wrong with his sensory apparatus—and he could hear the birds singing in the big Monterey pine outside the bedroom. He could hear the whispering leaves in the eucalyptus grove at the edge of the lot.

And he imagined, though it was only a wishful dream, that he could hear the sound of an approaching car, a car he would recognize by the fussy meshing of its numerous precision-machined parts. A German car. Toby Bridgeman's car. Toby was coming. His friend Toby . . .

. . . the only person in the world he called by that word.

He could remember quite clearly—for nothing was wrong with his memory either, but only, somehow, with his will—the very moment when he first suspected that a novel entity, a friend, had entered his life.

"*See it? See it happening?*" It had been midmorning at the lab, with Adrian hovering over Toby, breathing wetly through his mouth the way he did when he was excited about something, fiddling with the knobs of an oscilloscope while Toby peered through a microscope at a layer of bluish cells in a Petri dish.

"For God's sake, Adrian, choose a setting and let it rest. All I can see is a mess of blue goo and a couple of things that look like felled redwood trees."

Adrian fiddled a few seconds more, then backed away from the bench with an effort, his bony fingers still twitching. From a port on the face of the oscilloscope issued a double strand of fine wire, stripped and split in two at the end and gently introduced into the thin circle of cells—two hair-fine copper leads that when seen through the microscope were the tree trunks that Toby described.

Toby watched silently a moment. "There. A bud came off to the right."

"Yeah?" Adrian was as eager as a puppy.

"All at once. Rather like a tiny flower. Remarkable."

"Remarkable! Shit, it's terrific!"

"Quite." Toby lifted his gaze from the microscope and rubbed his eyes. "But of course it's what we expected."

"You little son of a bitch, why don't you be *happy*."

Adrian was furious. His glance skittered toward and then
away from Toby.

Toby slid his chair back and stood up. He paused for a
second—Adrian would never forget the suspense of that
moment—and then he reached out and grabbed Adrian around
his narrow, flabby waist. The shock on Adrian's face was
surely lost on Toby, whose own face was buried somewhere
near Adrian's armpit. Hugging him tightly, Toby mumbled,
"I am happy, Adrian. We did do it . . . and mostly you did
it."

"Yeah, okay, that's okay," said Adrian, squirming away
from Toby's embrace. "Hey, I just wanted to know."

"D'you know now?"

"Yeah."

"Good." Toby smiled brightly as he leaned away, and
Adrian watched his right hand creep up to smooth a nonexistent tie. "I'm not usually the demonstrative sort."

"Yeah," said Adrian warily. "So. This works, okay? So
what's next?"

The moment passed, and they resumed talking about work.

Adrian wouldn't let himself brood about the incident for
the rest of that day, or the next. But when the weekend came
it pressed itself on him.

He was at home on a Friday night, sitting cross-legged on
his rug, expertly fingering the strings of his classical guitar
and singing in a husky tentative voice a song of his own
composition he called "Marion's Blues."

She knew more than she could say and didn't say it,
So she went away and tossed those petals in the stream.

He sang well enough. And he played beautifully. That
time a long time ago when he'd yowled out a dirty old
drinking song to get rid of Toby's eavesdropping co-workers,

he'd been acting. And when he'd told Toby that he couldn't
sing and play at the same time he'd been lying. Acting and
lying were staples of his repertoire.

They looked for her and smiled when they had lost her.
They never knew she watched them, smiling from her
     dream.

His fingers bent to the strings and he played without words.

Not that he wasn't an authentic prick when he was at
work, which was to say most of the time. But tonight he
could relax awhile—he didn't have anyone to account to.
He'd eaten his frozen dinner, and he wasn't going anywhere,
having no taste tonight for the slings and arrows of the
singles bars. He was content to be by himself, playing his
guitar.

Through the plate glass walls of his darkened living room
he could see millions of lights spread out below his isolated
home in the Berkeley Hills. At any given moment on a
Friday night in springtime, between an hour after sunset and
an hour before midnight, he could see approximately 10.2
million houselights, streetlights, signs, and car headlights.
He knew because once he'd made a back-of-the-envelope
calculation which, although it allowed for the shape of the
bay and the trees that cut off part of his view, failed to
include such refinements as the topography of the slopes
immediately below his house. He wasn't obsessive; he'd just
gotten to wondering how many of those lights—lights like
glittering pearls—he could actually see on a clear night like
this one.

Those kinds of thoughts were easy and clean. They came
naturally, and while he might remember the result, especially
if it was numerical, he hardly ever remembered having the

thought, any more than he remembered what he'd eaten for breakfast on any given day.

The thoughts he did remember were different. They were full of fear and anger and determination. Full of hunger. They were the thoughts he had to live with.

At that moment he wondered why Toby had hugged him.

Toby wasn't queer, that was sure enough. And sure enough Adrian had liked it a lot when Toby had hugged him—and frankly that scared the shit out of him. He was always scared when he started to . . . to like feeling liked.

That little bastard. He had a lot of promise, no doubt of it. He'd already done what any brilliant-son-of-a-bitch programmer should have done, within the time Adrian had allowed for any anonymous brilliant-son-of-a-bitch to do it. And he'd done a shitload more. He was threatening to force Adrian into creating something grander than he'd imagined he could. Good ideas, hard work. All very well. But the measly twerp is coming into the lab two or three times a week and being *lovable*.

Adrian had had a lot of practice seeing through that kind of crap.

He couldn't see through it here. The thing was, there was no *motive*. Adrian wasn't a ticket to Baptist heaven or extra money in the bank for Toby, the way he'd been for his foster parents, endless sets of them. Toby had his plush job. He didn't even have to hang around the lab, like Adrian did; he could work at home most of the time. He could hardly spend the money he was making already, and he couldn't get promoted, so why was he being so *nice*?

Adrian stopped playing the guitar and laid it beside him on the rug. "Shit," he said aloud.

Maybe he just likes me.

Just like that.

It's funny to watch him get mad, the way he gets all

excited when I say shit this and fuck that and generally make an ass of myself. He likes it, it's as plain as the point on his pointy head. He must think it's liberating or something. The way he grew up, he probably had to ask his mother's permission to fart. "I say, Mommy dear, would you mind terribly . . . ?"

And the more worked up he gets, the more he starts spouting history and philosophy at me, a billion bits and fragments, just like all those brain-damaged high-school teachers lecturing me about bits and fragments that never did fit, that don't have anything to do with anything.

Adrian picked up the guitar. He grinned.

The more he talks to me—even if he's only doing it to try and get away from raunchy old Adrian—the more it starts fitting together. So I insult him some more, so he won't stop.

She knew things that he could tell her if she wanted,
If she wanted him to tell her, but she didn't
    know she did. . . .

The ceiling again, and the morning light burning his eyes. Adrian knew he really had to get out of bed. It was an important day, one he shouldn't miss. There was a message he had to give to his boss, Jack Chatterjee, one Jack didn't want to hear but one he was going to get even if Adrian had to write it on a piece of paper and roll it up into a tube and jam it up Jack's ass.

But first he had to sit up. Stand up. Walk to the door. . . .

Instead he stared at the ceiling. Toby was coming. Toby would save him. His friend would come and save his life.

◆◆◆

"Helloo, Dr. Chatterjee. Five minutes early!"

"Ah, yes. Thank you, Mrs. Dortmunder," Chatterjee whispered, forcing a smile. The woman never missed a trick. Jack Chatterjee's secretary was a brass-girdled blonde who typed faster than a line printer and had a voice like a rubber ducky. Nevertheless she could strike terror into the heart of any employee, creditor, or representative of the U.S. government who dared approach Chatterjee's office without an explicit summons.

He closed his office door firmly behind him and stood a moment, waiting for his racing heart to calm. The room was a hiding place, a cave, large and dark, carpeted in beige wool and hung with thick brown drapes. Abstract bronzes glinted from the walnut shelves, which otherwise held only a few leather-bound volumes, for show.

Had Mrs. Dortmunder been laughing into the phone just before she saw him? People made jokes about him, he knew. He was used to it. His mixed ancestry was apparent to

45

anyone who looked—he had his paternal grandfather's rough-hewn features, those of an English sergeant major, and his Hindu mother's walnut brown skin and sleek black hair, arranged in fussy wavelets. Moreover, he was cursed with a simpering accent, and he had the manners not of a captain of industry but of a cut-rate tailor, which had been his father's profession.

Chatterjee peered through one of the slit windows at the parking lot, reassuring himself that the lot was filling on schedule with his employees' cars; it was a minor daily ritual. He crossed to his desk with quick steps and perched delicately on the edge of his leather armchair. Across the bare expanse of his desk top he noted a faint white circle where a visitor's wet glass had rested on the wax, sans coaster. Irritably he shot his silk cuffs and smoothed the lapels of his gray pinstripe suit.

It was to be a time for brooding, then. What should be a day of triumph, the greatest day of his life, was to be an occasion of self-pity instead. He hated himself in these moods, but he was helpless before the imperative of his emotional nature.

There had been a time—as a new immigrant in high school in Los Angeles, as a student at UCLA—when their sneers, their laughter, their bland ostracism had hurt him terribly. At the age of twenty he was still crying himself to sleep.

Medical school was different, though. At Harvard everyone was equally alone, all alike isolated by desperate pressure and relentless competition. By the time Chatterjee began his own career in medical research, he was well accustomed to loneliness. His professional colleagues offered him no more companionship than ever, but at least they let it be known they respected him.

That had lasted until he had founded the Compugen Corporation, and made a success of it; then the respect turned to envy. His former research associates went so far as to hint that he had stolen the ideas on which his fortune was based. It was a false, a cowardly—even a racist—accusation. But it was a festering thorn.

For years Chatterjee had longed to do . . . *some*thing, something so original and so beneficial to mankind that it would silence the envious forever. He knew not what precisely, except that he had hoped, somehow, to conjure it from the depths of his corporate vats, from the intricacies of his microelectronic fabrication facilities. It had not happened yet. It seemed unlikely that it ever would.

He yanked open a shallow side drawer and raised a Tyger terminal to working height. He flipped the clasps and raised the little computer's flat view plate, then entered his personal identity code. He called up the confidential comptroller's report, an electronic document automatically kept current, to which only he and Compugen's financial officers had direct access.

Compugen's stock had gotten a boost two years ago with the announcement that the noted Dr. Tobias Bridgeman, an AI researcher well known to analysts who followed the industry, had been retained to work with Dr. Adrian Storey on the development of a revolutionary new computer. Since then the stock had never weakened, but had continued to inch steadily upward. And as the day for the official announcement of the new computer had approached, stock prices had begun climbing steeply.

Today was that day. Today at high noon.

No details about the computer itself had ever been released, but most industry watchers assumed, correctly, that Compugen was aiming for the next frontier, the fully self-replicating biocomputer. A steady flow of rumor supported the belief that the company was achieving its goal. For a year

the trade press had been calling the new machine the *Tyger
II*.

Tyger II. Chatterjee liked the name. Until only a few
months ago his marketing people had been pressing him to
christen the machine—known in-house only as Project E—with
some new and clever brand name in line with the company's
successful Pythons and Tygers. Some of the suggestions were
dull (Lyon) and some were awful (Dyno, Rhyno) and none
were in the least inspirational. Tyger II was best, thought
Chatterjee, partly because it ever so slightly downplayed how
revolutionary the inside of the new beast really was. Let the
name Tyger II reassure the buyer of continuity and the quality to be expected from Compugen products. Let the stuff
inside thrill the novelty seekers.

Chatterjee could be virtuously certain that he had personally done nothing to inflate the price of Compugen stock.
Many years ago, when Compugen was still growing and had
only the Python to sell, a rumor had started that the Python's
video screen could cause retinal lesions. It was a stupid story,
without foundation in medical fact, but sales suffered for
weeks while competitors made serious inroads. Ever since
then Chatterjee had done his best to control rumors about
Compugen, had even hired academic consultants who specialized in rumor control. (He suspected that the retinal lesion
canard had been launched by Data Major, Compugen's next-
door neighbor and chief competitor in the bioelectronic field.)
But he had not been able to control the rumors about Project
E. He admitted to himself that the unofficial news was so
good, so unremittingly good, that even though he had access
to the truth about what was going on in his own labs any
moment he cared to ask, he almost believed it himself.
Storey and Bridgeman were up to something big, something
that was going to work, something that was going to make
Compugen pots of money.

Or so rumor had it.

Chatterjee glanced at the financial report again. The European markets were holding steady, and the early returns from New York were also quite good, indeed too good to last out the trading session. But the coming weeks should be profitable ones, at least on paper. To anyone who didn't know Compugen as well as Chatterjee, it would seem that the company's future was one of unalloyed brightness.

He did know Compugen. Jack Chatterjee was very good at projection, the kind unaided by computers—what some call intuition—and he saw a crisis coming. What galled him was that in a desperate bid for unassailable respectability he had tied up millions of dollars of capital in a philanthropic exercise known as the Chatterjee Cognitive Research Foundation, and now he could not get at the money. This wonder of public relations was bound to Compugen by silken threads, so that any marketable advance made by it toward the understanding of human or artificial intelligence or the cure of mental disability would find concrete expression in a Compugen product—and indeed the foundation had already achieved notable successes in introducing novel diagnostic methods and ingenious new health monitors. Biochip implantations in the visual cortex could virtually cure certain kinds of blindness, while other biochips could regulate a variety of internal functions.

But the dream had soured. The foundation had cost the corporation, and Chatterjee personally, far more than it had earned back. The foundation itself was in fine financial condition, but Chatterjee *could not get at the money*! And in the past weeks it had become evident to him, his comptroller, and his corporate attorneys that the company would soon be in need of cash.

The reason was simple enough. There was nothing in the research pipeline, nothing that was even a glimmer in an engineer's eye to take the place of the Tyger II when it had exhausted its market potential. Adrian Storey had run out of ideas. Over a year ago Chatterjee had retained the best headhunters in the industry to search, in strictest confidence, for his chief scientist's replacement.

He'd made such a move once before—when he was looking for his own replacement, when he sensed that the creative spark which once had burned in him so brightly had dimmed. That time they'd brought him the name of young Storey, who'd gone on to create what Jack Chatterjee, not blind to irony, had chosen to dub *Tyger*. But now Adrian's flame too was beginning to burn low; Chatterjee knew it even if Adrian didn't. And the scouts had yet to identify a single available candidate who could begin to fill Adrian's oversized shoes.

Chatterjee could take comfort in only one aspect of the gloomy situation: he'd had the foresight to hustle Tyger II out the door while there was still time—before Adrian could twiddle it to the point of commercial extinction. Any hint of delay now would be disastrous. These machines were for sale starting *today*, and the retailers and the public had better believe it, even if Compugen's factory was still struggling to reach full production.

Yet even if current plans worked to perfection, Chatterjee knew without knowing, disaster would come anyway. He did not know why, he did not even know how he knew, he only knew it was there, waiting, in the dearth of ideas. Somehow he was certain, although he could not have put this thought into words, that the last great idea had already been born.

Suddenly Chatterjee felt peculiarly delicate, the membranes of his eyeballs oddly sensitive to the aridity of his office's conditioned air. Let us assume perfection, then—thus far we'll gamble—and make our preparations for what follows. Let us assume a minimum time to breathe, before the end.

He pushed the Tyger away from him and turned to the

intercom. "Mrs. Dortmunder, get me Arjunian at the law firm," he whispered.

"Yee-us, Dr. Chatterjee."

The world was a hard place. But on the bottom line, personal wealth was worth more than respect. He was prepared to act on that conviction, even if it meant forfeiting respect forever.

"By the way, has Dr. Storey come in today?"

"Noo, Dr. Chatterjee."

In the beginning Adrian had never been late for work. That had all changed long ago. "Please try to reach him at his home."

"As you say, Dr. Chatterjee."

He leaned away from the intercom. For the first time in thirty years, Jack Chatterjee felt tears pressing against his eyelids.

◆◆◆

After his Spartan breakfast Toby sat down at the dining-room table and began shoving papers around. Despite his shower and fresh clothes, he imagined that Ruth's scent was all over him.

He leaned back and stared unseeing at the ceiling. For some days he'd been seeking a theorem for relating parallel-processor computing power to the computation of certain classes of problems he suspected the Tyger II would be apt at attacking. Nothing had suggested itself, but at times it was best just to daydream. The only rule was, no dreaming about sex.

He wondered what Adrian was up to—he hadn't seen him in two days. Frantically brewing germs in a vat, no doubt, still trying to make improvements in a product that was already on the assembly line. Toby found the actual doing of microbiology highly distasteful; he preferred to deal with life, that sort of life anyway, in schematics.

In the beginning he'd worried that the two of them would

never make their collaboration work; it had taken almost six months of sparring before they settled into a routine. Most of the time Adrian worked alone on the big graphics screens or in the labs, while Toby worked at home, his personal computers having been connected to Compugen's mainframes by protected telephone lines. Several times a week they got their heads together in the graphics room, and it was there that the idealized creature the Compugen administration had labeled Project E was slowly coming to life.

With the virtually inexhaustible capacity of Compugen's graphics computer at hand, a gifted practitioner could draw any molecule, real or imaginary, allowed by the laws of atomic physics. When designing new organisms Adrian had found it useful to begin by sketching in just the kind of proteins he wanted—made of a few hundred atoms each, at most—then sitting back and watching how they interacted on the graphics screens. There would be plenty of time later to wonder how in the name of synthetic organic chemistry one was going to *make* the damn things—if they could be made at all—in useful amounts.

With luck, nature was already making something very like that growth factor or that hormone or restriction enzyme or whatever it was on her own—somewhere out there in the living world. In the brain of the Norwegian rat, perhaps. In the leaves of a viny parasite in the canopy of the Amazon forest. In the poisonous liver of a puffer fish. In the hind gut of an Australian termite. In the nucleus of an Antarctic protozoan. If some natural cell somewhere was pumping it out, odds were that a tame cell in a laboratory could be tricked into pumping it out too.

First Toby and Adrian had to create what they needed in computer simulation. Then Adrian, assisted by dozens of his Compugen subordinates, could tackle the problem of making it real.

On the computer screens the gaudy animated stuff of idealized Project E grew in close-packed sheets, a few cell-layers
thick; growing outward at the edges, the sheets left lacunae
bridged by strands sometimes only a single cell in width. The
pink and yellow and purple sheets grew one above the other,
forming laminates like a piece of plywood. Though Toby and
Adrian had written the algorithms that controlled the growth
of the patterns, they could not wholly predict the evolution of
each blossoming imaginary organism. They could only watch
its performance and wonder.

Information whispered through this system on discrete levels: once the structures were in place, digital computation
was carried out by the flow of (simulated) electrons along
specified paths, just as in an old-fashioned solid-state computer. The power requirement was miniscule, much less than
that of a refrigerator's light bulb, much less than a human
brain's.

The information that Project E used to build its own organs—
its memory structures, processing structures, switches and the
like—was encoded in synthetic DNA (simulated, of course,
by the graphics program). This information had to be translated into action using (simulated) artificial enzymes and
(simulated) structural proteins.

Toby had come to conceive of his task as devising a means
for Project E's different levels to communicate with one
another directly, instantly. The challenge was to induce an
individual colony of Project E cells to evolve on its own
terms—to ''understand'' its own purposes and adapt itself to
fulfill them. Thus computational operations, the only operations of interest to computer users, could directly trigger the
appropriate growth of needed new Project E organs. It was a
trick that only the more primitive individual living things
(real ones) had ever mastered.

Toby remembered the day they'd made their first breakthrough, in their work but principally in their willingness to deal openly with each other. It was the day Adrian took him to see the first live memory units budding under the microscope. He'd been thrilled at the sight—so thrilled he'd hugged Adrian to tell him how proud he was—but he hadn't dared to admit that the sight of artificial life sprouting in that dish had made him queasy. . . .

"Let's sit down," he'd said, the saliva rising at the back of his throat. "Not here. I'm starting to hate this place."

They'd abandoned the sterile electro-optics lab and the white-coated workers who peered at them curiously, and had gone into the research building's airy central atrium. They found a pair of wicker couches at right angles; Toby sat on the edge of one, while Adrian lay down and hung his leg over the back of the other.

Toby said, "The current clearly stimulates MGF, resulting in the formation of new memory structures—"

"Assuming the new memory stuff really works," Adrian interrupted. "Circuits and all. Statistics be damned."

"Let's assume the best. Don't let me rush you, but I can't see any reason not to proceed with the work on PGF, can you?"

Adrian lifted the second leg over the back of the couch. With his fingers knitted behind his head he was staring straight up at the clerestory windows in the atrium roof, three stories overhead.

After a moment Toby said, "Something on your mind?"

Adrian kept looking at the ceiling. "Toby, I want you to tell me what all that garbage is hanging off the end of the MGF code."

"Think of it as informational sticky ends," said Toby. "This program is going to have to link up with others."

"When we started this stage all we talked about—all I wanted—was for you to lay out a couple of simple feedback loops. We have a simple little precursor protein. We have a simple voltage trigger to split it into hormone-thingies. We just want a little something to make the memory grow. So why do I get the idea you're trying to reinvent sex?''

"I'm quite satisfied with sex the way it is," said Toby, smiling. "I'm doing away with death instead."

Adrian sucked his teeth and peered at Toby sideways. "I never heard that self-replication has to be the same as eternal life."

"No. But it does mean taking on the burden of self-directed evolution," Toby said. "A few higher species *do* actually do away with sex. None escape death. Sex speeds up evolution a bit, but death is what makes evolution go round."

"Yeah, yeah, get rid of the old to make room for the new. But who needs—"

"And that's why it's species that do the evolving, not individuals," Toby continued. "Perhaps it's even more accurate to say that it's life itself, all the life on the planet, over time, that responds to challenge by constantly evolving. The whole thing evolving at once."

"Yeah, and so what does that have to do with our custom-made cells? Nobody's asking them to do any evolving; they just have to sit there and reproduce when they're asked."

"The second law of thermodynamics—"

"This isn't a closed system," Adrian snapped.

"Do you recall the old saw about ontogeny recapitulating phylogeny?"

"Shit no." Adrian's face reflexively twisted into a sneer whenever Toby uncorked another four-bit concept he had not previously encountered.

"Well, the gist of it is that during embryonic growth an individual organism goes through all the evolutionary stages that led to the species. So a human embryo, for example, at

one stage looks like a fish, gills and all, and later an amphib-
ian, and so on.''

Adrian's nose unwrinkled. "I heard that once." He swung
his legs down and raised himself on an elbow. "Is that
true?"

"No, it's a nineteenth-century notion and so oversimpli-
fied it's practically trash." Not for the first time Toby wondered what this man had read at university. The way scientists
were trained in this country one might think that biology
sprang newly into existence with the publication of each new
college textbook—fully formed, without history, without an-
tecedents, like Athena herself. "I only meant to suggest that
the concept of *individual* evolution is after all not outlandish
or even novel. It's just that we call it development, not
evolution. Same Latin roots, by the way.''

Adrian sat up and put both feet on the floor. "I think
you're trying to tell me that what I've been thinking of as
add-ons, you think of as development, because just in getting
the new structures plugged into the net—"

"No, I'm really saying—"

"—there has to be directed development, relating the memory structures to the processors and so on.''

"—no, with respect to Project E, I really do think of it as
evolution.''

"Whatever word you want." Adrian waved his fingers
airily. "Same Latin roots, you know."

Toby laughed. "I'm serious. True, development is flexible, like evolution, and it responds to environmental pres-
sures, but there's a big difference in the level of programming.''

"Don't you really mean—?"

"Sorry, I mean the level *at which* the programming is
done. With the individual it's ultimately molecular, right
down there in the DNA of the fertilized egg; at best you
might have a metamorphosis or two written into the cycle,

but there's necessarily a preprogrammed limit to how big and complicated the brain can grow. And a preprogrammed limit on the range of possible behaviors.''

"And a preprogrammed end state. Death," said Adrian.

"Almost certainly programmed, yes.''

"Which you don't get in evolution. Which we don't need in Project E.''

"In evolution, the programming is at the level of the total system, organism plus environment—the world, which itself is always changing,'' said Toby, nodding.

"And in Project E the total system is however the stuff is being used, by whoever's using it.'' Adrian's excitement had not cooled.

"Quite. So that's where we've ultimately got to program. We can do it the messy old-fashioned general-purpose way, with a whole bunch of languages all talking up and down to one another. Or we can do something a bit more elegant, perhaps talk to all levels at once. To DNA at one end and to Mr. and Ms. User at the other. It's *our* organism, after all.''

Adrian shook his head fondly. "You're already writing it, twerp. Sneaking it by me. So that's what's with all the complication in the MGF routine.''

"You've found me out.''

"Do I get to play too?''

"I'll go home and fetch my schematics, if you like. Maybe it's not too soon to start drawing enzyme pictures.''

"You got a name for this superprogram?''

"Yes, actually. I thought I'd call it Program Interactive: Algorithmic/Juxtapositional.''

The big-words scowl returned. "Does that mean anything?''

"Not really, but it spells PIA/J.''

"I don't get it.''

"I'll tell you later.''

"Tell me now.''

Toby waved his fingers in a silent as-you-wish. "In the eighteenth century a biologist named Jean Baptiste de Lamarck theorized that all life evolves on purpose. He was brilliantly wrong, but the idea was so persistent that a century later it swayed even Darwin. And a century after that it came to influence a great Swiss developmental psychologist named Jean Piaget. Piaget was a kind of closet Lamarckian, a believer in this shadow heresy that acquired characteristics could be inherited, passed on. He was a dear tough old man, Adrian. I was his student when I was much younger, and I revered him." Toby tugged at his ear and looked at the bright, ugly, half-taught American across from him. "They say history repeats itself, Adrian, but it never does. I suspect the real value of knowing a bit of history lies in possessing this terrific stock of loony ideas—loony at the time they first make an appearance—but that with a little tinkering can be made quite workable."

"PIA/J, now I get it," said Adrian, ignoring the pitch for a liberal education. "But it isn't really going to do what you said."

"Not quite," Toby agreed. "For one thing, I don't think Mr. and Ms. User will ever actually be able to talk PIA/J's code. Unless they exchange smells with the computer or something." He grinned. "Now there's an intriguing thought. But as a practical matter they shouldn't have to. PIA/J will understand any high-level language we want."

Toby explained that as a kind of escape route or emergency entrance he would arrange things so that one could most readily communicate with PIA/J in ordinary LISP, the preferred language of the artificial intelligence community. PIA/J's internal language, however, would be quicker, richer, subtler, because the medium would be enzymic.

Its most primitive elements were already being worked out. Protein molecules, tailor-made by Adrian and contained in every discrete cell of Project E–stuff, were to be stimulated by the flow of electrical current. A high level of Memory Growth Factor in the memory system would induce Project E to build new memory units—that hurdle had just been leapt—and a high level of Processor Growth Factor would induce it to build new processors, and so on. Even with no knowledge of the precise nature of the needed computation, PIA/J should nevertheless be able to translate electrical activity into structural commands that the Project E–stuff must obey.

"So normally PIA/J is going to have no inkling of the nature of the computations it monitors," said Toby.

"So what? That's the user's business," said Adrian.

"Quite. But they'll be those times when building the proper structures depends on making judgments about the nature of the problem. That is, figuring out the user's *purpose*."

A good trick. And privately Toby wondered what would happen if PIA/J were ever to discover purpose in itself. . . .

He still wondered. He had more cause to wonder with every passing day. Though this morning he was home alone in his apartment he was not the only dreamer in the room. For two months a prototype Tyger II cartridge had resided in the middle of his cluttered dining room table. It was a bare steel rectangle, two by three inches wide and a mere quarter-inch thick, containing what the engineers called a *sloppy disk*, the crystal plate on which lived the Project E–stuff the marketing department had now officially dubbed *Epicell*.

A compound plastic tube connected the cartridge to its life-support unit, a miniature gurgling pump the size of a cigarette pack, and thin cables led to a full-sized keyboard and a two-dimensional color display, thin as a sheet of picture glass. The screen was all aflutter with an unreadable, constantly changing array of symbols.

The arrangement was awkward and messy, but as a prototype it worked fine. He'd heard that Tyger IIs were to be marketed with a miniature keyboard and a folding screen and a built-in life-support system in a package the size of a slim checkbook, and in a range of designer finishes—lizard skin, brushed aluminum, chinchilla, or something like that, whatever the consumer's pocketbook would bear. A few months thereafter, no doubt, Compugen would offer a range of peripherals—bigger keyboards, bigger monitors, printers, modems, "eternal life" support systems—toys to keep a user happy playing with the Tyger II for a long time. Nevertheless, all the computer's power would reside in the sloppy disk.

Toby didn't really care about all that, except as insight into the entrepreneurial mind. For weeks Toby had been running a limit test on the Epicell cartridge, trying to find out just how complex the bioelectronic life inside could grow before the Epicell goop showed signs of internal failure. Tyger II was being rushed toward the market so fast that the machine's true capacities had yet to be fully assessed.

Toby had a bank of cartridges chugging away in the Compugen lab, running more or less routine diagnostics, but he'd chosen to test the one here at home with geometry problems. Geometry was a sort of hobby of his, its smooth continuities affording him occasional relief from chunky binary code and the dull rigors of two-valued logic.

Toby had fed the little cartridge a few Euclidean axioms and then sat back to watch. After a week or two of unaided muddling the box had suddenly started making progress, having grown and integrated the appropriate new logic and memory units. Fairly leaping over the *pons asinorum*, the clever computer had soon propounded enough ancient theorems to fill a high-school sophomore's textbook. Toby was frankly startled by its achievement.

Then, unprompted, the Epicell–stuff began questioning Euclidean assumptions: what if parallel lines only *seemed* parallel at one place on a surface, and were convergent or divergent at another? In what sorts of spaces could such geometries be self-consistent? Toby had watched in fascination as the blob of plasma rediscovered geometries appropriate to curved spaces old Euclid, whose universe was four-square, had never dreamed of. At this rate, could topology be far behind? Or general relativity?

All of which was not to say the box was "intelligent." Everything it had done could be explained—if only in principle, and retrospectively—in abstract logical terms. Nevertheless, the Epicell material had shown something best described as ingenuity in its search for geometrical truth, and that was a sign of astonishing problem-solving power.

That no limit test had ever been completed on Epicell, however, was a sign of human haste—Chatterjee's tearing rush to get the Tyger II on the market. And the longer the limit test ran without sign of a breakdown, the more Toby wondered about his and Adrian's creation.

The phone rang. He walked across the room and scooped up the extension phone with his fingers, from its place of exile outside the bedroom door.

"Bridgeman here." He paced the living room, trailing the long cord, while Mrs. Dortmunder put her boss on the line. "Hello, Jack. . . . Very well, thanks. Looking forward to a grand show."

Chatterjee squeaked and hissed into the phone.

"I haven't noticed, really," said Toby. "I'll have a look if you like— No promises, but if I find him I'll do my best. . . . Yes. Good-bye."

Toby hung up. Jack had said he thought Adrian was throwing a tantrum. No one had seen him at Compugen in two days, and he wasn't answering his home phone.

Toby slipped on his blazer and left his apartment hurriedly, pausing long enough to set the alarm and lock his triple locks.

◆◆◆

It had been Jack Chatterjee's peculiar inspiration to combine the press conference announcing Tyger II with the first day of the new machine's initial sales conference. So what if the salespeople were unprepared to answer all the reporters' questions? Chatterjee was convinced their genuine enthusiasm would spread to the press. Indeed he was gambling on that sense of excitement combining synergistically.

The risk was less than it seemed. Distribution was already set to move Tyger II as fast as possible. The salespeople would receive thorough training within a few days, soon enough to become "experts."

Besides, Chatterjee was in a hurry.

Precisely at noon, without waiting for stragglers and with only brief preliminary remarks, he started the show.

The lights in the company's crowded auditorium dimmed. A burst of almost-in-focus color filled the giant screen behind the dais. A fully orchestrated stereophonic sound track rattled the speakers.

Compugen's media department had assembled a stirring montage of videotaped scenes portraying the design and creation of Tyger II. Spectacular computer graphics . . . assembly-line close-ups in red and gold light . . . happy young white-coated workers bent to their tasks and square-jawed executives marching briskly down busy hallways . . . seductive angles on the various models of the tiny Tygers, dressed in their leather and fur and metal "skins." All this was knit together by an on-camera interview with that handsome, charmingly British scientist Toby Bridgeman—and intercut with a few rather more distant views, in chiaroscuro, of the brooding genius Adrian Storey (he was shown peering into a microscope, his back to the camera). Finally, poured over the images like syrup over grits, was a slick professional voice-over narration. The whole show was so clichéd it was almost, perversely, ingenuous. Until the finale.

The final shot was a vastly enlarged and highly speeded-up series of frames obtained by synchrotron radiation, showing a growing, glittering bluish mass—a crystal of uniform polyhedral units—continually forming itself into tightly interlocking sheets. The sheets grew outward from the center of the screen like the widening branches of a snowflake, and eventually met other growing branches to form an open network, and then a denser, more packed layer, and then another layer on top of that, each planar structure echoing the shape of the basic polyhedrons on a grander scale. The spectacle was as sharply geometric as a Mondrian, as palely abstract as a Morris Graves.

The stuff didn't look alive, exactly. There was no quivering, no sinuosity, no hesitation to the movement of these synthetic cells, except for the random jostling flow of nutrient fluids (those swirling colors like a soap film) in which the whole structure was immersed. The little protein shells unfolded rapidly and rhythmically, like the unfolding and inflation of origami balloons, and one could imagine a rattling sound, like popcorn. But the only real sound on the tape was the music supplied by a video editor, too naïve to avoid cliché, the dolorous organ pipings of Albinoni's *Adagio*. Thus to baroque architectures of music the living machinery of Epicell erected its liquid geometries.

The newspeople in the audience began whispering to one another. "Is that what these guys are really selling? What is it exactly?"

The fruity voice of the tape's narrator supplied the answer: "Epicell. The life at the heart of a living computer. It may change all our lives, in ways we can as yet hardly imagine."

The projection went dark then, and a crisp circle of straw-colored light fell on a pedestal that rose from the floor of the dais. On the slender pedestal, almost too small to see clearly from the front row, was a shiny new Tyger II.

The salespeople broke into impassioned applause, and a few of the less jaded news types actually joined in.

Toby steered his blue BMW to a stop at the end of the muddy driveway, turned off the ignition, and sat contemplating Adrian's house on the slope below. It was after noon, and there was no sign of life. But Adrian's dented brown Saab was parked in the lean-to garage at the foot of the hill.

On the phone Chatterjee had insinuated that Adrian was being his usual juvenile self, trying to embarrass the company. Plausible, but the more Toby thought about it the more he wondered. Adrian had stayed away from work on other occasions, sulking, staging personal boycotts, but he had never failed to make his reasons clear.

Reluctantly Toby got out of his car.

It had rained off and on for a week, but the sun had been out all morning, and it was hot. He stepped gingerly down the steep track to Adrian's door, trying to keep his glove-leather Italian loafers out of the chocolate-mousse muck. The crooked house loomed before him, an image of its owner's mind—a corner broken from a hologram, capable of reproducing the whole jagged three-dimensional image in coarse resolution.

The site in the Berkeley Hills was bordered by wooded watershed lands, isolated from its neighbors; its original structure was a clapboard cottage, with a twenty-year-old coat of peeling white paint and a peaked roof of green asphalt paper now as lumpy as thatch. But erupting from the roof and sides of this ur-house was a forest of raw posts and beams, three stories of framework for a hedonistic redwood-and-glass bachelor pad of the future.

It would probably always be of the future. A couple of walls, half a floor, and a third of the roof had been completed, but the rest was a patchwork of crossbraces and tattered polyethylene film that flapped in the wind and did little to keep out winter rains. On a stormy night the edifice resembled nothing so much as Frankenstein's laboratory, open to the elements.

Toby knocked on the door. Hearing no reply, he stretched for the extra-high top step and went in. . . .

In the darkness below, Adrian heard the footsteps on the porch, the knock on the door. The alarm whistle screamed, and a few moments later fell silent.

Only Toby knew his alarm code. His friend Toby had come at last.

It seemed easy—he started to get up from the bed. Oh, but he was sore; the long muscles in his back were ropes of fire. He tried to inhale through his nose, but it was thoroughly stuffed. An acrid, nauseatingly sweet-sour liquid flooded the back of his palate. He fell back against the bed to rest again.

He had not moved more than an inch, and already he'd forgotten why he'd wanted to.

Toby's heels knocked the boards over his head. . . .

"Adrian?"

A gust of wind set the house timbers to creaking. The entrance, on the level above the cottage roof, was a corridor of unpainted plywood with a layer of dried mud on the floor. Toby went deeper into the house. He came to the partly finished living room, high-ceilinged, walled on two sides with glass, with a third wall faced in silvery insulation material. On the oak floor lay a magnificent Afghan rug, impacted with mud. Through the smeared windows a shaft of sunlight made the shambles plain.

On a table in the angle of the glass walls sprawled an old Tyger terminal and its peripherals, along with a handful of Epicell sloppy disks in various states of repair.

Beside the desk, a fat red Celestron telescope with a Nikon camera screwed to the eyepiece perched on its tripod, commanding a view of a thousand square miles of cities and bay. From the sharply depressed angle of the telescope, however, Toby judged it was focused on the back windows of Adrian's downslope neighbors. In another corner of the room sat a heap of professional-quality audio and video components, coated with dust and smeared with fingerprints. A tall metal Erecta-Shelf bookcase was stocked exclusively with engineering manuals and pornography.

The first time he'd been in Adrian's house Adrian had sat Toby down in the room's only chair, a chrome and black-leather construction impossible to climb out of, and made him look at his big color "art" books. Some of them—the Japanese prints, a few European items from early in the century—*were* art. All depicted scenes of considerable technical interest to students of human behavior. Toby had blushed madly as he'd turned the pages, making mental notes almost in spite of himself, meanwhile trying to appreciate the fact that Adrian was not trying to seduce him but was, in his inimitably cross-wired fashion, simply hoping to communicate that his own nature was as human as Toby's. In Adrian's nearly thirty years he must have had cause to doubt it from time to time.

Adrian had told him so in so many words. But the solution to Adrian's problems lay deeper than, say, introductions to a few friendly young women.

As Tyger II's announcement day approached, Toby found that Adrian was burdened with more and more to do while he had less and less. PIA/J was essentially complete; Adrian, however, struggled to perfect the protein structures of the novel life form known as Epicell—what amounted to performing a new act of creation on a deadline.

Toby tried to steal a little time to write up his own academicized description of what they'd achieved, but most of his time was taken up with the screeching boredom of interviews with Compugen staff writers, who were desperately trying to prepare supporting documentation and promotional material for the Tyger II. Near the end of one frustrating morning with a polite but persistent woman who was determined to get down on paper the amino acid sequence of every enzyme in PIA/J's repertoire, he'd had to shake himself loose with a phony plea to visit the loo.

He dropped into the graphics room instead and found Adrian staring at the screens—just sitting there, doing nothing. He looked exhausted, as if he'd been there all night, and Toby saw that his friend's cheeks were streaked with moisture.

"Could I talk to you, Toby? Somewhere away from here?" The plea seemed to come from a great way off in the darkness.

"Certainly, Adrian, anywhere you say."

"Buy me a drink."

"It's still morning," said Toby, genuinely surprised. Adrian rarely drank anything stronger than beer.

"Yeah?" Adrian's bleary eyes said that he didn't know what time it was and didn't care.

"All right, you're on." Toby's apartment was only a mile away, closer than the nearest decent bar. "Come over to my place."

Adrian followed Toby home. As soon as he got in the door he made for Toby's leather pillow sofa and sprawled on it, thrusting his big hands deep into the pockets of his ragged jeans. His heels lolled on the carpet, the frayed toes of his enormous feet rising almost to his eye level. Through the gap between them he seemed to be eyeing the cold abstract paintings on Toby's walls.

Meanwhile Toby bustled around, being a host, bringing a tray heaped with burned muffins and a pot of marmalade and a carton of reconstituted orange juice. "Eat, will you? You've not been taking care of yourself."

Adrian raised himself on an elbow. "What are you, some kind of Jewish mother?" He sounded surly, but it was as close as he could get to "thanks."

Toby smiled. "You might say so." Adrian couldn't be expected to remember his own mother all that well.

Toby, persuaded that much of his friend's fits of depression could be ascribed to overwork and undernourishment, watched happily as Adrian devoured a muffin, then downed a tall glass of orange juice, his Adam's apple bobbing mightily.

Satisfied, Adrian inspected his surroundings. With interest he asked, "You get a lot of girls on this sofa, Toby? They must go for the leather, huh? On their bare—"

"I don't invite women here," said Toby hastily. "That often."

"You billy goat." Adrian rubbed the leather cushions.

"When I get my place done—" He broke off, paused a moment. "Shit, it won't make any difference if I get it done or not. I scare them off. No matter how ugly they are, nobody's uglier than me."

The mournful goof looked so much like a sad basset that Toby had to suppress a laugh. "You're rather abrupt, you know. You can be a bit frightening. To people who don't know you."

"Not to mention the people who *do* know me."

"You wanted to talk, Adrian?" Toby asked, after a moment's silence.

"Yeah. That shitty little box. Chatterjee's kluge."

"You can't sell people what they can't see; they have to have a pretty box to keep it in."

"One deliberately crippled bag."

"Real problems?"

"Damn it, it's not *done* yet!" Adrian yelled.

Pure temper. Toby watched as Adrian squirmed on the pillow sofa, apparently unable to get comfortable. These past weeks Adrian's refrain had been *it's not done yet*, but that had also been his refrain in the weeks before the release of the original Tyger, or so Toby had had it on good authority— from Jack Chatterjee, among others—and it was apparently simply impossible for Adrian to be satisfied that any product was ready to go to market. Toby cleared his throat, hoping he wasn't being ostentatious about it. "I thought perhaps you had something else on your mind."

"Want me out of here already?" Adrian said sharply. He tugged his ankles toward him, twisting himself into a parody of Toby's neat half lotus. "It's my birthday," he said with a pout.

"Congratulations."

"I'm twenty-eight." Released from tension, his bent leg shot out sideways. He stretched out lengthwise on the couch, rolled on his side. "You don't think women are worth talking about?"

"Endlessly." Toby grinned impishly. "Don't tell me that's what really *is* on your mind."

"Why not?" Adrian demanded. "I look like a freak, but I'm all here. Everything *works*, it just doesn't get much *use*."

Toby rocked forward on his ankles, laughing. "Sorry," he said, "but it's true, we're so easily humiliated. I doubt that most women have the slightest idea." If Adrian wanted to talk about women, Toby could certainly humor him. "And those who do haven't any means of gauging their effect—the wreckage they leave in their wakes."

Adrian licked his teeth. "If they didn't fuck, nobody would talk to them."

"Spoken like a lonely man," said Toby. His grin faded. "It's that kind of thinking keeps you a lonely man, my friend. Not your slovenly costume. Not even your appalling manners."

"Don't stop there," Adrian said belligerently. "You're the expert."

"For God's sake, Adrian, women are people. Human beings. They simply wish to be treated that way."

Adrian twisted his face into a sneer. "Very amusing."

"Usually not. What reams of nonsense have been written about the biological urges of women." Christ, thought Toby, he's trained me to make speeches at the curl of a lip. "Yes, being human, they enjoy companionship—some of the time. Being human, many of them wish to reproduce themselves—but not all of them. I believe you've felt that particular urge, Adrian. I'm sure you have. And I don't mean sex. But because they bear the children, women are often stuck with raising them. Thus the vaunted 'maternal instinct.' "

Adrian was hanging on his every word. He really did

regard him as an expert. Toby felt a bit of a charlatan, because he wasn't sure he believed half of what he was saying. Women *were*—well, at least they did *seem*—different. When you studied the matter. But that was the last thing Adrian needed to hear. And the differences were certainly not those usually named.

He plunged on. "If you want to see biological urge run rampant, look at us men. Helpless liars, desperate to appear rational at any cost, in order to hide our shame. Where we cannot manage to disguise our obsession—having locked ourselves away in monasteries, or having driven our companions away, or in our last-ditch panic, or perhaps in despair—we reproduce ourselves on inanimate matter. Paintings. Statues. Blank sheets of paper which we cover with ink. Or like you and me, on thinking machines."

"Women do that stuff too."

"Of course they do; they really are very much like us. But I doubt they feel the same desperation."

Adrian thought about all that awhile. Then he said, "Shit, you left out my favorite part."

"Oh?" Toby, who had actually gotten quite excited but was calmer now, tried to sound nonchalant. "What part was that?"

"The part about love." Adrian rolled his eyeballs in mock horror. "All my foster mothers get to that part. Where you tell me I don't understand the meaning of the word *love*."

"Would I ever be so arrogant?"

And then Adrian had grinned at him. "Oh, you would. Despite your charm, you're an arrogant little fucker. . . ."

"Adrian, are you in?"

To Toby's left was a staircase. He descended cautiously—it had no railing—and felt for the string of the overhead bulb he knew was down here somewhere. The cottage below was as

dark as night; the dangling string brushed his face and he
batted at it, momentarily taking it for a spider's web. When
he pulled the string, the clear hundred-watt bulb threw stark
light on the cluttered counters and cabinets of Adrian's narrow kitchen.

The far end of the kitchen opened into the old cottage's
gutted interior, a labyrinth of sawhorses, loose planks, stacks
of Sheetrock, cans of paint. Toby went through, moving
slowly into the shadows.

He found a door on the far side of the maze, opened it a
crack, and peered in: Adrian's bedroom, unfurnished except
for shelves of bricks and boards and a mattress on the floor.
Adrian was lying on it.

"Are you all right, old man?" Toby asked.

Adrian was wearing the same clothes Toby had last seen
him in two days ago: a worn corduroy jacket over a plaid
flannel shirt, shapeless blue jeans, the same threadbare running shoes with splayed rubber soles, barely big enough to
contain his enormous feet. The smell in the room was suspiciously thick.

"None . . . of your . . ."—Adrian's mouth worked slowly
to form the words—"fuck-ing . . . busi—"

"Adrian, for God's sake," said Toby, pushing into the
room. He took Adrian by the armpit and tugged.

Adrian paid him no attention. Drunk? Sick? Toby was
strong for his size; he pulled harder, got Adrian to a sitting
position, finally managed to urge him to his feet. "How do
you feel? Can you stand up?"

Adrian pulled his arm away, irritably. "You're not my
nanny, you little Brit."

"Ah, you've decided to be reasonable. Out of those stinking rags, then, and into a hot shower. Come on with you, off
to the bathroom."

Adrian scowled and looked as if he were about to start a fight.

He's an ugly brute, thought Toby, looking up into his friend's unshaven face. Someone only a mother could love.

Adrian grunted and turned wordlessly away, stumbling out into the darkness, toward a bathroom hidden somewhere in the gloom.

Toby went to the bedroom's walk-in closet and shouldered the folding doors open against a drift of dirty laundry. In Adrian's meager wardrobe he found a brown tweed sport coat and a pair of tan chino slacks, wrinkled but fairly clean. In the pile of clothes on the floor was a permanent-press shirt, approximately white, and at the back of the closet, hanging from a ten-penny nail, a clot of neckties. Toby selected one of red silk, bearing the insignia of an engineering fraternity; the others were all four inches wide and made of something that looked like Spandex.

He found the bathroom by the sound of running water. "Put these on when you get out," he called into the steam, placing the folded clothes on the toilet seat. Adrian, invisible behind the frosted glass of the shower stall, made no reply.

Toby explored the rancid kitchen, searching for coffee. He located a two-pound bag of filter grind in the freezer compartment of the refrigerator, one of Adrian's favorite hiding places. Once, in the freezer of Adrian's personal laboratory refrigerator, tipped off by an informant, he'd found the manuscript of an article he and Adrian had written, which Adrian had claimed was lost by the post office.

He quickly boiled a pot of water on the big restaurant-style gas range and made a Chemex of passably good French roast.

He took a mugful back to the bathroom. Water still thundered from the shower head; the fog was impenetrable. He put the coffee mug on the back of the toilet, slipped out of his blazer, rolled up his sleeve, and reached a hand into the shower stall. A bit of fumbling, then he found the taps and turned off the water.

Adrian stared down at him, dripping.

"Are you quite sure you're all right, Adrian?"

Adrian blinked. "Think I got a bad cold, Toby."

"That's too bad. But not worth missing the fun for, is it? This is your day, Adrian."

Adrian looked at him solemnly.

"Well, dry off then. And get dressed." Toby struggled back into his jacket. "And do move along, will you? Chatterjee is having a fit."

Adrian frowned. "Greasy clam-ass. Idiotic schedules and flow charts. Turned my machine into the ultimate kluge."

"That's better," said Toby, relieved. Adrian was only sulking after all. "See you in ten minutes, upstairs."

Adrian grumbled something Toby took for yes. Toby went back into the kitchen and poured himself a cup of coffee, then went up the stairs.

Before he reached the living room he heard the telephone ringing. He hurried to it. "Hello?"

"Ah, yes, I had hoped to find you there." It was Jack Chatterjee's sibilant voice. "What's become of our friend Dr. Storey? Did he break a shoelace and despair of repairing it?"

"He's getting dressed now, Jack."

"The movies are over, Toby. I need *you* here in ten minutes, with or without our erratic genius."

"We'll be there together, Jack." Toby allowed himself a *soupçon* of crispness; he was still a consultant to Compugen, not an employee, and the distinction made a difference, at least to him. "Within a reasonable time."

After the merest hesitation, and without another word, Chatterjee hung up.

"Arrogant . . . sod," Toby said to himself, choosing the

obscenity over the racist term that came so naturally. Whatever he was, Chatterjee was no contemptible wog. Toby
carefully replaced the phone. He sipped at his coffee and
looked out on the glorious scene—the hills, the bridges, the
ships at anchor, the cities of the Bay white in the rain-washed
air, glistening in the spring sunlight.

He heard footsteps on the stair. Adrian appeared, his frizzy
hair rising above the floor's horizon, followed by his lumpy
face, and then by the rest of him, jacketed and trousered,
shirted and tied. His feet came last, white-socked and
track-shoed.

Toby smiled. Let it be, he thought, lest a too-respectable
appearance betray *le vrai Adrian*. "Ready to let yourself be
applauded?"

"Salesmen. What do they know?"

"More than the press, my friend. You're not leaving me to
face them alone."

"They won't listen to either of us. Fast-talking pricks."

"They love you, Adrian. God knows why." A few of
them do, at least. "Your picaresque charm, perhaps."

Adrian did not move. Insulted? Toby leaned forward, noted
that Adrian's pupils were slowly dilating.

A trick. "*Adrian*"—Toby's temper started to ravel at the
edges—"what the devil's the matter with you? Really, you're
not still moping?" He discarded his coffee mug on the table
that held the Tyger, ready to leave the house without his
friend. "You may fool others, but I—"

Adrian's eyes refocused, and his thick lips curled into
something between a sneer and a grin. "You're not so smart,
you randy little twerp. Still rushin' that cute piece of ass from
Atlanta?" Adrian leaned forward aggressively. "That why
you're in such a horny hurry?"

Toby colored. "Do watch your tongue."

Adrian stuck out a very long pink tongue and wiggled it suggestively, then abruptly crossed his eyes.

"Lord save us," Toby muttered. He took Adrian by the elbow and steered him toward the front door.

◆◆◆

Along with providing the usual facilities for the print media, Compugen's press officers handed out copies of the videotapes they'd just played to any TV reporters who asked for them, and offered satellite services to crews who needed it. The smaller TV stations would run the tapes virtually unedited, giving away publicity equivalent to hundreds of thousands of dollars of paid advertising.

Meanwhile, Jack Chatterjee herded everybody into the corporate lounge, where caterers had laid out an opulent display of canapés: clever unidentifiable tidbits wrapped in bacon and speared with colored plastic toothpicks, exotic marinated vegetables, expensive cheeses, miniature puff pastries filled with salty Asian somethings, little sausages swimming in sauce, sculpted mounds of pâté garnished with pimientos and sliced eggs, and a good deal more. While Chatterjee didn't encourage the consumption of alcohol, he could hardly forbid it, and there was an excellent selection of North Coast wines and champagnes. A hundred excited men and women crowded into the corporate lounge—all but those reporters with deadlines to meet—and rushed the buffet.

Harold Lillard from Boston stood at one edge of the crowd and happily munched on a Chinese sticky bun, staring through the windows of the lounge at the wide lawn outside. Harold was grateful for the chance to eat. His internal clock was still running on Eastern time; he'd gone to bed at nine last night, exhausted, and arisen this morning, red-eyed and restless, at four. His skimpy coffee-shop breakfast was too many hours behind him.

The lawn he studied so absently was new, striped in parallel stripes where thick rolls of sod had been laid down the previous autumn; it fell away in metrically perfect contours to the nearby shores of Aquatic Park, a remnant of tidal mudflats confined between the railroad tracks immediately to the east and the causeway of busy Interstate 80 to the west. Beyond the multilaned highway lay the sparkling waters of San Francisco Bay. The murky lagoon, bordered by imported ornamental trees and surrounded by a clutter of light industry, managed to project a sense of its origins: its muddy shores, patted slick by the webbed feet of countless coots and mallards and shore birds, stank of the primal ooze.

Harold didn't notice the smell. He noticed the heat. It was the end of March, and California was as hot as Massachusetts on a June morning. He wished he'd thought to bring his Palm Beach suits.

"What'd you think of the show, Harry?" It was Marv Butterfield from Los Angeles, swathed in a double-breasted black-and-white houndstooth-check jacket of some synthetic material. White cuffed trousers over saddle shoes. Pink shirt, white tie the width of a garrote.

"Great, Marv." *Is this the new wave? Is everybody going to dress like this out here?* "All the coverage should help us sell a few."

"Hell, this thing is going to sell itself," said diminutive Marv, sliding his palm along a wing of wavy blond hair. "It does everything by itself. 'The computer that learns as it grows and grows as it learns.' Got to hand it to the ad boys—how'd they think of a line like that?"

"Maybe it just came to them. That one piece of videotape, what was it, x rays? That was pretty convincing."

"Convincing? It was spectacular. The only thing worries me"—Butterfield leaned forward, whispering in mock conspiracy—"how long's it going to take Whisperin' Jack to figure out his sales force is redundant?"

"Marv, I've been hearing talk like that since I was a kid. Computers don't replace people. They make people powerful."

"Some they make powerful. Some they replace. But I won't argue with you, Harry. Either way, there's never been a computer like this one." Butterfield's glance shifted to the tables of food. "Guess I'll grab something to eat."

"Later, Marv." Harold slipped a hand into his trouser pocket and jingled a stack of quarters. Again he looked out the windows. The lagoon's colloidal waters seemed illusory in the direct sunlight, like the iridescent surface of a cup of coffee. Harold was normally insensitive to life's minor unpleasantnesses, but he could smell the fecund mud now, a sort of reminder of life's gloppy fundamentals. He slid a finger between his collar and his throat. Damn, it was hot.

Harold preferred New England, despite its savage weather. He knew what to expect there. Every time he came out to California, twice a year or so, people had changed again— new clothing styles, new haircuts, new buzzwords. Look at Marv.

Not that Harold was afraid of change, or he wouldn't have lasted a month in computer sales. But he liked to see change in the right direction. Progress was what Harold liked, not movement for its own sake. . . .

"Still saving quarters, Harry?" Jack Chatterjee had slipped up beside him unseen. The way he snuck up on people, you'd think he'd come to recover the idol's eye.

"For the kids' sake, Jack. Sets an example," said Harold. "I put the oldest daughter through Boston College on quarters."

"So you told me. When we met," Chatterjee said in that insinuating half whisper of his. "But not nickels or dimes. You had a theory."

"Yeah, the little stuff's not worth the effort. The kids bring me their small change, I put quarters in their banks. My fifteen-year-old just bought himself a slalom water-ski. Preseason sale."

"A wise shopper." Chatterjee revealed small ivory-colored teeth in a predatory smile, and patted Harold on the shoulder. "May they all—six . . . ?"

"Seven," Harold said diffidently. Not to mention the one on the way.

"May all seven be as successful as you, Harry."

"Any success I have is thanks to you, Jack."

"The fun's just beginning," murmured Chatterjee. Already his glittering brown eyes were scanning the crowd; they fixed on the CNN science reporter, a few yards away at the buffet table. "Later, Harry." Even as he stepped away his fingers lingered on Harold's shoulder, as if testing the quality of the brown wool suit.

Harold wondered if he should have worn a better suit. He'd never been a snappy dresser exactly, and as a representative of Compugen, in this suit . . . but he caught himself. That was Jack's way, leaving you to think you could have done something, anything, a little better. And he did it so subtly, maybe even unconsciously, he always made you think it was your own idea.

Ruth Slatkin from Atlanta wandered past, suppressing a tiny yawn with the tips of her delicate manicured fingers; the nails were lacquered blood red. She caught Harold smiling at her and smiled back. He took a step in her direction, suppressing a twinge of involuntary masculine response to this trim young saleswoman, who was barely older than his oldest daughter.

"Working too hard?" he asked sympathetically.

"Something like that," she replied dryly. "How's business in Boston?"

"Never better. I sold two of the DX models last week. Before I ever laid eyes on them."

"Oh?" Ruth's thin black brows lifted above her mascara-empurpled eyes. "Who got the early word? The security was supposed to be fantastic."

"Between you and me, ERMIT is the firm buyer." Harold jingled his quarters. "Government stuff. Hush-hush."

Ruth seemed unimpressed. She glanced around the uncomfortably crowded room. "Where's our star? All the years I've been with this company I've never known Chatterjee's shows to get behind schedule."

All her years with this company amounted to maybe three. But Harold had to admit, that was long enough, in this business. "I haven't seen Bridgeman or Storey yet, if that's who you mean."

"Toby did all the software. He invented PIA/J." She seemed to be taking his accomplishments personally.

"I like Storey too. He's a kick."

Ruth wrinkled her nose. "He's a *nut*, Harry. In Chicago year before last he tore down a twenty-foot screen just because his slides got mixed up in the projector. Fell all over him. I thought they kept him in a cage."

"Not exactly a company man," Harold said with a grin. "But if anybody's really responsible for the Tygers—one man, I mean—then Adrian Storey's the guy."

"That's not a selling point, Harry," said Ruth. "Not a

selling point at all. 'Scuse me. I was on the way to the john.''

He watched her leave, shrugged it off. Ruth had known nothing but the good times; she wasn't around when Compugen was heading for the slumps. Maybe Adrian was weird, but Harold and a few other old-timers liked him plenty—he'd saved them from the poorhouse.

He returned to the buffet and loaded a plate with sausages.

As Harold turned away from the buffet table he saw Bridgeman and Storey enter the room from the lobby. The crowd broke into spontaneous applause.

Jack Chatterjee appeared by their sides almost at once. "Ladies and gentlemen," he said, straining to lift his voice to a normal speaking volume. "No more speeches. But allow me to present the two fellows most responsible for building the machine that will carry our company forward into the next decade. Come and say hello, that's why they're here. To greet you. To get to know you." Chatterjee stepped away then, leaving the new arrivals to the mob.

A knot of admirers followed Toby to the buffet table. Harold hovered nearby, listening in.

"Joel Harris, ABC News. I need to ask you a good deal more about PIA/J, Dr. Bridgeman—"

"Call me Toby, please," said Bridgeman, smiling past the questioner at the loaded buffet table.

The reporter was square-jawed, tweedy, and rude. "About PIA/J. First of all, what does that stand for?"

"A little joke, really. You've heard of Jean Piaget, the Swiss psychologist? Surely you have. The letters themselves—but I say, is that smoked salmon? I must have some. Adrian, you have some of this too, you must be starved." Toby fastened his attention on the food and began filling a plate.

The crush was oppressive. By the time Toby turned in his direction, Adrian was on the edge of the crowd; somehow the mass of people had nucleated around Toby and, like a swarm of protein granules inside a cell, expelled Adrian as if he were an inert lump, a foreign object. Nothing personal.

Meanwhile Harold had circled the mob and come up on Adrian. "Dr. Storey, I'm Harold Lillard. From Boston. I don't know if you remember me, but I've been an admirer of yours for many years. You must be very proud."

Adrian blinked and stared down at Harold. Harold was an expansive man, but Adrian's height and expressionless gaze made him feel small. Adrian said, "What?"

"You must be very proud of your achievement. Designing Epicell. It's a wonderful step forward."

"Piece of shit."

Harold's friendly smile froze, and two newspaper reporters, the only other people left in Adrian's vicinity, decided they had better things to do. "Uh, not the Tyger II, surely? Everything we've heard—"

"Bullshit."

Harold's winter pallor turned pink, but he renewed his determination to be nice—nobody else was going to be. "This computer is truly revolutionary, Dr. Storey. It's almost as cheap as a Python, it's user-friendly, it expands without costing the owner an extra two bits." Harold jiggled his quarters enthusiastically, selling Adrian Storey on his own invention. "The potential uses of the Tyger II are virtually innumerable—in commerce, in science and medicine, in government and education. Every artist and writer will be able to afford one of these. You've ushered in a new era of—"

"Don't you know what shit is?" Adrian asked mildly, offering useful information. "Organic matter, typically brown and viscid. Don't get too close, it'll stick to you. It stinks." Adrian kept staring at Harold, as if searching his face for clues. "I smell it, you know," Adrian confided. "It's all around here. In my considered opinion, the rest are pretend-

ing. Come, come here.'' Adrian's knobby fingers clutched
Harold's arm in a painful grip; he turned away, dragging
Harold after him.

Adrian took big strides, but his rubber running shoes scuffed
the gray carpet. Harold had never noticed how pigeon-toed
Adrian was.

Adrian brought him to the wall of glass overlooking the
lawn and the lake. ''*See?*''—a whisper, almost a hiss—
''Dribble, dribble.'' Adrian's expression was fierce; he held
a bony finger to his rubbery lips and squeezed Harold's arm.
A sly look came over his features and he turned away,
fiddling with the latch of a sliding door with one hand,
keeping his movements out of Harold's sight. ''Disarm security. All opens before us.'' He pulled the door open a crack
and turned back to Harold, grinning. ''Heh?''

Harold, mesmerized by Adrian's bulging eyes and flaring,
static-charged hair, slid his glance sidelong to peer through
the crack in the door. Heat pushed into the room. The mud
smell was strong.

''*Eh?*'' Adrian jostled Harold's arm.

Harold had begun to consider whether the conversation
might be taking a nonproductive turn. He prepared to pull
away from Adrian's grip, but Adrian held him fast.

''Look at them. You understand now, don't you?'' Adrian
was peering suspiciously at the crowd around the buffet table;
Harold followed his gaze. Toby Bridgeman was talking a
mile a minute to a fascinated group of listeners, intermittently
glancing curiously in Adrian's direction.

No one else seemed to be paying any attention to Harold
and his friendly captor except Jack Chatterjee, surrounded by
his own knot of sycophants. Jack's dark brown eyes stared in
their direction with what seemed to Harold like a mixture of
concern and disapproval.

At the buffet, meanwhile, Toby had decided that even if

Adrian wasn't hungry, he was ravenous. Reaching around his aggressive questioner to get at the herb cheese, Toby's gaze fell full upon a striking strawberry blonde in a blue silk blouse. She seemed to be watching him with amusement.

He neatly shouldered Harris, the reporter, out of the way to get closer to her. "You're not one of these reporters, are you?" he asked. "You couldn't be—cynicism hasn't permanently twisted your smile."

"Very graceful, Dr. Bridgeman. My name's Joana Davies. I'm from the clinic."

"And my name is Toby. The clinic?"

"The Leigh-Mercy Clinic of the Chatterjee Cognitive Research Foundation," she recited, mocking the jawbreaking designation with the lilt of her voice. "Surely you've heard of us. We're just up the road."

He shrugged. "Something. Vaguely. And what do you do there, Joana. May I call you that?"

"If you like. I look after people."

"I see." Evasive. A nurse, then? He hesitated a mere fraction of a second, then went on smoothly, rather grandly, "Well, we're certainly honored by your presence." The gorgeous blonde had freckles, he noted, but her gorgeousness was unaffected thereby. With the lightest of touches on her elbow he moved her farther down the table, toward the champagne. "Are you interested in computers?"

She smiled thinly. "No. The clinic being what it is, we're forced to learn, though. Some software, simple programming."

"Champagne?" he asked. He reached for a glass of Domaine Chandon, which a smiling waiter pushed forward on the cloth. She shook her head once, economically. He set his plate aside and sipped at the glass himself. "What sort of programs do you write?"

"After two months of BASIC?" She smiled again. "I can write a good game of Hangman. Beyond that, well . . .''

"BASIC's a waste of your time," Toby said severely. "You'll pick up all sorts of bad habits."

"You sound offended."

"BASIC was written to make primitive machinery accessible to people who did not intend to make a career in programming. Machines are no longer primitive, yet the public seems to have gotten stuck with BASIC."

"You prefer something tidier? Logically?" She looked at him with eyes he could only think of as tawny. Perhaps it was the room's indirect lighting.

He nodded. "Before knowledge comes computation." Then, ruefully, he said, "But why am I talking shop?"

She cocked an eyebrow and said nothing.

"I mean to say, this is a fascinating topic, but really, I'd much rather pursue it at greater length another time. Would you like—?"

"If you wish," she said, interrupting him swiftly. "But I certainly don't mind talking about it now. In fact, Dr. Bridgeman, in view of various remarks of yours on that videotape, I'm curious to see if the man who so quaintly named a program *Piaget* has any sense of Piaget's real accomplishment."

Toby blinked. The gorgeous blonde had freckles and tawny eyes, and little tolerance for pomposity. "As a matter of fact, I'm very familiar with his work," he said defensively. "I even knew him, slightly, as a student. I admired him—as one admires any pioneer. . . ." He faltered, distracted.

Ruth Slatkin had materialized at his elbow. "I hope I'm not intruding," she said with edged sweetness. She leaned her dark head against Toby's arm.

"Ruth, how good to find you here," he mumbled, irrationally. In the midst of his mild confusion—this sort of scene had happened so many times in his life he'd lost count—he saw the skin at the corners of those tawny eyes crinkle. The woman was actually amused. "This is Joana, uh, I beg your pardon . . ."

"Joana Davies," she said, holding out her hand.

"Ruth Slatkin. So nice." They shook hands. Ruth kept her eyes on Joana, even as she turned her head slowly in Toby's direction, rubbing his shoulder with her cheek. Then she turned away, in a calculated attempt to dismiss the new-comer. "Tell me, Toby, how are the Europeans?"

"The who?" He remembered he was supposed to be meet-ing the mythical Europeans for lunch. "Oh, yes, well, I'll have to see, won't I?"

"It would be so nice if you could get away. I'm utterly famished."

"Ruth, I can't go just yet." He turned to smile winsomely at Joana Davies. But the gorgeous blonde was moving away, no longer looking at him, and what he could see of her face was quite without expression. Toby turned back to Ruth. "I owe it to Jack."

Her look was bleak. He glanced away. At his opposite elbow a man was asking him a question, something about Epicell, and with relief he launched into a rote reply: ". . . small packet of synthetic genes, designed by us, string of DNA. How's that herb cheese? Looks simply delightful. Mmm—growth program at the simplest level. Morphology a bit more complex. . . . Ruth, be a dear, get me one of those oyster things, will you? Thanks so much."

Mrs. Dortmunder stood in the doorway, bouncing on her toes and waving to Chatterjee. Chatterjee nodded and walked to the circle surrounding Bridgeman, and laid a hand on the shoulder of the man nearest him, who was laughing at one of Toby's pleasantries. Silence spread away from him, like ripples from a pebble dropped into a pond.

He waited until he had everyone's attention. "In half an hour we'll begin limousine service to San Francisco and the airports, for those of you who need it. Anyone wishing to make interview appointments or other arrangements, Public Affairs will be glad to help you. Now thank you all for coming. Enjoy yourselves."

Chatterjee abruptly fell silent. After a spatter of applause, conversation fumbled and resumed.

Ruth took advantage of the lull to whisper in Toby's ear, "I have to see you. Alone. Before another minute passes."

"I really must excuse myself," Toby said to the man who was talking at him, interrupting him in midquestion. Turning, he smiled his way out of the crowd.

Adrian watched intently as Ruth and Toby left the room. Then he walked to where Jack Chatterjee was standing momentarily alone.

"Something I must tell you, Jack. Can't wait any longer." Jack looked at him oddly as Adrian reached out and took him by the elbow. Adrian was quiet for a moment, as if searching for the right words; then, with an expression of secret amusement, he confided in his captive. "Semiotic restructuring requires retrenching on the part of all analyzers. Heh?"

Chatterjee's brown eyes widened. "I beg your pardon, Adrian."

"Do you need a demonstration?" Adrian abruptly released his hold on Chatterjee and lurched swiftly toward the buffet table.

Around the corner, in the lobby, Toby paused. "What is it, Ruth?" His smile was wary as he watched her approach.

She leaned toward him, tense and pale. "After last night, I thought you and I were special to each other, Toby."

"Ruth, my schedule today has been simply—"

"You're a liar, but you're making *me* face the truth." Under her vivid make-up her face was white, her expression quivering between anger and tears. She settled on anger. "Hell, why should I waste my time on you?"

He said nothing, waiting. His face was so composed, so interested, so polite, she could have read his expression as mockery.

She squared her tailored shoulders and took a backward step. "What a waxy-smooth surface you have, Toby Bridgeman. What charm. And so accommodating. You let me make of you what I wanted, didn't you? And it never touched you."

"Ruth, I'm terribly sorry if somehow—"

"Forget it." Emitting one barely audible little bleat, half hiccup, half sob, she turned and walked smartly away.

In the lounge, Adrian had shouldered a white-coated caterer roughly aside and dipped one long-fingered hand into a steam tray of sausage links. He took a handful of the dripping brown cylinders, brought them to his nose, and sniffed.

"Turds," he announced loudly. "Have one," he suggested to a man across the table. "Have several."

The man studied the sausages as if seriously considering the offer. Clear grease clotted with carbonized solids dripped onto the heavy white tablecloth. His eyes shifting rapidly, the man backed away.

In the lobby, Toby watched Ruth go. Slowly the tension between his shoulder blades uncoupled. Heavens, that had been awfully easy—he'd expected the worst. But these saleswomen were tough specimens. Thank God.

Then, from the direction of the lounge, he heard a woman's scream. He felt an urge to run and hide, and resisted it. Too easy. Too easy, after all.

Jack Chatterjee was moving swiftly around the end of the buffet. "Adrian, don't play with the food."

But Adrian danced away from him. "You then," he shouted at a frantic Mrs. Dortmunder. "Proportionate erosion of idiosyncratic ideologic expressionism vis-à-vis gynecologic ur-fact, am I right?" With that he lofted the sausages in her direction, lightly, as if free-throwing a basketball over the heads of the crowd. For an instant his lanky frame hovered in midpirouette, a balletic caricature, until the toe of one rubber-soled shoe caught in the carpet. He tumbled to the floor majestically, like a falling tree.

Meanwhile the tubes of meat spun in the air, spattering the crowd with drops of fat. Mrs. Dortmunder screamed again and dodged.

Toby Bridgeman rushed in, prepared for the worst that he could imagine—a scene with Ruth. At first he was desperately pleased to see that she was not the cause of the commotion. Then he saw who was.

Adrian was scrambling to his feet, holding out his big hands to ward off Jack Chatterjee. But Chatterjee had decided not to risk his dignity further. Adrian's legs buckled under him, but he recovered, and with an extraordinary rubbery stride he made for the glass doors.

Harold Lillard moved out of his way at the last moment, realizing that Adrian was walking right into him. Adrian bounced from both sides of the frame of the glass door before managing to squeeze through, tearing the shoulder of his jacket. At last he ejected himself onto the terrace. He half fell down the short flight of steps to the grassy slope below, stood weaving a moment, then set off toward the lake.

The neat stripes left by the sod formed a graph against which Adrian plotted an odd meander. His motion was not wholly Brownian, however, and after a minute of effort he reached the footpath beside the muddy shore. He did not stop there, but waded on into the soupy water.

By now men were running from the lounge to catch him. Adrian fell to his knees, his feet caught by the suction of the bottom, but he rose again and splashed forward another yard or two in the direction of the freeway. The water came up to the level of his waist, then got no deeper.

Adrian drifted to a stop, drained at last of his terrible energy. Waves of his own making sloshed against his mud-spattered shirt and jacket. He raised his ill-formed head and bellowed wordlessly at the sky, a sound that seemed to empty him of air—a baby's wail from a man's chest, the panicked cry of a mastodon trapped in the tar.

DIAPHASE

*Diaphase. The process of structural differentiation in an
epigenetic system.*
— Handbook of Bioelectronic Engineering
(revised), Blevins and Storey, *eds.*

◆◆◆

"Schizophrenia. That's what we're going with for the present." Joana Davies watched Toby across her cluttered desk top, her elbows firmly planted, her chin between her hands. On the wall behind her, in need of straightening, hung half a dozen framed diplomas and certificates, testimony to her rank and service in a long war. "It's not an ill-defined disease," she was saying, "it's just that many conditions can mimic the symptoms—other diseases, injuries, organic problems, drug reactions—and it takes a while to sort them out."

"And you have sorted them out?" Toby watched her as she watched him, outwardly friendly, inwardly wary. She'd fooled him. Fooled him, challenged him, laughed at him, walked away from him. She was a doctor, not a nurse. A bloody shrink.

Who can trust a doctor to tell the simple truth, he thought. Whitecoats, habitually making hasty and ill-informed assumptions about what a patient needs to be told, what a patient's family and friends need to be told.

This shrink, now—even in uniform she was skinny, pretty, with reddish blond hair and a sprinkling of freckles across her fine pert nose—had an engaging manner of bluntness, almost of dishevelment, of being behind in a busy schedule but relaxed about it. She wore her white coat casually enough—it was a clean but frayed garment—but she clearly cared about her appearance, about the impression she was making. Her neat corduroy skirt and plaid blouse said *smart*, said *sensible*.

Last week at Compugen her diaphanous blouse and clinging skirt had said *approachable*. It all made Toby suspicious.

Joana fished in a stack of folders and pulled out a file, flipped through several sheets of paper, ran her eyes down the page: "We don't have all the results back yet, but I doubt we'll be surprised." She leaned back, slouching in her rigid steel armchair, looking at the file. "Some neurotransmitter metabolites pushing upper normal, so we're repeating them, that's what's pending. If they point to excessive levels of dopamine, for example, that would help the diagnosis—and frankly, it would hardly surprise me. We've done EEGs: essentially normal. We've done brain tomography: no tumors, injuries, malformations. Brain angiography: normal. No evidence of drug abuse. He doesn't smoke, drinks very little. As for his general physical condition, muscle tone is poor but he's not overweight. He's got a mild sinus infection—a cold—but that's about it. Overall his equipment is what you would expect of a man his age who gets little or no exercise."

"He gets a bit," Toby said. "He works on his house, does heavy carpentry."

"Recently?"

Toby shrugged.

"That leaves his history. And his behavior."

"He's never been easy to get along with."

"So I gather. From the company personnel file and the information you gave us, we see that Adrian has few friends, is personally unkempt, keeps very irregular hours"—she was reciting from notes—"was raised in a succession of foster homes from age thirteen, when his mother died, his father having abandoned the two of them when Adrian was an infant." She looked up at Toby. "You gave us that, Dr. Bridgeman. I don't repeat such things carelessly."

"I really would like it if you'd call me Toby." A touch of warmth couldn't hurt, though he doubted he would be able to charm this one. "I suspect we'll be seeing each other often, if you're to be Adrian's physician."

"Okay, Toby. My name's Joana."

"I remember."

She glanced at him from under her brows as she riffled the papers in the file. A smile? A smirk? She dropped her gaze to the papers. "The rest is psychological stuff, scores on the MMPI, various perceptual tests. Symptoms: dissociation of thoughts and feelings, periods of catatonic excitement, suggestions of paranoia, possible hallucinations"—she leaned forward and laid the file on the stack—"in other words, a textbook picture."

Once more she rested her elbows on the desk top and cradled her jaw on the heels of her hands. "Have you spent a lot of time with Adrian?"

"We've worked together for over two years. Almost every day." Toby tugged at the lapel of his tweed jacket, setting the line straight. "The work has occasionally been very intricate, very intense. Adrian is not a graceful man. But he has the capacity to exhibit—felicitous phrase—grace under pressure. Perhaps *only* then."

"You admire him?"

"We're very different. Of course." He smiled, and the smile lines creased his face. "I'm very glib, I find it easy to think in the abstract. Adrian has difficulty expressing himself—in words, that is—but his powers of visualization

. . . astonishing. His experimental techniques . . . like magic at times.'' Toby leaned forward in the hard visitors' chair. ''You may not realize that when Adrian got his Ph.D., bioelectronic engineering wasn't a real discipline. Just a bag of tricks. He's one of the two or three people in the world responsible for changing that.''

She nodded, to reassure him that she was suitably impressed. After a pause, she said, ''You've mentioned only your professional relationship.''

''In our line of work that takes up most of one's life.'' He leaned back. ''Adrian and I rarely see each other outside the office.''

She watched him calmly.

He was silent a moment, fingering the knot of his green wool tie. Finally he said, rather shyly, ''Do you think it's odd, our mutual regard?''

''Not at all. I'm interested, though.'' Her tawny eyes, rimmed by pale lashes, invited his confidence.

''I had a brother, once. He . . . died. My parents weren't at home a lot when we were children.''

''Younger brother?''

He nodded.

''Do you feel in any way responsible for what happened to him?''

''Oh, heavens no.'' Toby's eyes flicked away to the corners of the haphazardly furnished office. ''He was grown by then. Off to war. Northern Ireland. Got himself blown up.''

''Then there's no question of responsibility,'' she said, inviting contradiction.

Toby looked at her sharply, and pink spots bloomed at the sharp corners of his cheekbones. ''Well, I'm certainly baring my soul for you.'' He shifted in his chair. ''Why not, then? Yes, of course, I don't think he really wanted to be in the army. But younger sons, you know . . . and I had failed to make it clear that I was serious about my research interests. Computers, silly fad . . . everyone in the family assumed I would inherit Dad's business, cheerfully take over when the time came." He cleared his throat. "So much for all that. We're here about Adrian."

"This is not beside the point, you know." She laid her hands on the desk top. "But we can go into it later. Toby, I seem to hear you saying you think Adrian's present difficulties are exceptional, not part of an ongoing pattern."

"I simply don't think of him as a madman."

"Schizophrenia is not hopeless. Far from it. If you're right, Adrian may be a promising candidate for therapy." Her calm gaze had not wavered. "Toby, don't let me put you on the spot with this. Maybe you could help Adrian. It could be time-consuming."

"Please go on."

"Leigh-Mercy is an expensive hospital. Your Dr. Chatterjee's clinic doesn't make it any easier on anybody, by the way. Unless it's an experimental procedure, the patient still pays—"

"In no sense is he 'my' Dr. Chatterjee."

She acknowledged his indignant denial with a nod. "Sorry. What I was getting at was that almost all our patients arrive with family attached, family that can pay." She allowed herself a rueful grin. "Family's often their main problem, of course. But in my other practice, in Oakland, I see a lot of poor people with family, and a lot of street people without. Two things I've noticed, maybe they're obvious: yes, money makes a difference in quality of treatment. But contact makes at least as much difference. Progress is rare when there isn't somebody on the outside pulling for the patient—family, good friends, anybody in the real world who cares. And except for money, Adrian's more like street people."

"Well, I'm his friend."

She said nothing, waiting calmly.

"I'll do whatever I can," he insisted. "I've moved to become his conservator, you know. The hearing's next week."

Joana pushed her chair back and stood up. "Yes. I'll be there; the state requires it. I'm glad you did, Toby; it's good news for Adrian."

He stood too. Then he said, "If you mean you'd like me to help you personally, I will. But I want to impose a condition."

"Oh, what's that?"

"I intend to ask lots of questions. And I want you to be straight with me."

She did not hesitate. "I'll agree to that." Abruptly, she held out her hand.

As he took it, it occurred to him that they were on the level already, eye to eye, both of identical height. She really was quite pretty.

Joana's smile was polite, reserved. As she withdrew her thin, strong hand she said, "But do remember who's the doctor, Dr. Bridgeman—I mean, Toby."

Surprised, he laughed. "I promise."

Later that night he carried the telephone to his balcony, cradling the handset on his shoulder as he stared at the sprawling lights of the town, spreading up from the Bay into the hills. Somewhere up there she lived. But her phone rang a long time without an answer.

Finally a male voice came on the line, merely repeating her number.

"Is Joana there?" asked Toby.

"I'm sorry, sir. This is Dr. Davies' answering service. May I take a message?"

"Don't bother." He hung up.

It was early yet, and he was restless, brimming with unspent energy. He decided to go to his racquetball club, see if he could pick up a game, see if there were any new members he should make an effort to meet.

◆◆◆

Joana sipped rich coffee from a raku mug, savoring its warmth. Outside, the rain began to fall. She set the mug on the hearth in front of the small bright fire; the tiny sound of its ceramic grinding against the stone was a signal to her subconscious that all was well, that she was home.

It wasn't the coffee or the deeply shadowed living room— the beams and dark paneling more felt than seen in the firelight—or the cozy fire itself that made this old place homey. This wasn't even Joana's house. Her apartment nearby, comfortable as it was, was only a place where she lived.

What made this place her home was the woman who smiled at her from the other side of the hearth. The woman held a baby in her arms, and she was seated in a spoke-back rocker, a mate to the one Joana sat in, in which she moved smoothly back and forth like a gentle pendulum.

"Let me hold him," said Joana to that smiling face, the face that was like a mirror to her own.

"Surely he's worn you out." But her twin sister held out

107

the sleeping boy, and Joana gathered the shawl-wrapped
bundle into her arms.

"He's fine now, Susana, isn't he? All well." Joana looked
down into the miniature face. She brushed the fingers of her
right hand lightly across the downy skull, across the bright
pink crescent scar that looped over the dome of the bulbous
head from behind the infant's left ear.

"I wish I were completely certain." Susana knelt before
the hearth, probing the coals with an iron poker. She placed a
billet of split oak on the glowing logs. "But I worry about
things, like the way he twists his mouth to the right, the way
he works his tongue."

"Paterson tells me he's developing quite normally."

"That's what he tells me, too. Even precociously, he says.
Still . . ."

Joana put her lips against the boy's hair, inhaling the sweet
waxy odor. A month ago the baby had undergone emergency
surgery for a blood clot on the surface of the brain. The cause
of the clot was simple, freakish: as he'd nursed at his mother's breast his five-year-old sister, asleep with her head in
Susana's lap, had awakened in terror in the midst of a bad
dream. The girl had fallen asleep while playing with her
mother's heavy bracelet; waving her arms violently, she'd struck
her baby brother with it.

The bruise was barely evident, and for several days the
increasing paralysis of his right limbs and the right side of his
face was too subtle to arouse Susana's suspicion. But Joana
saw that the infant's fumbling was unnatural and insisted on
tests: they revealed a break in a small vein under the skull, a
pool of leaking blood. . . .

Craniotomy for subdura was swift and efficient, but the
surgeon emphasized that whether or not there was residual
damage was uncertain. The outcome would not be clear for
half a year or more.

"There's hardly a more resilient organ than the brain, in an infant," said Joana firmly. "Our heads don't fossilize until much later."

Susana smiled back. "Thanks, Jo. Maybe Teddy wouldn't be here now if you hadn't spotted what was going on." She took a branch of dried rosemary from beside the stack of wood and tossed it onto the burning oak. The shrub crackled and blazed, filling the room with the incense of the coastal hills. Susana leaned back in the rocker. With a mischievous grin, she added, "He never would have been here at all, without your prompting."

It was true, Joana had talked her twin into getting pregnant the second time. Part of Joana's concern had been for Susana's older child, Margaret; Joana had persuaded Susana that the only child of a single parent bore special burdens. "I was actually trying to give you a gentle push in the direction of marriage."

"Do tell." The attempt had failed miserably. Instead, Susana took the advice about a second child literally, and went and made one.

"You've really been good with Margaret," said Joana, swaying the sleeping child in her arms. "On top of ordinary sibling jealousy, what a thing for her to deal with."

In the fireplace a cluster of rosemary twigs exploded softly, bringing reflected sparks to Susana's pale eyes. She studied her sister. "She meant to do it, though. Didn't she?"

"Probably," said Joana, still rocking the baby. "That's the honest answer."

"Which is why you brought it up," Susana said testily.

"Margaret didn't know she meant it. And you really have been very good about not blaming her."

"Overcompensating? Spoiling her? Letting her get away with murder . . . ?" Susana stopped, caught her breath.

Anger briefly shadowed her face, flitted away into the dark. She laughed shortly. "My, what a person will say."

"Maybe you think you're too good for those feelings."

"Don't bait me, sister. I'm dangerous." Susana abruptly got up and left the room.

Joana heard her scraping and banging around in the big open kitchen. She waited quietly, without tension, hugging Teddy to her breast. She knew her sister well enough to know her anger was dissipating, flowing away into purposive activity, while she let her emotions cool.

After a few minutes Susana reemerged from the shadows with a fresh pot of coffee and a plate of small elaborate cakes, made of layers of chocolate and nuts and pastry. She put the plate on the hearth. "My students' work. Tell me what you think of the triple-chocolate torte."

Joana smiled. "Your version of sweet revenge?"

"My version of an apology. I got mad because you made me admit something out loud that I was trying to keep a secret."

"From yourself?"

"No. I knew it, Jo. I do know myself." She sat down, but did not begin rocking again.

With the baby snugged securely into her left side, Joana took the narrow wedge of triple-chocolate torte in her right hand, carried it to her lips, bit into its tip. She felt the physical response of the glands high in her jaw, the saliva rushing hotly to the scene of the chocolate incursion. She restrained herself mightily to keep from eating more than just one bite.

Susana watched her, smugly satisfied.

"Well, I acknowledge that I'm a fool for chocolate," mumbled Joana.

"I know your soul," said Susana throatily. "It's mine too."

Joana struggled to recover her dignity. She put the cake back on the plate. "The urge to kill your siblings is not only understandable, Susana, it probably once had survival value as well."

Gently, Susana interrupted. "It's not that I'm avoiding the subject. Or even that I'm not interested. But it is late, sweet sister."

"Okay. Just remember that Margaret's thought processes were probably much less conscious than mine. The times I wanted to kill you! And I was old enough to know just what I was doing. And you probably wanted to kill me just as often."

"Probably. You've still got that scar on your knee, where I swung the bicycle chain?"

"Oh yes, I'll always have that." Joana's brow knitted at the remembered pain. "You know, I never figured out until a couple of years ago why you did that. It was Ralph, wasn't it?"

"Of course, you little dunce. Did you think I was going to sit by the road with a broken bicycle while the two of you went off into the hills and did things? Deliciously dirty things—or so I imagined. Without me? I told myself I was protecting you."

Joana was smiling, but tears came into her eyes. She looked at the baby in her arms. "So you protected me. Have you ever thought about the ways we split up our life?"

Susana leaned back, watching the flames. The shadows danced among the beams and posts. The architecture was dark, heavy, yet with a sense of rhythm in the spacing of the redwood members, the slate shingles, the leaded panes of glass, that suggested Japanese clarity as much as Celtic sentimentality.

Joana envied Susana this house. It was a beautiful house, and Susana had earned it, not with any help from their

parents, not by an advantageous divorce or any other com-
promising arrangement, but by her own unaided success. She
was the author of two best-selling cookbooks, and she personally produced her own syndicated TV-strip cooking show,
which also assured a steady income from the classes she
conducted at home in her remodeled kitchen.

"Was it so bad, Jo? We couldn't go on trying to trick each
other's boyfriends"—Susana laughed, a throaty murmur—"not
without getting very kinky."

"I don't mean that. I mean the way it's turned out you've
done all the gutsy stuff. And I've done all the heady stuff."

Susana shook her head, her red gold hair glinting in the
firelight. "You're making it too simple. It takes brains to get
a bunch of prissy technicians to produce a TV show on time
and on budget, whether you think so or not. And it takes guts
for you to hang in there with all those hopeless weirdos you
care so much about."

"Maybe I really mean, you have all the fun." This time
Joana failed to hide the edge to her voice. She hugged the
baby tightly to her breast. "I'm feeling sorry for myself. My
apologies."

Susana looked at her, mildly surprised. "Rare enough,
you're entitled. But don't fool yourself about me, okay?"

Joana nodded, but she was unpersuaded. Though there had
never been a moment when she hadn't empathized completely with her twin, known just how she was feeling,
supported her in it, there were many things about Susana she
couldn't really understand. How had this sunny California
surfer girl, this daughter of a staid lawyer and his socialite
wife—in every way Joana's double—turned into such a symbol of unconventional, go-it-alone success?

Susana, never married, had never been convinced she must
forego the experience of motherhood simply because she'd
formed no permanent liaison with a male. At the age of

twenty-nine she'd picked a man she liked, inquired discreetly into his family history, then appointed him father of her firstborn. He'd never known any but the most transitory aspects of the honor. She hadn't told him the rest, fearing an outburst of startled paternalistic pride. And then, some years later, after Joana's unwitting prompting, she'd seduced the man again—deciding there were advantages in both children having the same father (at least it might simplify the inevitable explanations).

Whenever Joana tried imagining herself in the same situation, assuming the same responsibilities, she was appalled. Nevertheless, she envied Susana's children; she envied her the having of them, and the hope of them as well.

The rain came down harder, a spring storm only now beginning to arrive in full force, pelting the diamond-shaped panes of glass and the dark shrubbery outside.

"I met a rather charming man today," said Joana, studying the baby's delicate eyelids, tiny shells of flesh fringed with fine lashes.

"*Rather* charming?" Susana's voice was droll. "Another of your dotty lame ducks?"

"This one's not a patient. Friend of a patient. Rather British."

"Eh, wot." Susana grinned. "Do tell."

Joana looked up almost shyly. "I can't get involved, I'm afraid."

"You're always afraid, Joana. So am I. Just get the guy drunk. Carry him off." Susana became enthusiastic. "I know an inn near Jenner, a new place, pines and surf and calico sheets on the feather beds. How can he resist?"

"Really, it could be a serious mistake. Because of my patient. His friend."

"Oh, well, that certainly sounds plausible," Susana said archly, "though I don't know why." Her sister said nothing.

Susana leaned to toss another stick on the fire. Flames leaped in the window glass, danced against the liquid night. She watched her sister rocking her child. "I wish I could share Teddy with you, Joana," she said abruptly.

"You do share him. And Margaret."

"No, you know I can't, really." She got up from her chair, yawning. "You're on your own that way." She stood in the firelight, watching the flames, her pale eyes gleaming. "Well, Jo," she said, after a long silence, "you always do the right thing."

Joana smiled ruefully. "You make it sound like a curse." She got carefully to her feet. "You'd better take back your son. Before I get attached."

Susana leaned close to take her baby. As she did so she brushed her twin's cheek with a kiss.

♦♦♦

Harold Lillard parked his black Cadillac in the ERMIT Corporation visitors' lot. He'd signed in with the guard at the main gate, and now, clutching a cardboard pass, he walked toward the guardhouse in the inner fence.

ERMIT's several hundred employees occupied a brick building built in the 1950s, four stories high, spread over the equivalent of a city block but set on a dozen rolling acres of wooded land near suburban Concord. Looming amid thickly clustered trees were great outcroppings of mossy granite, rocks which had hidden Yankee snipers when the British made their fated march on Concord's Old North Bridge.

Within the past week spring had decided to arrive all in a rush. It was a fine warm day. Oaks and elms and maples were still mostly bare but budding out furrily; here and there a willow glowed electric green, and forsythia bushes made splashes of yellow in the morning sunlight. The air smelled of loam.

Harold should have been smiling. In the slim briefcase he

carried in his left hand were two Tyger II computers, fresh from the factory; he'd happily anticipated delivering the new machines to his first customers in person. But he suspected that he was coming down with a cold. And family matters had put a damper on his enthusiasm.

Marian's pregnancy was starting badly. Each of the previous seven expectancies had had their characteristic joys and difficulties. Indeed, Harold sometimes wondered whether Marian's impatience with Donna was related to how violently she'd been sick while carrying her, or conversely, whether her indulgence of Paul had anything to do with what an easy pregnancy he'd been. But never had she been plagued with sickness so early.

Harold had been bold enough to suggest that she ask her doctor at St. Luke's if there was some sort of diagnostic procedure to determine whether the developing fetus was normal—he'd read of amniocentesis, and some other test with sound waves. But it was too soon for that, and at any rate Marian refused to consider it. Since there was nothing she could or would do about the outcome—except become more depressed, if it looked unfavorable—she didn't really want to know. Harold could hardly argue with that.

He'd have to give all this some serious thought later on. Meanwhile here was the inner gate, and Stan Kubiak waiting to escort him inside. Harold smiled broadly and waved through the chain link fence, while inside the hut the guard punched some apparently complicated program into a keyboard, which eventually allowed the door to swing open.

Stanislaw Kubiak was a rotund man with a bald head and a biblical growth of curling black beard, the head of Section F of ERMIT's Mathematics Division. Harold had no clear idea of what Section F did, though he knew it had something to do with devising ways to encode electronic communications. Or breaking other people's codes. Or maybe both. ERMIT itself was only slightly less a mystery to Harold; he knew it was one of those not-for-profit think tanks supported by the government, an outgrowth of a World War II project in electronics research run by MIT. ERMIT did a lot of work in C^3I—command, control, communications, and intelligence— and it seemed like every worker in the place had his or her own personal computer. They'd been very good customers. Harold anticipated delivering lots of Tyger IIs to this address.

"So, Harry, come to gyp the government again?" Kubiak took him by the arm and led him up granite steps through swinging doors, which opened onto a broad, busy corridor running the length of the building. Waxed linoleum echoed under a myriad of scurrying feet. Whenever he visited ERMIT Harold had the feeling that he was back in high school, that Stan Kubiak was a hall monitor escorting him to the principal's office.

They chatted amiably as Kubiak led Harold deep into ERMIT's inner recesses, Kubiak pretending to complain about Compugen's high prices, lousy equipment, and poor service, while Harold countered with a jolly diatribe about ERMIT's obfuscatory paperwork and dilatory payment schedule—fancy phrases he'd learned from Kubiak himself. Several turns of the corridor and flights of stairs later they arrived at a featureless conference room, somewhere in the interior of Section F.

"You know the drill, Harry, I've got to lock you in here while I round up the other fellows. Back in two shakes. Before you get unpacked."

Kubiak was too optimistic. Setting up a Tyger II meant little more than laying a nine-inch-long folding leather case on the table and flipping up its lid to reveal a keyboard and a tiny video monitor. Harold had a separate monitor and a larger keyboard in his briefcase, but he was hoping to impress Kubiak's individual colleagues with Tyger II's diminutive friendliness, in hopes they'd be tempted to buy personal units.

Since he had two machines, Harold decided to let the four-color sample graphics run on one of them. He pulled the other one out of its skins, so he could make a few basic points about the maintenance of bioelectronic computers.

By the time Kubiak's "troops" arrived—a dozen young men in slacks and white short-sleeved shirts and one primly skirted young woman—Harold was ready to begin his lecture on the care and feeding of Tyger II.

"This computer runs on sugar," Harold announced to the assembled group, beaming as broadly as if he'd invented Tyger II himself. "Ordinary glucose. But don't try to feed it home brew."

He poked his thick finger into the narrow, shallow box that lay open on the top of the conference table and tapped a slender green canister, labeled "NF" in raised white letters; nestled beside it were a blue canister labeled "Ox" and a gray one labeled "Waste." The cylinders were smaller than triple-A flashlight batteries. The rest of the interior was a diminutive package of plastic tubes, miniature fans and pumps and the rechargeable batteries to power them, and an old-fashioned integrated-circuit card with wires and connectors which served to mediate between the computer's protein-aceous innards and the hardware of the outside world.

"The nutrient fluid in this canister contains most of the synthetic enzymes used by the growth program," said Harold. "A supply adequate for two or three years, under normal conditions. So they tell me. Don't worry, we give you enough of them to last longer than a human lifetime. Replacement is a simple procedure that takes only a few seconds, and when the canister needs replacing you'll know it: Tyger stops whatever it's doing and flashes at you, 'I'm hungry.' "

The ERMIT employees laughed shyly. One of them asked, "What about waste disposal?"

"Pretty much the same," said Harold. "The machine tells you, 'Got to go.' " They laughed again. "Oxygen filter too. It just says, 'Gasp.' " Harold smiled. "I admit I'm paraphrasing."

He described Tyger II's internal arrangements, explaining at some length that the computer's homeostatic program monitored and regulated temperature, humidity, delivery of nutrients, removal of waste, all with no help from the user. Not that it should be allowed to freeze or fry—there were a few idiot lights on the front panel that warned of abnormal conditions—but basically the machine took care of itself.

Twenty minutes later Harold slid the leather cover back onto the open box and raised the miniature monitor. As soon as it was in place it began to display alluring graphics: HI, I'M TYGER II.

"End of basic lecture," said Harold, pleased with himself. "Now you all know how to use your new Tyger IIs. Can I answer any questions? Reasonably nontechnical, I hope," he added with a spare-me smile.

While he was waiting for questions his nose began to tickle, and he rooted in his trousers pocket for a handkerchief. He found it just in time to sneeze.

"Uh, I'm a little uncertain about security," said one of the younger men. "The machine appears to interface easily with all sorts of other systems. Does it have any built-in data protection features? I mean that in certain applications—"

"Right," said Harold quickly. The kid had fourteen colored pens in his nerd pack and an obvious craving to do things right. "We at Compugen like to think Tyger II is the ultimate user-friendly machine. Nothing special-purpose." You don't want to tell me about the business you're in, thought Harold, and I don't want to hear about it. "So you folks will have to provide security on your own. Somehow I think you'll be good at it.'' He was rewarded with soft chuckles.

"Despite my better judgment, Harry, I'm moved to admit that your machine is a pretty little bauble.'' A sardonic grin lurked somewhere under Kubiak's beard. "But just how long will it be before we can expect to get some use out of this thing at professional levels of data manipulation? We have a charming picture of cells dividing and multiplying and organizing themselves inside like a little embryo, but do we have to wait nine months to get results?''

"Ha, ha, that's good, Stan. Nine months.'' Harold thrust his left hand deep into his trousers pocket and gave his quarters a good jingle. He had a momentary fantasy of giving the Pope two bits' worth of advice. "Nine hours is more like it. This isn't just a number cruncher, Stan, it's a problem solver. Remember, the PIA/J program works at the cellular level. Then you've got a more or less standard operating system. You've got the LISP format you ordered, or we can give it to you in FORTRAN or whatever you want. It's up to you. Give this baby something to chew on and it will go to town.''

"Though it's my understanding PIA/J itself communicates by manufacturing proteins,'' said Kubiak, persisting. "Isn't that rather tedious?''

"Not natural proteins,'' Harold corrected him. "Artificial enzymes. Made to order. Sure, the process is slow, that's why it takes maybe half a day for PIA/J to build you what you want. Maybe longer, if you really try to stump it. But that's your own little demon architect down in there. Once the structures are in place, they work faster than any electronics ever could. Tyger II is denser than brain tissue, so they tell me. You don't even have to turn it on. Just feed it a problem.''

"Precisely where does all this growing and structuring take place?" asked the woman in the group.

"I'll show you," said Harold. He slid the cover back, then reached into the exposed computer, slid a lever a few millimeters to one side, and with both hands gingerly lifted out an object resembling a microscope slide. "At the factory they call this a sloppy disk. Always making wisecracks."

Between his extended index fingers Harold held up a thin sandwich of crystal plates, no more than two inches square. As he tipped it back and forth in the pinkish fluorescent glare, a glittering latticework of hairlike filaments became visible in the plane where the two protective plates pressed against each other. "That grid consists of microtubules for transporting gases, nutrients, waste products. And the I/O ports, of course. Can't see the goo yet, except with a microscope. But it's in there. And sooner or later it will expand enough to be visible. Or so they tell me."

Kubiak watched closely as Harold realigned the glass sloppy disk with its positioning grooves. As Harold shoved the disk back in, a row of nipples along one edge met a row of soft plastic tube mouths and wire pins. He swung the small lever back to complete the connection. "There. Isn't that simple?"

One of the onlookers piped up. "How do you turn it off?"

"You don't," Harold replied. The damn thing didn't use as much juice as a firefly, why bother to turn it off? "You don't have to."

Kubiak again: "So, Harry, if I feed it a problem, as you say, then it will just go on working?" Kubiak looked at him shrewdly. "No overtime? No fringe benefits?"

"Yeah, Stan, that's what I'm telling you. I'll be back next week to take your order for the next two dozen."

"We'll let you know. Thanks for dropping by." Kubiak extended a hairy hand and indicated the door. "I'll escort you back to the outer world."

The two men paused in the hall and looked back into the room. Kubiak's staff was gathered around the two Tyger IIs, punching keys, chattering excitedly. Kubiak said, "You made a hit, Harry. If this thing is half what I've heard it is, your company's going to win big."

"It's the other way around, Stan. What you've heard isn't the half of it."

"Any word on Storey's condition?"

"You heard about that?"

"It's a small community. Word travels fast."

"Then you probably know more than I do. The man just needs a rest, is what I hear. He worked himself into the ground, building Tyger II."

As they neared the outer doors, Kubiak asked Harold a final question. "What really is the functional capacity of this thing, Harold? Did Bridgeman have anything to say about the theoretic limits?"

Harold laughed. "I never talked to Bridgeman directly. But they tell me he's been running a test on the prototype back there, seeing what happens when the sloppy disk gets filled up. I hear it hasn't even grown big enough to see yet."

"Maybe they haven't fed it a worthy problem. Perhaps here at ERMIT we'll find something to test your Tyger's limits."

"Oh, you will, Stan. I have faith."

They parted at the inner gate. Harold made his way across the warm asphalt to his Cadillac, sniffling, thinking about his next appointment at a high school in Bedford, thinking about Marian, about the new life growing inside her body. He reached into his pocket and jingled his quarters. The sound comforted him.

◆◆◆

Waking early on a Saturday, Toby gauged the weather and decided it was just right for a day on the beach. But he required a spectacular beach. He knew of one that never failed him, in sun or storm.

The coastal hills of northern California are made of clay and limestone and coal and odd bits of maroon and green rock churned up from the floors of ancient ocean beds—stuff so thoroughly mixed by grinding catastrophes over the eons that it takes a bold geologist to confidently order the strata. For most of the year the hills are brown, dry, and dusty, their minimal covering of grasses shriveled and gone to seed and tinder, and in late summer the tinder often burns, ignited by flickers of lightning or the carelessness or malice of passers-by. During the winter rains the hills slough off the job of being hills and, sliding down over themselves, seek to become river bottoms.

The Russian River patiently contends with this restless landscape, running its milky green water over gravel bars and

123

boulders of mudstone and volcanic rock, under basalt cliffs, through prim fields and farming towns worthy of Norman Rockwell paintings, alongside forty miles of Highway 101 before turning westward.

On this bright spring morning Toby Bridgeman and Joana Davies, driving north from the cities of the Bay, met the river west of Santa Rosa and joined it on its way to the sea.

Somewhat to Toby's surprise, Joana had agreed to his offer, made only yesterday in the sterile confines of her office, of a day in the country—during which, he managed to suggest, they would discuss many things relating to Adrian's case. So far today they had mentioned Adrian only in passing. He was physically well, Joana assured Toby, and Toby agreed that he seemed in good health. Then a silent conspiracy arose between them, to escape Adrian and the world's pain.

The blue BMW sped past neat vineyards flourishing under a desiccating sun, then slowed for weekend traffic in the tacky river resorts that clustered in the midst of the hills, nestled under dusty redwoods. Then the car accelerated along the wide river road. Toby's stereo tape player filled the airy, leather-cushioned interior with a Brahms piano concerto. Joana seemed content to listen, and Toby was uncharacteristically shy.

In the last few miles before the sea, the hills on either side of the river valley grew smoother, more rounded; the chaparral gave way to grass, tall redwoods retreated to dark ravines, and lines of giant eucalyptus, planted by farmers a century ago as windbreaks, arose like columns of gray smoke on the brows of the hills. Even in the depths of summer ocean fogs touched the hills with green, and in the spring sunshine the grasses were as bright as glowing neon, with orange poppies dancing like flames and purple lupine shadowing the road banks.

Very near the sea the river widened and became frisky, its closely spaced wave crests heaving rhythmically over a sandy bottom.

"Toby, what's that in the river? Are those people?" Joana leaned to look past him, over the guardrail.

He glanced sideways. "I think they're seals!"

Dark heads rode nose high as seals surfed in the cresting rapids; sleek brown flanks flashed in the sunlight as they let the current roll them in the sand. At the river mouth the animals turned and drove back up the channel for another spill down the wide, shallow water slide.

"They're as playful as children," said Joana, delighted at the unexpected sight.

Where the fresh water spilled in tan currents into the salty Pacific, a long sandbar cut across the mouth of the river. Facing the sea and sand, the tiny weather-beaten town of Jenner clung to grassy headlands. Toby drove past the town and parked on the bluff to the north.

He and Joana took their basket and cooler and blanket down the breakneck path to the wide beach. The sparkling morning was free of any whisp of fog, but a cool steady breeze blew onshore, bouncing grains of sand across the dunes.

The beaches of the North Coast are graveyards of trees; Toby and Joana found shelter in the angle of an immense driftwood log of uncertain species, its bark long ago stripped and its wood bleached and rendered furrily soft by the patient attentions of salt and air. Hidden from the wind, warmed by the sunlight that glistened in the salt-charged air, Toby and Joana shared a picnic lunch of pâté and sourdough French bread, sharp cheddar and *cornichon* pickles. The wine was a buttery Chardonnay, grown and finished a few miles up the river.

At first they talked about inconsequentials—food, mostly,

exchanging notes about their favorite restaurants, groceries, wineries, country inns. For several generations Toby's family's business had been the importation of fine wines and liquors, doing well enough to have earned appointments to the royal family. He had often spent holidays in France and Italy, in Bordeaux and Champagne and Tuscany, where even as a boy he'd been widely feted for his father's name's sake, and these experiences added a cosmopolitan authenticity to his considered discussion of wines. For her part, Joana had learned a good deal from her expert sister (the first Toby had heard of her) about so-called California cuisine, fresh local ingredients presented in a Continental manner—garlic and herbs, artichokes and avocados, fresh-killed lambs' and piglets, almonds and avocados and lush tomatoes—all the bounty of the most diverse agricultural region in the country. It was the sort of talk that went well with good food, and for the moment that was all they needed.

After lunch they walked a long time on the beach. The day kept insisting on itself, on its own brightness and beauty. It produced prodigies: a pod of sei whales charged the bar, rolling on the sandy bottom, spouting and blowing in the shallow surf. Toby and Joana watched, their fascination tinged with concern that the whales would beach themselves, but after a short back-scratching excursion the whales turned and steamed majestically back out into the deep.

The day was not done with spectacle: now it brought out seals in profusion to play in the ocean surf. They stuck their heads out of curling breakers and stared at the watchers on the beach, ducking back again just before the water crashed against the shore, to reappear half a minute later in another oncoming wave. Low-flying squadrons of pelicans strafed the wave tops, gulls wheeled and screamed overhead, cormorants dived, sandpipers scurried daintily in the foam.

Joana and Toby strolled the coarse golden sand. He rolled up his jeans and they both carried their shoes, picking their way around beached jellyfish and strands of kelp, letting sheets of foam caress their ankles.

She was used to directness. She thought it a good moment to ask him how it was that he found himself unattached. He admitted he wasn't single, exactly. Intrigued, she pressed for details. He gave her the story of his married life, abbreviated version.

"Would I recognize her?" Joana asked.

"Perhaps from the advertisements. She used to have more speaking parts, but I suppose accents aren't the rage they once were. I've seen her a few times on television, draped over the hood of a car, or in the background when they're selling perfume. It's always a bit of a start."

"Children?"

"No—um, actually I took care of that permanently. Thought it more fair to her."

"Still, neither of you care to make the divorce final?"

"I know, it's bad practice, everyone says so. But we've always been friends, still are. Simply not mates."

"You make it seem quite civilized."

"No, sheer laziness. And perhaps an insufficient sense of the eventual danger."

They walked quietly a moment. Then she said, "Meanwhile, it's an awfully good excuse, isn't it?"

"Oh, yes. Occasionally I've used it to avoid becoming involved. Not when I really cared for someone, though."

She laughed, delighted. "When you care for them you tell them the truth?"

"Yes. What's so amusing?"

"The truth—that when it's over it's because you're bored with them?"

He looked at her, his face turning pink. "Actually, I

intended to say . . ." His words trailed off. After a moment he said grumpily, "Do you have the feeling this beach has somehow come to resemble a doctor's office?"

They walked in silence for a moment. She said, "I'm sorry. I was out of place. But thanks for telling me the truth to begin with."

"I should like to be honest with you in all ways."

"Good." She glanced at him and reached out to touch his shoulder. His skin was warm under his shirt's thin cotton. Her touch was brief, a gentle apology. "In fact, perhaps I see you in a—new light."

"It *is* a weakness, I'm quite aware of that. I would quickly settle matters if it were important."

She smiled privately. "How different you are from my sister! But how much the same." She told him about Susana and her children. "In your determination to avoid entanglements both of you tackle what look to me like pretty formidable complications."

"One doesn't have to tackle them. They leap from the woodwork."

"Like Adrian did," she said quietly.

"Indeed, yes."

"Is he really very much like your brother?"

Toby laughed. "Nobody could be more different." Why had Toby taken such a liking to Adrian? He remembered his boyhood, which suddenly, as he thought of it, seemed a long time ago.

Twenty years ago, whenever Toby's father was off on some terribly important piece of diplomatic business somewhere in the antipodes, in Africa or the Near East or the Indian subcontinent, and his mother was quietly but rather abstractedly attending to the spirits-importing business—which had to pay for Dad's aristocratic style—Toby had been left to take responsibility for his little brother, Thaddeus, seeing to it that he got his breakfast and a packed lunch before he went off to day school, seeing that his uniform was reasonably clean, seeing that the bullies stayed clear. Of course on weekends none of that counted—when the little beast had gotten into Toby's watercolors, mixing them all together, or invaded Toby's armies of toy soldiers, mucking up the neat ranks of type-metal Napoleonic French and English and Prussians. Toby'd whaled the tar out of him then. Still, Toby had had a proprietary attitude toward the miserable brat; he'd wanted to see Tad make something of himself, on the playing fields or in the classroom.

Well, the lad had done both. But the day came when Tad, at twenty-one a very junior lieutenant in Dad's old regiment, had forever let Toby down—by getting himself blown to pieces in a stinking slum in Northern Ireland, a stupid piece of ill luck and bad judgment.

"Were you in the army too?" Joana asked.

"No, I favor my mother. I was too short." He paused. "I didn't want them to take me, of course, but I could hardly admit that to anyone, could I?"

They were nearing the northern end of the beach. The bluff closed in, cutting across the sand; invisible from below, the road followed the edge of the cliff. Campers and an old pickup truck were parked in the view area overhead.

A tumble of dark boulders high enough to hide a standing man spilled from the bluff onto the sand and into the ocean. Water swirled around the bases of the rocks, white foam against the black.

"Want to turn around, or climb the cliff?" Joana asked.

"What's that fellow doing?" said Toby, ignoring her question.

Beyond the boulders, just visible from where they stood, a beefy young man wearing a red baseball cap and a greasy down vest was lying belly down on a rock, facing the surf.

Beside him a tall fishing pole was planted in the sand, its line draped in a long flat curve into the surging water some yards away. But he was no simple fisherman. What had caught Toby's eye was his hunting rifle, an old bolt-action 30.06.

Toby followed the fellow's line of sight, and saw a playful young seal poking its head out of a wave. The rifleman tensed, but the seal was gone instantly. It reappeared a few seconds later, in the following wave, but apparently found the ride lacking in excitement and rolled under the water.

The guy was trying to shoot seals. Perhaps he'd already taken a few potshots; from more than a hundred yards away the report would be inaudible over the sound of the surf.

Toby stood still, and Joana looked from him to the gunman. "Toby, perhaps you'd better . . ."

There were no carcasses on the sand, however.

"Just a moment." He walked slowly forward, approaching the man through a frame of tall rocks. Not until he was within a few feet did the man turn, startled and guilty. He had a round red face and an uneven blond mustache. He was in his early twenties at most, still a boy. He tried to roll sideways to hide the gun with his body, but he must have realized he'd been seen. Toby looked at him only a second, then turned and circled back toward Joana.

They began to walk slowly back along the beach. "Don't look around," said Toby. "I'll walk behind you for a moment."

They trudged stiffly through the powdery sand, nervous and quiet.

"Is he pointing the gun at us?" Her voice was thin. "It was dangerous to confront him."

"He didn't seem that dangerous. I only wanted him to know he'd been seen."

"What are you going to do?"

"Report him to a ranger. If he has any sense, he's already

on his way out of here." He moved up beside her, laying his arm across her shoulder. "He must have climbed down the bluff from the highway. One wouldn't display a rifle on a state beach."

"Why would he do that? Do the seals take his fish?"

"A simple sadist. The fishing line was probably baited to lure them in."

"Some of the fishermen cut the beaks off pelicans." They walked in silence, hoping the man had made his getaway.

"We're well out of range, I think," said Toby. "For that old rifle." He stopped and turned. The end of the beach appeared to be deserted. The battered pickup was leaving the view area.

"I admire what you did, Toby." Her voice was warm.

He grinned at her, his green eyes sparkling. "You know, of course, that if you hadn't been here, I almost certainly would have pretended to myself that I hadn't seen him."

"You are determined to be honest, aren't you?" She smiled and took his hand. "Careful—martyrs are no fun."

At the visitors' center in Jenner they talked to a young, sunburned state park ranger. She promised to put out the word, but said there was little chance the sniper would be found and not much that could be done unless he were caught in the act. Shot and bludgeoned seals and sea lion pups were found on the beaches more often than most people wanted to hear.

Toby and Joana stood beside the car, watching the intense yellow sun slip a little lower toward the metallic seascape. If they started for Berkeley now it would be dark by the time they got there, but both of them thought it too early for the day to end. Toby suggested dinner, down the coast at Bodega Bay or Point Reyes—the long way home.

"Let me make a phone call first." Joana went back to the

phone booth at the corner of the lot and made her call. Toby sat in the driver's seat, the door open, his feet on the ground—feeling the sand in his shoes—and watched her curiously. When she came back she said, "My sister told me about an inn just north of here. It's small, but they have room for us for dinner. We can walk a while, until it's time. If you'd like to."

"Indeed I would."

Toby sat back in his chair as satisfied as he could remember being. Lamb chops—the lamb raised on the salt grass of the coast hills—and dill potatoes, green beans in virgin olive oil, a piquant salad, a shared bottle of subtle Merlot . . . not that he was concentrating on memories. The present moment was in fine balance, not spoiled by concern for the future, untinged by regret for the past.

Throughout the meal Joana had watched him steadily, her eyes made golden in the candlelight, her hair gleaming like fine strands of warm metal. Somewhere in the darkness outside the lace-curtained windows the wind sighed in the pines, and beneath the cliff the surf groaned against the sand.

Her fingers crept forward to brush his knuckles, and his face grew warm, and he responded with a longing that had more to do with hearth fires and kind words than with lust.

"You're a lovely creature, Toby. As I suppose you've been told many times."

"Never often enough. Why does it surprise me that *you* should say it?"

She smiled. "Because I'm too sensible for such things, of course." She stretched her hand farther, stroking his palm with her fingertips. "And aren't you rather a cad?"

His mouth twisted into a puzzled grin. "I certainly don't like to think so."

"I'm not being a shrink now. I'm just someone who's attracted to you for painfully simple reasons."

He took his hand away and looked down at his wineglass, rotating its stem idly between his fingers. "I don't know what to say." He looked up at her. "Suddenly I feel—*little*."

She smiled. "Bless you for that. *I* feel like a fool."

"This isn't something you do regularly?"

"Awkward attempts at seduction?" She swallowed a laugh. "There's a first time for everything."

He looked up, his green eyes sparkling under dark lashes. "It's a long drive back. Plenty of chances to change your mind."

Her skin grew rosy under her freckles. "Too late for me. They had a room here, too. I reserved it."

"Ah."

"So it's up to you."

"Supposing I am a cad?"

Her voice was husky. "I guess for now I don't give a damn."

The room was tiny and cold, but there was a fever heat on both of them, desire held hours in suspension, now homing on its goal. They kissed a long time, deeply, standing one step from the hall door where it had closed noisily behind them. Clothes came off slowly, a piece at a time, amid the muffled laughter of mouths that would not part. The flow of cold air from the ill-fitting window insinuated itself between them, glided over glowing skin.

"Baked Alaska," Joana mumbled. Her laughter filled his mouth.

He chuckled. "Mm, you've got goose bumps. All sorts of interesting places."

The floorboards squealed once, sharply, as they bounded into the high brass bed and promptly sank deep into its down-filled mattresses, disappearing beneath the layered sheets and quilts and comforters.

Fumbling and giggling beneath the covers.

Silence.

Rising commotion.

The bed walked two inches away from the wall before stillness returned. Then a hand shot out and pulled down the covers. Toby's. He gasped for air. Joana sighed, nuzzling his throat.

The room was so dark that the starlit ocean was visible through the glass, a dark gray line against a darker horizon. A single bright star glimmered in the vaporous night.

They lay quietly for a minute. Then Toby hopped out of bed—the floorboard squealed again—and disappeared into the closet-sized bathroom, pulling the door closed behind him. Yellow light suddenly spilled from the crack under the door.

Joana heard a hollow pop and the clink of glasses. The door opened slowly, nudged by Toby's shoulder. Dazzling light lapped his contours. Naked, a half smile on his shadowed face, he took a tentative step into the bedroom. He held his arms in front of him rather stiffly, for in each hand he carried a flute of golden champagne full almost to the brim.

"Wonderful! How did you get that up here without my seeing it?"

"A word to a prurient waitress. I'm not completely lacking in resourcefulness." With his heel he pushed the door almost closed behind him. His limbs were radiant in the single plane of light that cut the room vertically. Watching him, Joana forgot that he was a small man; he was so well proportioned— his articulated muscles moving cleanly under taut skin, without the exaggerated bulges of the undersized body builder—that in the odd light he might have been of any size.

"God, Toby, you really are too beautiful."

"And soon I shall be frozen to stone." He passed into the darkness and the floorboard squealed. Never taking his eyes from the brimming surface of the champagne, Toby set his knee on the bed. He carefully handed her a glass and turned, letting his legs slide beneath the quilt. "Aah, salvation."

"Oh, is that what they call it?"

"Cheeky. Here's to wild moments."

With covers pulled up to their chins they sipped the ticklish wine. When the glasses were empty they were set carefully on the floor; the covers came all the way up, and the sinuous movements began again, slowly, as if the creatures in the bed were swimming under water.

"What made you change your mind?" he whispered, his lips pressed against her ear. Her massed hair was sweet in his nostrils, springy against his cheek. "You weren't going to have anything to do with me, I could tell."

"My secret. Nothing to do with you." She stretched her thighs against his hand. "No, what a lie. Everything to do with you."

"It will be different Monday."

"To hell with Monday. Don't talk now."

He did very little talking before morning. She did rather more.

◆ ◆ ◆

There was orange industrial carpet on the floors of the new building and designer colors on the walls, but the Chatterjee Foundation's clinic at Leigh–Mercy Hospital had the smell and feel of hospitals everywhere. Toby waited in the hall for Joana to finish with her midafternoon therapy group; he preferred the sunny hallway, with its wall of multipaned windows overlooking a grassy courtyard four stories below, to the soulless, have-a-nice-day decor of the psychiatric ward's waiting room.

It seemed to Toby that as the world grew more crowded, more and more of it looked just like this—sterile rooms whose windows looked principally upon other windows.

Down the hall a door opened and the members of Joana's group emerged. They looked listless, thought Toby, perhaps because the big event of their day was over. Beyond a vague sense of their variety he had no clear impression of any of the dozen men or women, because he avoided looking at them.

Not that they seemed overtly strange, but he thought of them as—we¹l, *crazy*.

An irrational reaction, he knew, but there it was.

Finally Joana came into the hallway. Sunlight through the windows caught the coppery highlights in her hair, made plain the smile lines around the corners of her eyes and mouth. Her bright print cotton dress, with its bold pattern of blue abstracts, was almost clingy. Her frayed white coat hung precariously on her spare shoulders, a bare acknowledgment of hospital discipline. Only her nameplate and the clipboard she held loosely in smudged fingers gave her profession away.

"There you are, Toby Bridgeman," she said, with a cheerfulness that sounded forced. "Ready to hide in your closet?"

"Hullo, Joana." He hurried to join her as she walked briskly down the hall. "You make it sound shameful. Like Peeping Tom."

"Ah, ah, watch what you say. You know us shrinks, alert for any sign of human weakness."

"Then it's as bad as I've always feared."

Her smile was weary.

They turned a corner, leaving sunshine behind. Joana fished a ring of keys from the large pocket on the front of her skirt, selected one, and inserted it into the knob of what looked like an ordinary closet door. She opened the door and flicked a switch.

The tiny room held two metal chairs; its only illumination was from a plastic Donald Duck night light stuck into a shoulder-height wall socket. A dark sheet of opaque glass took up most of one wall.

"This is it?"

She nodded and looked at him quizzically, as if offering him a last chance to back out.

Yesterday, as they were driving back from Jenner, Toby had decided to test Joana's promise to answer all of his questions. He'd announced that he wanted to be let in on the minutiae of Adrian's treatment; he wanted to observe her sessions with him.

That the court had approved Toby's conservatorship made the request not entirely unreasonable, and after mulling the request overnight, she had reached her decision. He could observe once—more than that would be unethical—and he would stay out of sight; it wouldn't do to give Adrian the impression that his only friend in the outside world was somehow conspiring in his commitment. Toby was to fully discuss his impressions with her afterward.

"Does anyone on that side really believe it's only a mirror?" Toby asked.

"We tell them what it is," she said briskly, "and we tell them that occasionally other staff members will be observing. Most people forget about it. If they can't, we move the sessions and do without the spying."

Again the faintly accusatory tone. Toby wondered if he'd done something to irritate her. Perhaps she was just having a hard day.

"I'll be back in a moment," she said.

As she turned to leave, two men approached. "Ah, Dr. Davies," said the older. He was a solidly built Asian-American, fiftyish, with thick black hair cut short and plastered flat across the top of his square skull. "You do normally interview the patient Storey at five P.M.?" He glanced at his watch.

"Dr. Lee. Yes. The afternoon group sometimes runs long. Let me introduce Dr. Bridgeman."

"Dr. Lee," said Toby, taking his hand. This one wears his white coat buttoned all the way to the throat, thought Toby, and it's spotless: some thick, sleek, stretchy material. "Y. N.

Lee, MD, Director, Chatterjee Cognitive Research Foundation, Leigh-Mercy Clinic," says the badge—the typographer having managed to cram all that onto one piece of blue and white plastic.

"And this is Dr. Ormsby," said Lee.

"One of our new residents," said Joana for Toby's benefit, as Toby shook hands with the young man, whose dark beard was perfectly Freudian. Turning to Lee, she said, "Dr. Bridgeman is a consultant for Compugen. He's with UC, in—development."

Toby noted that she did not specify which of the university's campuses was his current *mater;* perhaps she hoped Lee would assume it was the medical school in San Francisco, which did indeed have a department of Human Development.

"Consultation?" Lee asked.

"Research. Preclinical," said Toby, in his best clipped British. "Davies here. Been most helpful."

"Certainly. Good," said the doctor, unconsciously mimicking Toby. "Well, Ormsby here—like him to observe. Please carry on, Dr. Davies."

"Make yourselves comfortable, gentlemen," said Joana as she turned away. "I'll have the patient here shortly."

Toby insisted that Dr. Lee precede him. It was a deadly politeness, since whoever had the misfortune to occupy the inner chair was trapped until someone else opened the door. As for Ormsby, Toby decided that Dr. Bridgeman's presumptive status required that the resident stand.

"What kind of research are you doing, Doctor?" Ormsby asked, and Toby replied, "Brain." After the second such exchange Ormsby gave up. Dr. Lee preserved his dignity and his silence.

They waited in hot and awkward silence. How she must have enjoyed shunting us three busybody males into a dark closet, thought Toby.

Finally lights came on next door. Joana ushered Adrian into the carpeted room, furnished with a soft fabric sofa and chairs and, in one corner, an incongruously bruised oak desk. The room's pearl gray walls were bare of anything that might have emotional or intellectual implications, undecorated except for a single framed poster, Oregon's snowcapped Mount Hood. Joana guided Adrian to the couch, then sat in one of the chairs near the desk.

It took Toby a moment to get used to the thin, flat voices, conveyed by a poorly positioned microphone in the room and an inadequate speaker inside the observation booth. He saw that Adrian was complaining; the complaint was not in words so much as in the slump of his shoulders and in the expressions of outrage and hurt that played over his face.

Adrian did not look good. Perhaps Toby was made extra sensitive by the presence of professional observers in the room with him; perhaps he was imagining that he saw Adrian as they saw him. Still, Adrian's sallow complexion, sleep-distorted mass of hair, and crumpled hospital pajamas (but no paper slippers—rather his dirty track shoes now untied, their broken shoelaces trailing)—all spoke of a deteriorating self-regard, which had not been robust to begin with.

". . . George went on a long trip," Adrian was saying. "Biologicals intervened. Catastrophe. Missed connectivity."

"It's all right for you to be upset with me for being late," said Joana. "Can you acknowledge how you feel?" When Adrian stared at her silently, she prompted him. "Tell me."

"All right. All right. Scratch it. George went on a long trip?" Adrian's tone of voice was questioning, but his facial expressions were oddly matched to his words. He grimaced wildly, then smiled.

"So it was George who went on a long trip," said Joana cautiously. "Tell me about George, then."

"Tell me George," Adrian repeated, parrotlike. "Male

name, English. Metaphorical referent." He paused a moment, and Toby, watching, could not resist the notion that gears were grinding in his head. "George looked for the beast. Beast, where is thy honey tree? The beast smirked. George, know thyself. Reflexivity inappropriate. Level jump. Restore. Burn the tree to ashes. Take the honey. Short cut embodiment of diasynchonicity, leading to infrastructural appreciation of dualities. Level jump. Reset."

Inside the closet, the three men listened intently. "Typical schizophrenic word salad," Lee said brusquely. "The challenge is to analyze the content."

"Man sounds almost like one of these modern art critics," said Ormsby. "Interesting to know where he picked up the vocabulary."

But Toby, surprised by what he heard, said nothing. Why would Adrian use those phrases? Those exact phrases?

Joana waited patiently while Adrian, silent now, antically contorted his face. When she was certain he had nothing to add, she asked, "Why did George burn the tree?"

Adrian laughed. "*George* didn't burn the tree! Upper-level translation error. Reset. George. Beast. Honey. Ashes. Tree."

Inside the observation booth Lee twisted to eye the resident. "Dr. Davies attempts to draw out the patient by inviting him to discuss his obvious anger at her tardiness. He responds by erecting ever more elaborate verbal defenses, telling a story about a nonexistent fellow named George. An evocative metaphor: a name for a saint or a king, a slayer of dragons, a rescuer of princesses."

"An oppressor of colonists," Toby added dryly.

Lee grunted something that might have been approval. "Plainly the task is to penetrate the mythological cloak in which he swathes his sexuality and aggression."

"The patient is evidently a learned man," Ormsby observed sagely.

"An intelligent schizophrenic poses particular difficulties for the physician," said Lee, turning away. "Consciously or otherwise, he may quickly deduce the therapeutic methodology and use his knowledge to subvert treatment."

Toby looked sidelong at the humorless Lee. He did not know which perplexed him more, the notion of Adrian as a learned man or the notion that an engineer would deign to match wits with a psychiatrist: Dr. Lee severely underestimated the contempt of the true-believing reductionist for anyone who took the word "mind" seriously. Maybe that in itself was a form of defense.

". . . George found the honey trees. There were three green trees and one dead. The beast laughed. Bug it! Connec . . . connec . . ." Adrian began making a gagging sound, then sat up, became rigid. His eyes bulged. He stopped breathing.

Joana tensed; her gaze flickered to her watch and back to Adrian's face, timing the fit. "How do you feel, Adrian?" she asked in a firm, unemotional voice.

Adrian's face twisted, through a wonderfully sunny smile into a nose-wrinkling scowl. Then he seemed to relax. Looking at Joana alertly, he began to speak rapidly. "The central difficulty resides in the question of whether the epigenetic properties of the model organism must be reflected in an isomorphic simulation at level two, or whether a sufficiently powerful *general* algorithm, process- rather than goal-directed, can be used to . . . to get the honey. *Nicht wahr?* George is surrounded. Level jump. Beasts are sucking him. Reset. Don't burn the tree."

Joana said, "Adrian, are you afraid? Do you think someone wants to hurt you?"

Toby leaned forward in his chair.

"Did you say something, Doctor?" Lee asked sharply.

Toby realized he'd just said *no*. "Knows what she's doing, Davies," he said. "Analytic strategy. Superb."

"Yes, of course," said Lee, looking away.

But in fact Toby knew Joana was barking up the wrong honey tree.

The three men emerged from the closet, sweat-soaked and ruddy. Joana met them in the hall. Lee took her aside for a moment, and Toby heard only polysyllabic words, drug names that meant nothing to him. Lee seemed irritated. Joana's face was drawn.

After a few moments Lee turned to him, saying, "Good to meet you, Doctor. Drop by and tell me about your research one of these afternoons."

"Pleasure," said Toby. He gave Lee's wide, moist hand a quick jerk, then brushed fingers with Ormsby. "And you, Hornbeck."

He turned to find Joana looking at him sidelong, her color restored, restraining a smirk. "Very persuasive—Doctor," she said archly, as the others walked away. "I was afraid I was going to have to explain you to Lee—and that he would not have approved." She started toward her office, and he hurried to keep up with her. "Anything to share?" she asked him.

"I'd like to drop in on Adrian. I wonder if—"

"We have a deal," she said sternly. "Talk to me first."

"We *are* running rather late. No visitors at mealtimes."

Her nostrils flared, but she conceded the point. "Just a visit?"

"I do know how to honor an agreement."

She looked at him, exasperated. "All right," she said testily. "I suppose I should apologize for getting so far behind today."

"I won't hear of it. There is one thing you can do for me, though."

"What's that?" she said wearily.

"Have dinner with me."

"Oh, Toby, normally I'd like that," she said, almost contritely. "But I don't want you and me to get mixed up with the two-of-us-plus-Adrian. Does that make sense?"

"You're asking for the impossible." He touched her hand lightly. "I've some ideas about Adrian that may prove fruitful. I'm not practiced in forensics. I need time—not to mention peace and quiet—to explain myself. Humor me."

The strain of indecision showed itself in the stretched skin across the tip of her nose. "Okay," she said at last, less than delighted.

"Eight o'clock?"

"Okay."

They made the arrangements, and Toby went off toward the ward, hurrying down a hallway now awash in direct yellow light from the late-afternoon sun.

He knew just what he wanted to say to Adrian.

"Hullo, Adrian. How's your cold?"

Adrian peered at him quizzically. He said nothing.

"All better, then," said Toby. "Glad to hear it."

Adrian smiled. "Toby!" Then the smile turned into a twisted parody of itself, an obscene leer, and just as quickly his face was blank again. The low sun played over his sallow skin, casting a hard shadow horizontally against the white plasterboard wall near Adrian's bed, where he sat perched like an exhausted penguin. His bony fingers played absently over the weave of the stiff white sheets.

Toby's heart went out to his friend, helpless in the grip of an obscure compulsion. "Adrian . . ." He paused, wondering if after all he were betraying his promise to Joana. But whether he was right or wrong he could do Adrian no further harm. "*Run* George," he commanded.

"George went on a long trip," said Adrian without expression. "He met the beast in the woods. 'Show me the honey tree,' said George. 'I will eat you first,' said the beast. 'Have some cheese,' said George. The beast ate the cheese. 'Are you hungry?' George asked. 'No,' said the beast, 'I have eaten cheese.' 'Show me the honey tree,' said George. The beast showed George the honey tree. George got the honey—"

"Very good, Adrian," said Toby. "Just as I—"

"The beast sucked George dead," Adrian added.

Toby was silent a moment. "Oh, really?" he said quietly, more to himself than to Adrian. "A new wrinkle—"

"Semantical analysis essential to syntactical decoding at crude chunking level," Adrian observed.

"Quite," said Toby. "We'll get to that, Adrian—"

"Reset," Adrian suggested.

"—but not just yet."

◆◆◆

The restaurant was a tiny converted railroad station, a mission-style construction of whitewashed stucco with a big central dome. Redone in thirties *moderne*, the decor tended toward potted cacti, Indian rugs, and old Santa Fe Railroad posters: smiling Navajos against red mesas, blue skies with cottony cumulus clouds. Beneath the dome a blond fellow in a black velvet suit tinkled away on a grand piano, crooning Cole Porter, while in the corners of the square wings diners chattered at one another by the light of crystal paraffin lamps.

Toby stared surreptitiously at Joana, hoping she wouldn't catch him at it. Oh yes, he was thoroughly taken by this All-American Girl—her knowing gaze, her blunt honesty, her intelligence, and of course her refreshingly pretty face, and her body, just the right size and shape, not quite taller than he was, slender yet very well defined—so that part of his mind was coolly calculating what would continue to impress her, charm her, keep her seduced (now that he had been well seduced himself), while another part of his mind was sternly telling him that, with him, sexual attraction was virtually a constant and should not interfere with his intention to help Adrian, his friend.

He sat upright, self-consciously dissecting a savory filet of mesquite-grilled shark, stealing glimpses of her freckled nose. Her tawny eyes—looking up after a last nibble at a tentacle of squid—snagged his gaze.

Smiling, she leaned back and pushed a hand through her stiff hair. "I may as well go the rest of the way with the apology, Toby. I've been so edgy. Especially when I learned Dr. Lee was going to be peering in on me today, hounding me about drug treatment. Diagnose it, prescribe Brand X, that's his theory. Sanity through chemistry. And I'm not as confident of Adrian as I was—from one session to the next, everything is different."

"I wondered about that," said Toby.

"Do you sense it? It looked so simple. Now we're getting nursery rhymes and structuralism."

"Is it time to talk shop? You seem to have demolished that cephalopod."

"I devoured it. Delicious. Therefore yes, tell me *your* brilliant theory."

"My brilliant theory." He pushed his chair away from the table. "You can stop worrying about the content of all that stuff Adrian's been spouting."

She shook her head, puzzled.

"The content is trivial. It's from a fairly primitive language program he and I were working on a while back— warming up, really. All that nonsense about George, honey trees, all that. We were trying to get the computer to tell us a comprehensible story. A lot of the mythology is implicit. Built in. By us. If you want, I'll show you the reams of printout we got from it."

"Lévi-Strauss? Winnie-the-Pooh?"

He nodded and grinned. "I'm almost embarrassed to admit it, but yes, George is a teddy bear."

"But Adrian's *using* it."

"No, he's just reciting it, I think. But the real point is the confusion of levels. He even makes it explicit. 'Level shift.' He keeps saying it. I think that's the important concept."

She looked at him suspiciously. "You're feeding me a forty-year-old theory of schizophrenia, Toby. Next you'll be talking about double binds."

"Ah, yes, the good Dr. Bateson. Well, there is a historical connection, to be sure—through information theory—but I had in mind something much more immediate. A computer, any information-processing system, functions as a hierarchy. At one level you've got electrons shuttling back and forth along physical paths. At another level you've got programs that control and assign meanings to patterns of opened and closed switches. And on top of those, programs that communicate, and revise meaning, by interaction with the outside world." He cleared his throat. "As you know."

"At least I know what a hierarchy is," she said dryly.

He was unperturbed. "Then you understand that when you want the machine to do a fast Fourier transform or tell you a bedtime story, you can't be concerned that the machine may have to do fast Fourier transforms or tell *itself* stories in order to carry out your request. In that context you can't be concerned about machine language, or assembly language, or anything but the top level, the level at which meaning is communicated. You've got to be confident the machine is going to maintain hierarchical separation—isn't going to start chasing some endless loop because it's confused the content of a sentence with an instruction about that sentence. *Principia Mathematica* and all that."

"You're saying that Adrian is recapitulating specific experiences in the recent history of his work?"

"Specific design problems. I think he's modeled Epicell onto himself, as it were. He's trying to say, 'If I fix this, things will run smoothly.' But he's operating at very primitive levels of discourse. And he's getting trapped."

"This is going awfully fast, Toby. Are you saying Adrian thinks he's a computer?" She stared at him.

"No." He smiled then, apologetically. "Or only in a manner of speaking. We're all computers, Joana—information-processing systems, if you prefer. Granted, that's not all we are. But Adrian's trying to do what can't be done, certainly not by a human being. He's trying to understand the processes of his own brain."

Toby was silent, and Joana watched him as silently he sipped at his wine, twirled the glass in the flickering light, studied the focused flame in its depths. Finally he said, "With Epicell the problems were peculiarly intense. Through Epicell, through PIA/J, the Tyger II has a program which allows it to build its own physical hardware in response to top-level demand. Like asking a child to build onto his own brain in order to solve harder maths problems."

"Children build onto their own brains all the time."

"Thoughtlessly. As children do. But with Epicell, Adrian—Adrian and I—had to think about it. I don't know much about how the brain develops, Joana, but I know how Epicell develops. The explanation fills volumes, the process itself takes practically no time." He smiled again, mocking himself. "But I'm a flighty sort. When I'm away from the office I don't think about Epicell very much."

"Unlike Adrian."

"Unlike Adrian. He's a brooder. A perfectionist, never satisfied. The Compugen people took it away from him before he was ready to let go."

"And you think he hasn't let go of it yet." She sat a moment, pursuing a leftover fragment of tentacle about her plate with the tip of her fork. "It sounds plausible," she said at last, putting the fork down firmly, as if reminding herself not to play with her food. She studied Toby's face, with its eager-to-please expression. "You seem to be suggesting that, as his therapist, it's time I intensified my education in computer programming."

"I'm said to be a good teacher."

"I can make a little time available."

"I promise to devote it to your education."

She laughed. "In programming?"

He twisted his shoulders into an elaborate shrug. *"Bien sur."*

He pulled to a stop in front of her stucco apartment building, north of the campus. He looked past her to the floodlit century plants beside the entrance of the building's central courtyard.

When he looked back at her, the lines around his eyes had deepened. "So. There's the simple explanation: man becomes obsessed with his own creation. But it may well be worse."

"What do you mean?" she demanded.

"I don't think there's anything to the content of the George stories. What if I'm wrong? Adrian has been creative. He uses words we never included in the primitive program."

"Such as?"

"Poor George got 'eaten' now and again. He never got 'sucked dead.' ''

"Very graphic. Atavistic, in fact." She seemed almost pleased. "That one should yield to my kind of analysis."

"Oh, indeed." If it's only a symbol, he thought, as he watched her face in the light from the streetlamp. But he said it only in his mind. For Joana, he displayed his most charming smile.

"Will you come in?" she said. "Even though it's Monday night?"

"I'd like that very much."

"You have to promise to help me get up at quarter to six."

"I'm an early riser."

"Mm." She leaned toward him and kissed him.

Later his roaming fingers found the scar on her knee. "My, that was a bad one. How did you get that?"

"My sister gave it to me. Trying to prevent moments like this."

◆◆◆

On Monday night Harold Lillard came home late to find Theresa playing with the family's Tyger II, using the machine to create her own animated cartoons. She was adept at programming in LOGO, a language particularly good at simple graphics, so Harold had seen to it that the model he'd brought home talked LOGO. It also talked something like English, making use of an add-on voice synthesizer Harold had provided, a gizmo more expensive than the Tyger itself.

Theresa had the plates and pads of the little computer down on the floor beside the beat-up wooden toy chest in the corner of the family room; she was lying on her stomach, her chin in her hands, her elbows poking through holes in the sleeves of her favorite hand-me-down sweater. Her bare legs waved gently in the air, rocking on knobby knees, like inverted pendulums.

The big screen Harold had brought to go with the miniscule computer was displaying patches of bright color. Theresa watched it awhile, then reached out and tapped at the

detachable keyboard, making adjustments. Harold crept closer
to get a better look. He thought he recognized the characters
in the cartoon—they vaguely resembled the stuffed toys that
surrounded Theresa on the floor. The voices were familiar
too: the toy leopard (he could tell it was a leopard by the
spots) was clearly Marian, with a voice that was gentle, firm,
and somewhat distracted, and Harold guessed that the stuffed
dog was supposed to be him, gruff and nervous. Smaller
yapping creatures were Theresa's brothers and sisters. Theresa had portrayed herself as a sinister thing that vaguely
resembled a rat.

"Who took the car keys?" yapped the dog.

"I'm going to eat his toes," hissed the rat.

"That's nice, dear. But be careful," purred the leopard.

Theresa cackled. With a few taps of the keys she set the rat
to chasing the dog; around and around the screen they coursed,
leaving their paw prints in an ever widening spiral.

Harold smiled, then sneezed. His cold was growing worse.

His daughters ignored him. Thinking fondly of his youngest, he turned and went upstairs to change into his old
clothes.

The child had grown up around computers; Harold had
been bringing them home since before she was born. She'd
treated the new machine as nothing special when he'd pulled
it out of the box, and Harold had not bothered to expound
upon the technical details of biochip CPUs, or why a Tyger II
was different from a Tyger I or any other computer. She
would not have been impressed. But in the week that the tiny
new Tyger had sat around the family room, Harold had been
pleased to see that it had weaned Theresa wholly away from
the television set.

Now, when Theresa and Donna came home from school,
her older sister—who had never shown the least interest in
computers—watched game shows and reruns and afternoon

movies at one end of the room, while at the other Theresa spent her time in front of the Tyger II.

Harold thought the voices really were remarkably good. And the action was as convincing as any he'd ever seen on a computer screen. It was a clever gadget, and he was proud of it.

Upstairs in the bedroom Harold emptied the day's collection of quarters onto the dresser and pulled his work clothes out of the closet. He paused a moment, sitting on the frayed bedcover, staring dreamily at the faded wallpaper. Then, with an effort, he forced himself to get on with his chores.

In the midst of cleaning up his garage workshop Harold became engrossed in the instruction manual for his new power lawn mower. An hour later Marian found him sitting on the cold concrete floor beside the machine, contemplating the cutaway diagram of its two-cycle engine.

She pulled him to his feet, clucking at his forgetfulness, and tugged him into the dining room, where the children were already shoveling down their dinner. "I told them to go ahead. I'm sorry, Harold, but I called and called."

He nodded, unperturbed. Harold usually started the meal with a blessing, but he did it to please Marian, and he thought God would not be terribly displeased if she and the children asked grace for themselves once in a while.

The Lillards ate in silence, except for the sound of chewing and swallowing, Harold's soft sniffling, and Theresa's occasional loud snorts.

"Theresa," said Marian, "if you have to blow your nose, excuse yourself and leave the table."

"Yeah, don't be snotty, kid," said Anthony, grinning at her over his plate of macaroni.

"I'll eed your does," Theresa threatened nasally.

"Oh, *gross,*" said Donna, melodramatically slamming her fork to the table, staring at her sister in disgust.

"Eed yours doo," Theresa offered.

"*Moth*er!"

"Theresa, stop that this instant. And the rest of you," said Marian.

Theresa sniffled. " 'Scuse be, please." She slid off her chair and went into the kitchen.

Marian looked at Harold, who was gazing solemnly at his plate with watery eyes. "Harold, do I have to do it all myself?"

Harold sniffed. A moment later a strenuous honking sound issued from the kitchen. Harold slowly focused his dreamy gaze on his exasperated wife. "What is it, dear?"

She took a deep breath and let it out slowly. "You haven't touched your dinner."

"Oh. Sorry. Guess I'm not hungry, dear. I think my cold's getting worse."

"Harold, why don't you just go and lie down? Maybe you'll be hungry later."

"If you wouldn't mind. Got to get an early start tomorrow," said Harold, pushing his chair back.

"You go ahead. I'll be up in a minute."

Harold smiled absently and rose. He staggered a little as he went into the hall, toward the stairs.

Theresa came back into the dining room and hopped onto her chair. Hungrily she eyed the pile of macaroni on her plate. She speared a couple of the short round tubes and carried them toward her mouth. As she loudly sucked the yellow cheese sauce from the noodles, she eyed her brother wickedly.

"I know what you're thinking, brat," he said. Then he burst out laughing.

"Oh, *gross!*" Donna howled.

Harold, face down on the bed upstairs and sound asleep, was wholly unperturbed. Nothing penetrated his consciousness before morning light seeped into the room.

The sunshine, broken into a million shards of light by the new leaves of the young poplars outside, poured through Harold's Compugen Corporation office windows. On the credenza opposite his desk was a leather-framed triptych of photographs, color glossies of Marian and the kids taken two summers ago at the lake. Harold sat behind his desk and stared at the snapshots, daydreaming.

On his telephone keypad a red light was blinking, indicating that his secretary urgently needed to communicate with him at his earliest convenience. The light had been blinking for half an hour.

Last week had been busy for Harold, and this week promised to get busier with every passing day. Harold had already demonstrated the Tyger II at a half a dozen locations on the seaboard—a sail loft in Marblehead, grimy classrooms in the shadow of Bunker Hill, law offices in the Back Bay, a weaver in New Bedford. The Boston school system had bought three of the bottom-of-the-line models—they were cheaper than filmstrip projectors, after all, and a lot more fun—and Harold had personally delivered them just yesterday. He'd even spent his own money equipping Theresa's classroom with a half a dozen of them.

Lately he'd begun to realize that he'd better let up a little, before his sales staff became unhappy; after all, the boss had no business stealing their customers. He certainly didn't need to do their jobs for them. He'd get his cut either way.

Harold would have to explain to them that he was out on the street for the sheer fun of it, because it took him back to the good old days. He'd see to it they all made their commissions, as if they'd closed the sales themselves. And soon, he knew, he'd have to start handling his desk work. But he was still having too much fun: Harold's calendar indicated that he'd scheduled another busy day, starting with a trip to the Navy base in Connecticut.

He should have left an hour ago. He was prepared—despite his terrible head cold he'd forced himself to get up early, arrived early for work, somehow managed to clear most of the paper off his desk by nine—but when the time came to leave, he hadn't moved. He hadn't answered the intercom, hadn't answered the phone, hadn't answered his secretary's knocks on the door.

For the last hour he'd been staring at the family pictures.

More knocking, insistent pounding. The door swung open. Harold's secretary, backed up by the office manager and the regional vice president, peered cautiously into his office. "Harold? Harold, we'd very much like to talk to you. Do we have a problem . . . ?"

But Harold didn't reply. His eyes were wide open, but his mind was somewhere else.

The long central atrium of Compugen's research building was full of morning light from the clerestory windows high overhead, the only outside windows in the building. Tall ficus trees in pink clay planters stood against the rough-plastered walls; the irregular tile floor was dappled by leaf shadow.

Toby arrived at midmorning. His leather heels clicked on the hexagonal red tiles of the oddly deserted hall.

Though researchers with something to discuss often lounged in the atrium's blue-cushioned wicker chairs, chatting in genteel comfort, Toby and Adrian had more often locked themselves into the dark computer graphics room to fiddle with arcane variations of protein architecture on the giant video monitors; there, watching the sculptural images twitch and rotate in vivid false color, they could put the world out of their minds. Toby had rarely visited Adrian in his laboratory. He was not unobservant, but at times he had a delicate

159

stomach, and there were some things his subconscious had warned him he'd rather not observe too closely.

This morning the normally crowded microelectronics lab was closed and locked; peering through the wire-reinforced glass, Toby could see sealed forced-air benches, hooded gleaming optical instruments, racks of idle electronics. The place had been cleaned up thoroughly, then deserted.

Toby went to the next door, the one with the warning symbols and emergency phone numbers pasted to the glass near the doorknob. Inside, a black teenager wearing a ragged white coat, his hair in dreadlocks, was mopping up a spill of some sticky yellow liquid.

Toby moved on to Adrian's office. The door was locked, but Adrian had given Toby a key. Toby went in.

The office was a small laboratory in itself, normally cluttered with glassware and electronic instruments, and with books, papers, and computer printouts as well, detritus spreading over every flat surface, including part of the floor. But Toby saw that someone had sorted through Adrian's papers—likely the redoubtable Mrs. Dortmunder, acting on Chatterjee's orders—and evidently she'd made off with everything she recognized as sensitive and arranged the rest in neat piles. When Adrian came back to work it would take him weeks to get things disorganized again.

The office had a window, made of two layers of reinforced glass, but it didn't have much of a view: it looked into the building's P-4 facility, a small laboratory designed for maximum biological containment. Equipped with airlocks, decontaminating showers, and a corner where dangerous organisms could be handled by means of rubber gloves thrust into sealed boxes, the P-4 facility had never actually been used for any serious purpose. In fact, Compugen was not even required by law to maintain it, although Chatterjee cited its existence whenever it was politic to stress Compugen's safety protocols.

Through the window Toby could see Adrian's personal refrigerator, where he kept beer, unfinished manuscripts, old copies of *Penthouse,* and several sealed, frozen tubes containing strains of undifferentiated Epicell, which Adrian jokingly referred to as his "starter yeast."

Toby walked through the unlocked air lock door and reached for the padlock on the refrigerator. He slid his copy of Adrian's key into it, mildly surprised at the resistance. The key wouldn't turn.

It was a new lock. Irritated, he went through the second air lock into the biology lab on the far side of the P-4 facility. The place seemed deserted, except for the self-styled Rastafarian teenager nearby, who was still swiping at the puddle on the floor.

The boy glared at him. " 'Ey! Wha' *time* is it?"

Startled by his vehemence, Toby peered at the truculent face a moment before consulting his watch. "About ten after ten," he said mildly.

"All righ' . . . ," said the boy, tiredly, as if Toby had passed some sort of test. He went back to his mopping.

Toby said, "Excuse me," and gingerly stepped around the spill. The boy stared after him, radiating silent, furious, unfocused contempt.

The large room was a maze of long benches, with shelves reaching to the ceiling. The aisles were narrow, barely wide enough for two people to squeeze past each other sideways. At the far end of one bench a woman sat on a high stool, listlessly dabbing with a paper towel. "Hullo? Sara?" Toby walked toward her. "Where is everybody?"

She looked up, startled—mouse-brown hair, red-rimmed brown eyes, tears streaking her cheeks—then quickly plucked a tissue from a box nearby and turned away.

He halted a few feet away. "I didn't intend to intrude," said Toby. She shook her head sharply, not looking at him.

He stood awkwardly, glancing around. Through the spaces in the shelves he could see that he and the woman and the sullen teenager were the only people in the large room. The laboratory was filthy—piles of stained tissues and paper towels on every bench, sinks full of soapy gray water, empty cardboard cartons blocking the aisles. Beside one sink were half-dried pink and yellow scraps laid out on a towel, the remains of a dissected mouse. The place smelled of formaldehyde and ammonia.

The woman turned to him. "Chatterjee called them in to discuss their new assignments." She sniffed. "They all hated Adrian too, but they kept their mouths shut. I protested, Dr. Bridgeman. Which is why I'm here and not there."

"Toby, please. We're not strangers."

"Yes we are." She wiped at her face once more, then tossed the tissue aside. "Did you ever once really *see* this place?" she asked bitterly. "On your way to play with your pretty computer graphics?"

"I must admit that I've—"

"They left *me* with it," the woman said. Her face darkened. "My Ph.D.'s from Stanford, I did three years of postdoc at Tübingen. Every week there are fifteen pages of classified ads in the back of *Science*, crying for specialists, and I had to come to work in this shit-pile." She glared at the teenager. "Jimmy, you can get started on those cartons now, you don't have to wash the whole floor."

The boy gave her a disgusted look and let the mop fall, its handle hitting the floor with a sharp crack. He turned and grabbed an empty carton from the bottom of a stack, ignoring the tower of cardboard that collapsed behind him; he made for the door in majestic sloth.

The woman slid off her stool. Sara Brewer was small, with square features and a thin, wide mouth. "Look at that animal."

Toby's gaze followed her pointing finger to the mouse parts beside the sink.

"Look at the brain. He botched it. I've been doing brain sections practically since I was out of high school. That's why they hired me, I thought." She squinted at Toby, her red-rimmed eyes blazing. "A year ago, when I first came here, I threw away a dissection he'd abandoned. It was almost a week old. He came in the next day and screamed at me for fifteen minutes, loud enough for the whole building to hear. I was a 'menstruating bitch' with no conception of experimental technique. *Nobody* presumes to clean up after Adrian Storey, he told me, *nobody*. Well, nobody does now."

"Do you know who changed the lock on his refrigerator?"

"Chatterjee's orders. Something in there you want?"

"Oh . . . some magazines, that's all. Nothing important."

"Mrs. Dortmunder will find them for you."

"Quite."

"By the way, this one died of polio. I assume you've been vaccinated."

Toby involuntarily cringed away from the scraps of flesh. He scowled at her, then laughed, a humorless bark. "Bit of a joke, eh? Polio's specific to humans."

"And other primates," said Brewer. "One strain gets mice."

"Yes, of course," said Toby. "I suppose I do know that."

She glanced at him quizzically. "But that's not what this mouse died of. This mouse died of a synthetic. An analogue." She rummaged in a drawer until she found a package of rubber gloves. She began pulling a pair onto her small hands. "The RNA is mostly the real thing, of course, except the genes that code for the coat proteins. Those are practically one hundred percent artificial; you and Adrian could probably get a patent on them. Synthetic polio. Congratulations." She gingerly gathered up the animal's greasy remains, deposited them in a plastic bag, and carried them to a steel trash receptacle.

He remembered now. Polio had once seemed a promising candidate for the Epicell matrix design. Toby could recall Adrian listing its advantages: it was the smallest well-understood animal virus, a spherical, membraneless particle only three hundred angstroms across, its coat consisting of repetitions of a single protein. It was genetically stable, slow to mutate. Like viruses generally, it reproduced by invading cells—nerve cells, in its case—shutting them down, appropriating their protein-manufacturing equipment to its own purposes. Behavior that was unnecessarily complex, from Adrian's point of view; still, he suggested, much could be learned by observing polio's organizational strategy.

They'd set about fooling with its genes, trying to get the same structural result with an even simpler protein. Adrian did the dirty work, as usual. Toby's input was theoretical, strictly on the level of information theory and pretty graphics. They'd learned what they wanted and moved on to other protein structures. Toby hadn't thought about the polio project for a long time.

He watched Sara Brewer deposit the mouse remains in the trash receptacle. She tossed the gloves in after, and locked the lid. Turning to him, she said, "Well. To what do I owe the honor?"

"Sara, I'm terribly concerned about Adrian, as I'm sure you can understand." Toby ventured a smile. "I'm looking for any possible clue to his illness."

"He's schizo, isn't he?" She seemed surprised. "Pardon me if I'm insulting a friend of yours, Dr. Bridgeman, but Adrian was—is, I mean—a very disturbed man. Nobody was surprised to hear he was in the hospital. There were twenty researchers in this laboratory, ten more in microelectronics, many of us with good reputations in the field before we came

here. He made life hell for all of us.'' She laughed sourly.
"But we were *very* highly compensated. Why else would
anyone stay?''

"He does like to do everything himself,'' Toby said lamely.

"And he *does* take all the credit. Cleaning up he leaves for
others.'' She gestured angrily. "Would anyone with a shred
of self-respect work in this environment? Compugen should
be grateful I don't turn them in to three or four different
government agencies.''

"Perhaps that's what I'm trying to get at,'' said Toby.
"Do you believe he might have caught something? Infected
himself with something?''

"Who did you have in mind?'' she said sarcastically.

"I'm quite serious. This pseudo-polio, for example.''

She paused, then spoke carefully. "No, I think not. Nothing exotic, anyway. Not polio.'' She looked away, fussed
with a set of stainless-steel tongs. "I guess I was joking, a
little. Contamination of experiments is the worry here, not
infection. That clever strain of yours is completely attenuated
in humans, it could never get out of the gut.''

"I see.''

"That's what comes of his kind of reductionism, you
know. He thinks biological molecules are nothing but miniature electromechanical devices. He thinks living organisms
are nothing but machines.''

"And you don't.''

"I'm no vitalist. But life isn't that simple.''

"Of course not.'' Toby was at a loss; he doubted he would
learn much more from the distraught Sara Brewer. "What's
to become of you?'' he asked her.

She half smiled. "Thanks for asking. I suspect that if I
stick around I'll get to do lots of cleaning up. Instead I'll
quit, which is what they really want. And I'll get paid lots of
money to reaffirm my nondisclosure agreement. And then I'll

go off and find myself a medical school where I can get some real work done.''

"I sincerely wish you luck.'' Toby looked into the woman's taut, intelligent face. "Perhaps I could ask a favor of you. I need to do a little reading on brain chemistry. Perhaps I could have your recommendations?''

"Certainly.'' She smiled more fully. "If you don't mind taking advice from a janitor.''

That afternoon Toby laid a stack of books and periodicals from the university library on his tabletop, carefully avoiding the wires and tubes of his prototype Epicell computer. He took the top book from the stack, leaned back, and stretched his short legs to rest his heels on the edge of the table. Over the top edge of the book, through the dining room window, he was aware of the Berkeley Hills hovering distantly in clear afternoon light.

He opened the book but ignored its text; for a long time he looked at the photographs and studied their captions. His mind wandered through dark forests of arborized neurons, which intertwined their black branches against a background of pictorially undifferentiated tissue as red as a tropical sunset. He contemplated the dense cables of nerve cells that connected the body's sensory organs to its information-processing structures, that connected these structures to each other, and that channeled the resulting signals to the muscles.

As he often had before, he wondered how it all managed to work so well for so much of the time. In the face of such intricate near-perfection, the argument from design paled to nothing. Only the cybernetic processes of life itself, striving blindly over the eons, could have created something so unimaginably complex as this ''meat machine,'' with its neuronal components as numerous as the stars in the Galaxy—a

hundred billion or more of them—the connections among the
neurons numbering ten thousand times that.

He glanced over at diminutive Epicell, spewing its symbols onto the little picture-frame screen. Idly, he reached out
and tapped at the keyboard. The screen flickered and went
blank, and words were displayed: HI, I'M TYGER II.

"No, you're not really," Toby whispered, amused. It
wasn't Tyger II, it was half-naked Epicell, but it didn't know
that because it couldn't sense its own lack of a Tyger II
chassis. It was only doing what it had been told. It hadn't
been provided with sensory apparatus, or a language program, or any means of communicating with its environment
except through the keyboard and screen. Its universe was
purely mental, consisting solely of the edifice of abstractions
it had constructed on the foundation of a few axioms Toby
had fed it weeks ago.

What, after all, was a mind without a body to do? It was a
thing of pity, helpless, unknown, perhaps unfathomable.

Toby tapped another key, and the screen filled with equations in an odd symbolism. They stayed in place, arrested for
his perusal. He peered at the screen awhile and realized he
understood very little of what he was seeing. He tapped the
key again and the display advanced. A few seconds of study
told him the new screenful was wholly incomprehensible.

He put his feet on the floor, leaned forward, and tapped
repeatedly, now backing up the display, looking at earlier
results on which Epicell's latest bright ideas were based.
When he finally found notation he could recognize, he uncon-
ciously clucked his tongue. The eager machine had indeed
carried its attentions into the footless halls of topology, but in
order to express itself it had created its own notation, and
what it had discovered there was beyond Toby's amateur
ability to judge. He would have to call in someone from the
university to tell him what was going on.

All this from a smear of proteins on a plate.

Toby tapped again at the keyboard, and the prototype went back to its lonely business. He returned his attention to his book. Of course the human brain—somebody's human brain, anyway—was capable of everything this machine was. And the human brain generally was capable of incalculably more. In fact it seemed that only *idiots savants,* poor creatures otherwise mentally crippled, displayed the sort of astonishing feats of memory and calculation that were any computer's proudest achievement.

Odd how scratching for food, safety, a mate, seemed to tie up most of the circuitry most of the time. Nice if a way could be devised to switch around that.

Enough daydreaming. He turned back to the acquisition of facts.

◆◆◆

"Mee-uster Ar-*joo*-nian is on the phone."

"Thank you, Mrs. Dortmunder," Chatterjee said. He pressed the button on his speakerphone. "Well, Mike? Are we making any progress?"

"So-so. Whaddya want first?"

"What have you learned about Dr. Bridgeman's activities?"

"He's screwing Storey's psychiatrist, if that's worth anything."

"That's interesting news, Mike."

"Hell, she works for you. You probably know more than I do."

I wish I did, thought Chatterjee. "She doesn't work for me, Mike. The foundation's affairs are completely separate, as you know all too well. Do you see any threat to us there? Is he snooping into financial matters?"

"Doesn't look it, Jack. I think he just got the hots for this gal when he was visiting the hospital, so he's visiting the hospital a lot these days. The only possible problem, he's

169

also asking a lot of questions about the way Storey ran his lab. I can see some potential stickiness there if word gets out to OSHA or the EPA or some other busybody agency, but I believe you've got a containment going on that, am I right?''

"Yes, yes. Putting that aside for the moment, Mike, what can we do about reducing the costs of these stock transactions? And still expedite them through the, uh, most efficient channel. . . . I trust you know who I'm talking about.''

"Yeah, I checked. There's nothing on your gentleman. Believe me, the SEC's already done its best. And even if there was, Jack, what could we do with it? My advice, as a friend, not as your lawyer, my advice is, play along with him.''

Chatterjee was silent. Mike Arjunian, Compugen's corporate attorney, had his own reasons for wanting to "play along" with Chatterjee's long-time broker: Arjunian's personal savings were tied up in Compugen and his own fortunes rode with Chatterjee's. Perhaps Chatterjee really had no choice. "Thank you for your help, Mike. I want you to be assured I'm personally doing the best I can for you.''

"I really appreciate that, Jack. I really do.''

"Good-bye, Mike.'' Chatterjee abruptly hung up.

He stared at the message he'd received just before being interrupted by Arjunian's phone call. His New England sales manager, Harold Lillard, seemed to have contracted some sudden and debilitating illness, possibly psychotic. Chatterjee did not have the slightest idea what to make of the news. He only hoped Lillard hadn't put all his savings into Compugen. Perhaps there was something to be said for quarters after all.

He turned his attention back to the excruciating task of trying to dump his own and Arjunian's Compugen stock, and that of a few other favored cronies, without bringing the Securities and Exchange Commission knocking on his office door. Internally, things were secure; Bridgeman seemed to have found something relatively harmless to occupy himself, and after this morning's meeting the employees were living in a fool's paradise of promised bonuses and exciting new research programs. All of which would last another two or three weeks, if they were lucky.

Selling stock was only part of Chatterjee's problem. He also had to stash the proceeds offshore where it would be safe from the Feds when they eventually caught up. Which they surely would.

Even after the news of Adrian Storey's "nervous breakdown," Compugen stock was still riding high on the success of the Tyger II. But Chatterjee had had to give away more than half the gross of what he'd been able to sell, in bribes.

That in itself didn't gall him. What rankled was that, in return for silence and the judicious spreading of false rumors, his own broker, his old buddy, was the most insistent bribee!

"Harold, the children are here. Gary. And Paul. Young
Marian. Agnes. And the little ones. They want to say hello to
their father."

Harold said nothing. He lay stiffly among the starched
sheets, staring at the acoustic-tiled ceiling, unconscious of
the brooding dark faces of his wife and offspring clustered
about his bed. Tubes fed into the veins of his arms, and into
his nose; sensors sent discrete signals to quiet monitors,
where traces of green light confirmed that Harold still breathed,
that his heart still beat, that his brain still produced random
bursts of its own peculiar electromagnetic energy.

The older boys clustered protectively around their mother;
though they bulked large and determined, they also seemed
slightly embarrassed, as if their father were showing appalling manners in refusing to answer her, as if she were humili-
ating herself by trying to talk to him.

Agnes turned to Gary and began questioning him, *sotto*

voce, about his visit to the family lawyer, but Marian turned on her. "Not in front of him," Marian said.

"Sorry, Ma, I didn't think that it . . ." Stricken, she glanced at her father, then turned away. Her sister put an arm around her as she started to sob.

"Come on, Mama, it's better we don't make a fuss," said Paul, almost whispering.

Marian ignored him. It had been her dogged strength that had kept the family functioning thus far through the course of Harold's short, terrifying illness. In the midst of her fear she had never lost the certainty that had guided her all her life, that God had a clear idea of everything that was happening and why, and that it was her task merely to smooth the mundane wrinkles in existence as she came to them, much as if she were ironing an endless sheet. "Harry, I know you can hear me. Just see if you can answer."

Theresa, standing near the end of the bed between the tall shapes of her two oldest brothers, reached out to pat her father's knee. Neither he nor the monitors showed any sign that he had felt her thin hand. She withdrew it, and sniffled.

Anthony watched Theresa, twisting his hands behind his back. When she looked at him he smiled shyly.

"The doctor will be here in a moment," said a nurse from the doorway. "Will you all please wait in the visitors' lounge until he has completed his examination?"

Marian bent and gave Harold a quick gentle pat, then turned to the door. The children filed out slowly behind her.

The visitors' "lounge" on this floor of the vast and ancient medical center was a wide place off a busy hallway. Nurses and interns rushed past, while ambulatory patients clad only in blue wrappers tied in the back staggered along, clutching the walls, and overhead a defective public-address speaker fuzzed something about "Dokr Jkbwsky to rdgrphy. Mr. Srrmlls pick up wide kutsy tlfn. Nzz Bnnnz sjry *stat*."

Marian and the children settled themselves on the furniture of worn green plastic and tubular steel. Agnes, a twenty-year-old version of scrawny Theresa, stood at the corner of the hall; she nervously pulled out a pack of brown cigarettes and lit one, avoiding the disapproving glance of her mother.

An old black woman was the only other occupant of the waiting area. Wearing a pink fake-fur ski jacket and dirty orange stretch slacks, she hunched in a chair on the opposite side of the room and stared curiously at the Lillards, meanwhile sucking noisily on a Players' cigarette and spilling the ashes in her lap.

In uneasy silence the Lillards waited for the doctor to finish his examination.

With his opthalmoscope Louis Sherfey peered into Harold's open eyes, searching for characteristic signs of known neurological disease. Or drug addiction. Or brain death.

He found nothing of interest—no evidence of high blood pressure, tumor, vitamin deficiency, collagen abnormality, diabetes, no congenital abnormality. Harold's eyes might have been made of glass.

Sherfey straightened and pocketed the instrument. He glanced again at the charts and monitors, grunted, and walked out of the intensive care unit without a backward glance at his patient.

Sherfey was a wizened gnome whose tanned and freckled pate was barely covered by a gauze of thin white hair. A professor of neurophysiology at Harvard Medical School, a senior member of the hospital's Department of Medicine, he was one of the country's most distinguished students of the human brain.

He was less at home with human emotions. Alerted to the Lillard case by the regular staff, Sherfey had taken a personal interest, partly because the hospital's other physicians admitted they were stumped. Sherfey found Harold Lillard's unique catatonia baffling. Clinically fascinating. There was a good deal to be learned from it, he was quite sure.

He located the patient's family in the waiting room. The thick middle-aged woman was the wife. Odd shape. Pregnant? At her age? Life was various indeed. "Mrs. Lillard, I'm Lou Sherfey. Would you come with me to my office?"

The woman stared at him, ensconced on the plastic settee, surrounded by her stark-faced children. "My feet are tired, Doctor. Talk to me here, why don't you?"

"Certainly, as you wish." Sherfey was unperturbed. "Doctor Arthur asked me to look into your husband's problem. Tomorrow I'd like to move Mr. Lillard to the neurophysiology wing, just across the street. We can keep him under closer observation there, and we're specialized for this sort of thing."

Gary, who resembled his father the most of any of the boys, said gruffly, "What's that going to involve? I mean financially?"

"I'm afraid you'll have to check at the front desk," said Sherfey. "Surely the employer has insurance?" When Gary said nothing, Sherfey turned back to Marian. "Mrs. Lillard, I hope you understand, this case is clearly unique. There are a few sensitive matters—"

"They can hear it."

"Of course." Sherfey gave Gary a warning look. "Your children seem to be responsible young people, and I'm sure it will come as no surprise to them to learn that Mr. Lillard is gravely ill. Very gravely ill."

"When will he die, then?" the woman asked flatly.

"Of course, we'll do everything possible with the considerable resources at our disposal—"

"Doctor—"

"—but I'm afraid there's some possibility your instincts

may be correct.'' He insisted on getting the standard reassur-
ances out of the way.

"When?''

Sherfey told the simple truth: "At any time.''

The furry voice of the public-address system filled the
silence: "Dkr Brnt, xtsn thrdeedree. Dokr Nmboodrir to
'tholgy. . . .''

Then Theresa began to cry. When she sneezed in the midst
of her blubbering, Sherfey reflexively groped for the wad of
tissues he carried in the pocket of his white coat. He thrust
out a Kleenex and she took it, bobbing her head in thanks.

Marian ignored Theresa. She leaned forward, and Paul
quickly bent to take her elbow.

Sherfey said quickly, "That's really not all I had to say,
Mrs. Lillard.''

"I have to call Father Berneri,'' she said. "We can talk
later.''

"Oh goodness, there's certainly plenty of time for that,''
said Sherfey.

His pitiless words cut through her unspoken grief. She
settled back into the sagging plastic.

"If, as seems likely, your husband should die of his
affliction before we are able to ascertain its exact nature, we
will be in urgent need of your assistance,'' Sherfey continued, regretting his harshness, trying to disguise his impatience. "I'd like you to assure me of your willingness to
provide that assistance.''

"What do you want?'' she asked.

"Brain research is a tremendously . . . *challenging* . . .
field, Mrs. Lillard. But it can be an extraordinarily difficult
field to pursue. Not because of the technical hurdles alone, I
assure you, although those are indeed daunting.'' He realized
he was going at Marian Lillard as if she were a foundation
president instead of a grieving spouse. He was out of practice

at this sort of thing; usually the interns did it for him. "The ethical considerations, these are far more, um, confining."

From the opposite side of the room the old black woman snorted. The sound might have been derisive; it was hard to know, for it ended in a tearing cough.

"Your husband's situation is unique," Sherfey repeated warmly. "Nothing in his medical history or personal situation of the moment gives a clue to his catatonia. There is no sign of infectious disease. No test we have administered gives us so much as a hint of any known organic problem. Yet the neurological specificity of the syndrome is undeniable. We certainly would like to have a look . . ." On the thin edge of disaster some instinct saved him. He attempted a friendly smile.

As her children looked on, mute, numb, she said, "Go ahead, Doctor. You take all the time you want with Harold. Look at his brain. I'll sign the papers."

He was mildly surprised, but very pleased. The woman seemed to have known what he was getting at. Just to be sure, he pressed her. "You understand we're discussing an autopsy . . . ?"

"Of course I do. Harold always said he thought it was a social obligation to give his body to science. It's in his will. If you want me to sign something, I'll sign it." She sighed. "But let me call Father Berneri now, if you would be so kind."

Without another word, Sherfey got out of her way.

◆◆◆

Susana's Sabatier blade nipped up and down within milli-meters of her fingertips as she minced peeled garlic cloves to fine shreds. "It's a hell of a romance, sister. The man won't even bother to get unmarried."

"Neither will I," said Joana from the direction of the sink, where she was peeling carrots. "From my job."

"An evasion if I ever heard one."

"Well, who are you to talk? Wasn't Eric quite happily married when you got him to—" Joana broke off awkwardly, aware that Margaret had just entered the room.

The red-haired little girl trundled confidently to a counter that held an old-fashioned cookie jar. She tugged a stool into place, hitched up her green corduroy overalls, and climbed to the top. Just as she reached for the jar, Susana, who had barely glanced up, said, *"One."*

Margaret eyed her mother askance and gave out an exag-gerated sigh, but she fished out a single chocolate-chip cookie, carefully replaced the lid of the jar, climbed down, and

179

walked away. As she reached the archway to the dining room she turned to Joana. "Now you can tell secrets. 'Cause I'm not listening."

Joana waited until the child had gone. Then she said, "Ha."

"It's not easy to keep anything from her," said Susana. "I doubt the transgression you were about to charge me with is any secret."

"She knows her father was married to another woman?"

"She knows he's married now, and that he has children of his own." Susana looked up, assuming a mock-sweet expression. "But he lives very far away, and though he wants to come and visit her, it's just not possible. Not this year."

"I see."

"Do I detect disapproval?"

"Look, Su, I'll zip my mouth if you'll zip yours. Let me have Toby my way."

"No argument. But who's being had?"

"I assure you, it's mutual."

"I'd love to believe it. Okay, okay, I'm dropping the subject." She swept the minced garlic into her hands and slapped it onto the pork roast that lay in the pan, vigorously massaging the naked pink flesh. "Let's get this in the oven and have a drink."

Ringed by mossy terraces and cloaked by shrubbery on the steep hillside, the garden and the back of the two-story house were well concealed from neighboring houses and from the street. Joana and her sister took fresh margaritas to the brick patio in the small garden, and there settled into a long niche in the retaining wall.

Susana pulled her full peasant skirts across her knees. "So when do I get to meet your irresistible philanderer?"

"Soon. We've been spending three and four hours a night

at his place—doing nothing but programming.'' Joana grinned. ''Well, almost nothing. Torrid, eh? I've started to hate it, if you want to know. At first it was kind of fun, and I thought I was humoring him, which was pretty stupid. Then I realized I was doing it to prove I could.''

''What do you have to prove to this guy?''

''Nothing. And he doesn't ask. But I want to prove I can do it, Su, because—I just do. Anyway, while I practice he reads neurophysiology. He's got this charmingly naïve notion that when we can put his knowledge of computers and my knowledge of the human psyche together, we'll miraculously cure his friend Adrian. Tom Swift and his Digitized Psychiatrist.''

''Head trips,'' said Susana sourly. ''Remember what that son of a bitch of a zoologist did to you?'' It was a rhetorical question; Susana was looking into the shadows, sipping from her drink.

''Toby's a fountain of ideas,'' said Joana, blandly ignoring her. ''Half of them are nutty, and he realizes it himself the next morning. Some of them strike me as extraordinarily insightful—and there's absolutely no way they could ever be tested. Some of them are good and useful. Meanwhile I try to keep him calmed down while I learn his damned LISP.''

''He lisps?''

Joana laughed. ''LISP is a computer language, the one the artificial intelligence people use.''

Dutifully, she tried to convey the intellectual attractions of programming to her sister: conceptually simple, programs quickly grew intricate and surprising, but the surprises were instructive, and the intricacy was at least aesthetically pleasing. In the beginning it had seemed like play.

But Joana's ten-hour days on Leigh-Mercy's psychiatric ward, alternating with even longer days in Oakland, left her

weary. She doubted she would be able to give the new hobby
the energy it demanded much longer. "Tonight's the first
time I've skipped Dr. Bridgeman's class. I've been missing
you."

"About time you had a proper dinner." Susana took a
mouthful of the icy margarita and shivered. The April night
was cool. "Hmm. What about the object of all this attention?
The patient, what was his name?"

Joana sighed. "Adrian. I don't know what's going on
there. He's not improving. That's about all I can say. Lee
talked me into some new tests, synchrotron radiation imaging—
a new kind of x rays they do at the university. With an atom
smasher."

"That should be good for him, getting his atoms smashed,"
Susana muttered. Her margarita glass was empty. She studied
it.

"You went through that one pretty fast," said Joana.

"Let me freshen yours."

"In a minute. Wait for me, okay?" For a moment neither
woman spoke. "I saw Paterson today," said Joana. "I heard
Teddy is going back in the clinic."

"Yes, there are some things . . ." Susana let the sentence
trail off.

"Anything I can help with?"

Susana's lips bent in a quick smile, and tears started in her
eyes. "Just come see me every once in a while, okay?"

Joana slid forward and took her sister's hand.

"*In both sensitization and classical conditioning a reflex
response to a stimulus is enhanced as a result of the activa-
tion of another pathway.*" Toby was certain that sentence
had a very simple content, but the more times he read it, the
harder he concentrated, the more it seemed to dissolve into
euphonious nonsense.

He put the book aside. He checked the Epicell prototype, off on its own trip. He played with his Tyger I, trying to amuse himself with tiling games. No fun. He was bored.

He was also hungry. There were several things he could do about that. He could cook something, ghastly thought. He could go to a restaurant and eat alone, feeling foolish and restless. He could skip dinner and play racquetball instead, if he could get a court and a match. Exercise usually killed his appetite.

He drove the two miles to the club in the marina. It was as busy as usual in the early evening, but he was lucky. After spreading the word and hanging around watching others play for half an hour, he picked up a game with a man whose partner had quit early.

He knew the fellow well enough, and they were both fair players, so Toby didn't have to waste a lot of time calibrating his game. He went at it hard and thoughtfully, investing all his physical and mental energy into sending the ball where he wanted it to go, snagging it when it came at him, trying to steer it where his opponent wasn't. The sound of the ball hitting the racquet, hitting the wall, over and over, served him as a sort of mantra.

After forty-five minutes of close, hot work he emerged pleasantly exhausted, having narrowly won one and narrowly lost two. He shook hands with his partner and waved good-bye. He walked up the carpeted stairs to the balcony bar. He took a cold Beck's beer to the rail and leaned against it, looking down on the glass courts below, daydreaming.

"Wanna sit down?" It was a woman at one of the tiny round tables beside the rail. "You can see just as good."

"Well—thanks," said Toby. He could hardly have turned his back on her. He pulled a chair to the other side of the table and smiled. "I'm Toby."

"I know. I asked. My name's Darlene." Darlene had a

wide, pretty smile, and light brown hair permed into loose curls. Her V-cut purple leotard clung tightly to her large breasts, which hovered near the surface of the table; she was either cold or she had something on her mind.

"How nice to meet you," said Toby. Get up now and leave, he told himself sternly; this is the last thing you need. "Haven't I seen you here before?"

"Yeah, I just joined last month. Mostly for the weights. I noticed you right away," she confided, without a trace of coquetry. "But I haven't seen you for a couple of weeks."

"Yes, well I, umm . . ." All he had to do was mention Joana's name, it was that simple. Cursing himself, he gagged on the truth.

The conversation lurched on, and in time Toby learned that Darlene was an aerobics dance instructor, temporarily unemployed, and that she had two ambitions in life, one of them being to remain as happy and satisfied with herself as she was at that very moment, the other—a close second to the first—being to acquire "washboard abdominals."

Before midnight, lightheaded on three strong beers and an empty stomach, knowing that was no excuse, he found himself in the bedroom of her apartment.

Early the next morning he discovered that Joana had left a message on his answering machine: "Call me when you have a chance. It's about Adrian. I love you."

◆◆◆

"George can't do it." Adrian stared impassively at a
button on his pajama shirtfront. Cast adrift from its button-
hole, it had left a gap through which doughy skin gleamed.

"Shall I do it for you, Adrian?" Toby asked.

"No. George wants to." Adrian's gaze remained fixed on
the unbuttoned button. Both hands, resting on his knees,
trembled rhythmically. Aside from their slow vibration, Adrian
was motionless.

Toby said nothing. He knew a grinding struggle was going
on somewhere behind the mask, that anything he had to say
would be an irrelevant distraction. He stared at the gap in
Adrian's shirtfront as intently as Adrian did. Adrian's belly
fat mesmerized him; incongruously he thought of Darlene's
washboard abdominals.

Adrian's abdominals resembled the laundry more than the
washboard. His hands moved now, oscillating in regular little
circles, closing in on the button. They surrounded the neigh-

boring cloth, brought button and hole into near proximity, then mashed blindly against each other.

Several seconds passed without further progress.

Toby waited as long as he could; then he reached out and took Adrian's hands in his own, trying to still them. They quivered like small animals. Adrian's nervous tremor transmitted itself, and Toby could feel his own tense forearms and elbows wobbling in minute circles, slaves to positive feedback. He gently pushed Adrian's hands aside and flicked the white plastic button through the thread-wrapped lips of the hole.

Toby leaned back then and looked up at Adrian's face. Adrian was still expressionless, but tears wobbled on the rims of his eyelids. "Who are you?" he demanded.

Two orderlies arrived and, with brisk apologies to Toby, began arranging the passive Adrian on a gurney. Firmly they strapped his arms and legs to the stretcher. Their impatience was overlaid by a thin shellac of good manners, of the sort found only in the better-paying private clinics. Adrian said nothing; a tear escaped the corner of his eye and slid down his temple, into his ear.

"Where is he going?" Toby asked.

"The doctor wants another look at his CSF."

As they trundled Adrian into the hall, Toby turned to stare through the blinds at the high, thin fog. Summer was coming early. Inside and out, the world was toneless and flat.

Joana put her head through the door of Adrian's room. "I have a few minutes. My office."

He followed her past the bright windows, down the shadowless corridor. Behind them the orderlies wheeled Adrian away, turning off sharply at an intersection to disappear into the depths of the building.

Joana waited for Toby beside her office door. She closed it

behind him, stepped around him, and pressed herself quickly against him, letting her lips linger on his mouth.

"Mm, that was a long night." She stepped away. "Sit down. I'll just be a minute." Ignoring the blinking lights on her telephone, she turned to her file cabinet, moved a dying strand of Swedish ivy out of the way of the middle drawer, and began rooting through the ragged-edged papers crammed inside.

"You should put all that on a computer," he said idly.

"And have just anybody know where to find it?" She found the document she was looking for and yanked it from the file drawer, further shredding its frayed margins.

"Let's hope that doesn't have to last long," he said, smiling.

"That would be nice. Did you see what I meant about Adrian?"

"What do you make of it?"

"I don't know. Parkinsonism is typically a sign of damage to a specific area of the brain—"

"The substantia nigra."

"Yes, very good," she said, smiling coolly. "Perhaps you've also read that biochemically it would seem to be quite incompatible with schizophrenia."

"In fact that does ring a bell."

She slid into her chair, slouching as usual, her gaze skimming the pink sheet of paper. "Maybe we've all been wrong. The onset of this was incredibly rapid. I hope the new tests will tell us something." She set the file aside abruptly. "Hate to say it, but it's a busy day."

"I understand. Give me another moment." It was a bad time to introduce another wild theory; he tried to sneak up on the subject. "How would you go about identifying a viral infection?"

"That's where he's off to. Lumbar tap."

"So the orderlies said."

"We look for antibodies; usually they're easier to spot than the virus itself. There are various way of labeling them. When Adrian was admitted we did an immunoassay on his cerebrospinal fluid. CMV, for example—cytomegalovirus—has been implicated in schizophrenia." She tapped the sheet of paper she'd been reading. "Negative for CMV. Also negative for the viruses we know can cause specific neurological disorders—flu, herpes, polio, so on. But we're trying again. Spreading a finer net."

"How about a new virus?"

"An unknown? That's another matter. Looking for an unknown is tough. It can take months, years. Forever." She leaned forward, inserting her chin into the socket of her cupped hand, and gave him a suspicious stare. "Okay, Toby. Another bright idea?"

"What if I could give you the amino acid sequence and fully characterized structure of a novel protein? Viruslike. Could you test him for it?"

"Maybe. I don't know. I'm not a biochemist."

"Adrian's lab is a cesspool," he said. "In my uninformed opinion he could have caught half a dozen diseases there, including most of those you've just enumerated. I admit the staff disagrees with me. But I believe Adrian may have become infected with one particular . . . organism."

"Toby," she said quietly, "you promised not to play doctor."

"I assure you, I've said nothing to Adrian," Toby protested.

"That's not the point," she said firmly, sitting up straight. "Adrian is not an experimental toy, he's a suffering human being—"

Stung, he interrupted. "Indeed. It was I who—"

"—but not the *only* suffering human being. And each of your cute theories that I take half seriously, it ends up costing me and my other patients, of whom there are many, more of my *time*."

"I have no wish to see Adrian stored in a padded cell for the rest of his life." The bridge of Toby's nose grew pale.

Her nose, meanwhile, had turned pink beneath her freckles. "That was a rude, ignorant remark."

He puffed out his cheeks, then sighed. "I apologize. But if what happened to Adrian were in Dr. Lee's hands instead of yours . . ."

For a moment she said nothing. Suddenly she said, "Where were you last night?"

Toby felt his cheeks grow warm. It would have been the simplest thing in the world to lie. How often had he practiced smooth deception at just such a moment? Why, he'd forgotten to turn off the answering machine, that's all. Or he'd left the phone on the balcony. Or he'd come home so exhausted he'd have slept through a thunderstorm. In a pinch, if it would help to admit to a lesser sin, he could claim he'd been drunk.

Instead he blushed. His tongue felt like it had been shot full of Novocain.

Joana said, "I shouldn't have asked. I wasn't going to." She stood up. Then she sat down again. "I'm sorry."

Glowing, Toby watched her. "It's I who—"

"Please don't say anything at all, Toby. I don't think I could take your honesty at the moment." She stared at the ceiling, tears pooling in her eyes. "Maybe some other time." Savagely she wiped her coat sleeve across her face and shifted her teary gaze to the immunoassay report. "So what about this goddamned—*organism* of yours?"

He withdrew a folded sheet of computer printout from his inside jacket pocket. "Here's the sequence and a line drawing of the protein backbone," he said quietly. "I understand you can make specific antibodies from a short piece of synthetic peptide. The technique has been used to trace uptake of previously unidentified proteins in neuronal pathways.''

''Really,'' she muttered, taking the printout. ''Are you suggesting we section Adrian's brain?''

His face darkened. ''I—''

''There's a word for people who don't know how much they don't know, Toby. Sophomoric.''

He shifted uncomfortably. ''Touché.''

She stood again, shoving the desk chair away impatiently. ''Well, I'll give this to neurophysiology. Do you have a name for your pet virus?''

''It's not a virus, exactly.'' He got to his feet. ''But yes, it has a name. Epicell.''

''Sure. Epicell.'' She distractedly brushed an imaginary wisp of hair out of her eyes. ''Now get out of here, please. And I'm going to ask you not to visit Adrian anymore. Not for a while.''

''Why?'' He was offended, genuinely surprised. ''Unless you find that protein, nothing's changed.''

''The problem is your attitude. You keep telling me you understand that Adrian is a human being, but your definition of a human being is different from mine. I don't think we're nothing but 'information-processing machines'—''

''I never said—''

''—*and* I don't think that emotion, cognition, motivation— all the richness of human thought and feeling and action— can be reduced to a circuit diagram.'' She spoke loudly, and her eyes glittered with anger.

''Nor do I. Joana, I've personally—''

''Toby, you *do*. You believe in artificial intelligence. You're trying to create it. It's all a very challenging game, believe me, I appreciate that now. And I thank you for the—education. But clearly you're projecting your own fantasies onto Adrian, with this continued insistence that he has somehow been magically transformed into a . . . a . . .'' She stopped.

He shrugged, frustrated. ''All I've done is suggest he's got an infection. At least you could test—''

''I'll do as I said.''

He cleared his throat. ''I'll be available if more information—''

''Thanks. I'll call you later, Toby. Now I'm sorry, but I really am terribly busy.''

''I'll be at home,'' he said, but she said nothing and would not look at him. He left. He had rarely felt less charming.

As soon as he left, her tears started afresh. Why had she brought that up? Why couldn't she just lock the nasty thing in its box?

She stared at the paper he had given her. She'd been quite unfair, of course, using Adrian against him just at that moment. Although she also knew she was right—it *was* best that he stay away from Adrian, until the real cause was identified.

But *him*! Though he hadn't promised her anything, he'd implied it. He was like wax in a woman's hands, taking the form that was pressed on him. When Joana was with him, he was with her. When she went away, he found somebody else. Maybe his wife still thought they were married!

She picked up the phone and tapped out the number of the clinic's molecular biology department. She'd acted as if it were a complicated thing to test for Toby's novel protein, but it wasn't. Not these days. In a few hours they'd have the peptides; overnight they'd have the antibodies. By tomorrow afternoon she'd know if this—Epicell—was in Adrian's spinal fluid.

What would she tell Toby if he were right?

She stared at the phone, waiting for someone to answer.

Sadness swept over her. What would she do with herself tonight?

She knew. She'd start on all the work that had been piling up while she was playing his damned computer games. After all, she wasn't one to waste time.

And what would he do with himself?

◆ ◆ ◆

"Good afternoon, Sherman. You're looking cheerful to-day. As usual." Stanislaw Kubiak looked magisterially down upon his portly colleague, who brooded over a cup of the ERMIT Corporation's weak cafeteria coffee.

"If I were given to vulgarity, I would suggest that you do something anatomically unlikely to yourself," snarled the other man, not looking up.

Kubiak sniffed. "How fortunate for me that you are in fact too cultured a gentleman to suggest any such thing," he said nasally, setting his cafeteria tray down across the table. "Could it possibly be that you are encountering deciphering difficulties?"

The florid Sherman Gass said nothing, but his face glowed a brighter pink. He slurped at his coffee, then swiped at his rosebud lips with a napkin.

Kubiak smiled. "You don't appreciate progress, Sherman. I've known that a long time, but your resolute Luddism continues to dismay me."

193

Gass ponderously shifted his weight. "I appreciate progress in cryptanalysis, Stan. These new computers of yours are toys."

Kubiak grinned. "Sherman, Sherman, my friend, this humorless intransigence—it lacks subtlety. You're practically conceding defeat. You and your caged nerds in G persuaded yourselves we would never succeed. But a mere fortnight after we picked up those little beauties, all our problems have been solved."

Gass's rosy cheeks brightened, and he smacked his thick lips. "We'll find your weaknesses soon enough. You're not talking one-time pads, Stan, you're talking heavy traffic, field communication systems. You need reliability, you need redundancy." Gass showed yellow gapped teeth in what passed for a smile. "You'll be easy to crack." He shoved his chair back.

"Before you have to rush off," said Kubiak casually, "do me a favor and glance over these. I'd like your opinion." He held out a dozen pages of computer manifold, covered with equations.

Gass glared suspiciously at Kubiak, then grabbed the papers. His glance skipped lightly over the first couple of pages, but by the third sheet he had slowed and begun to read, to think. He turned the last page slowly.

His features were gelid. He slammed the sheaf of papers to the tabletop. "You had this already? All this has been a game to humiliate me?"

"Sherman," Kubiak said gently, "I had very little to do with that printout you are abusing. The Tyger II computer, working by itself in its spare time, has produced a general solution to its own methods of encryption."

"A machine did this? That's an absurdity. This is original work of the highest order!"

"Believe me, I sympathize." Kubiak abruptly grabbed for his napkin and sneezed into it. "Beg your pardon."

"*Gruss Gott,*" Gass snarled, loud enough to attract the attention of others in the cafeteria. "Something must be done about it!"

"Thank you—and I agree." Kubiak smiled. He blew his nose vigorously into his napkin. "I have something to show you."

"Really, Stanislaw," said Gass with disgust. "Why don't you go home to bed before we all catch our deaths?"

"I will. But first you must come with me."

Squinting, Kubiak peered through the eyepieces of the microscope at a complex structure of copper struts and girders, gleaming plates and transparent aqueducts, as extensive and seemingly as massive as the skeleton of a modern skyscraper. Hung in the midst of the framework was a glittering field of crystals, a ten-story futuristic sculpture.

"Ah, here it is," said Kubiak, proud of himself. "Sherman, look at this. I swear it's twice as big as it was the last time you were in here." Kubiak rolled his chair aside so that Gass could peer through the binoculars of the Zeiss microscope.

Gass was silent for a long moment. Then he grunted. "Thirty percent increase at best."

"Pick-*eee*. With that attitude you'll never learn to write truly magnificent grant proposals." Kubiak looked on as the man continued to stare silently into the microscope. "Wiggle the stage a little," Kubiak suggested. "See the way it breaks up the light? Like a diffraction grating. It's quite beautiful, really."

"Simple crystalline structure," Gass muttered, unimpressed.

"Oh, give me that back." Kubiak, rolling back to the microscope, pushed his colleague aside. He gazed at the magnified array of threadlike wires and glass microtubules for several long seconds before lifting his bald, bearded head. Rising from his chair, he reverently detached the sloppy disk from the microscope slide and reinserted it in the exposed Tyger II on the electronics workbench nearby. He carefully closed the tiny machine's cover.

Kubiak straddled his chair backward this time, resting his hairy forearms on its back, a posture that simultaneously suggested informality and a readiness to move fast. He looked past his pudgy colleague serenely, as if gazing into the future—though in fact he was looking at a smudged plasterboard wall hung with crude Government Printing Office posters exhorting him to safety and discretion. "You know, Sherman, I'm not sure we really need all that reliability and redundancy in the system itself. What if we just equipped the troops with Tygers? You a betting man?"

Gass looked offended. "Are you serious?"

"Forget the bet, then. Remember that on this fine spring day I predicted a revolution. A Tyger II in every pocket, and the American fighting man's secrets will be safe forever."

"You won't tell the Russians, will you, Stan?" Gass mounted his most withering sneer.

Kubiak redirected his benign gaze to Gass's pudgy features. "Damn it, Sherman," he said softly, a crease appearing across the front of his bald dome, "why didn't I think of that before you did? Sometimes I think I wasn't really cut out for this work." He sniffed irritably.

"Really, Stanislaw—"

"I'm quite serious. Maybe there's a reason the government pays your salary after all." Kubiak tugged at his flowing beard, something he only did when scheming. "I think I'd better put in a call to my friend Lillard. I wonder if Professor Bridgeman is having any luck filling up his sloppy disk?"

◆◆◆

Adrian, lightly sedated, mumbling of adventures with his breakfast tray, was strapped into a wheelchair and rolled into the parking lot. There he was transferred into the back of a university car waiting to take him on the short ride up the hill. Joana got in beside him, logy with fatigue. If she were to become this involved with all her patients, she'd burn out in a month.

The Lawrence Berkeley Laboratory sprawls in the hills above the University of California campus, the dome of its 184-inch accelerator squatting like a stupa on a wooded ridge, its other big machines nestling discreetly among the trees. The hot spring weather had brought the coast deer to the edge of the hills to raid suburban gardens. Joana saw a doe and her newborn fawn watching from the dry shade of a eucalyptus grove as the car climbed Cyclotron Road and entered the main gate.

The driver stopped in front of a circular building housing the electron storage ring. Two attendants greeted them at the door with a gurney at the ready, but as Adrian unfolded himself from the front seat he said firmly, "George wants to walk."

Joana nodded to the driver, a strapping young student, who got out and helped her steady Adrian; supported between the two of them, he walked with elaborate caution into the building's cool, cluttered interior, while the attendants with their gurney followed at a discreet distance. Joana looked around curiously and saw what appeared to be a half-empty warehouse, its space randomly occupied by a jumble of pipes and squat pieces of electronic equipment, big blocks of concrete and thick plates of iron. The hum of machinery was a blanket of white noise, penetrated only by a distant chiming.

Most of the building's interior was filled with a ring-shaped structure, a recurving concrete wall, but tangent to it were straight sections terminating in concrete-block rooms. The attendants led Adrian toward one of the nearer doors. A sign beside it said "Cave E."

From the cave emerged a pudgy middle-aged man, blinking. Graying blond hair stood out thickly from his head; he resembled a sleepy hedgehog, Disney-style. "Who are *you*?" Adrian said with real interest, startling the hedgehog so that he took a step back toward his den.

Another man was hurrying up to them from somewhere in the interior of the place, a distinguished-looking fellow in his fifties, with a neat dark beard streaked with gray. "Golly, Dr. Davies, you beat us to it," he called cheerily. "I'm Sam Hansen," he said, thrusting out his hand. "We talked on the phone."

Joana shook his hand. Hansen's white socks and high-pitched voice threatened to betray his dignity, but that suited Joana just fine. At least he was human.

Hansen introduced the furry medical technician, who would ensure that Adrian was properly aligned in front of the x-ray machinery. Coaxing and clucking, the technician led Adrian into the cave and settled him on a steel bench. Adrian appeared to be listening in fascination.

Hansen gestured to Joana to follow them inside. Inside the cramped room he patted a stainless steel pipe bristling with calibrating knobs. Cheerfully he described the operation of the machinery. "The beam from the synchrotron here is just a nifty source of x rays, no different from the x rays you folks use in your CAT scanners, except terrifically *intense*, plus they come in really short bursts and they're *monochromatic*—we tune 'em to just exactly the frequency we want—which means we don't do near as much *damage* to tissue."

"Who *are* you?" Adrian demanded, focusing on the excited voice.

"He's a friend, Adrian," said Joana, laying her hand on Adrian's shoulder; it seemed to calm him.

She asked Hansen to continue. Though she tried to follow his explanation, she felt herself mentally drifting. What was it about this painted metal, these templates of glass and aluminum, these clamps and straps locking Adrian's head into the target position—this whole bright, grim room of steel and concrete, with its eager experimenters mumbling at each other—that made her deeply uneasy, that brought her near to anger? Why the irrational suspicion that none of these people thought of the gangling body on the stretcher as more than a giant hamster?

She struggled to maintain her clinical detachment, but what she felt in the presence of research scientists and their arcane devices was not much different from what most of her patients felt in the presence of ordinary physicians like herself. Toby had confided that he'd had the same reaction to her the first time they'd met—suspicion and resentment in the face of "strong juju," as he'd put it, in that sometimes bizarre British slang of his.

Perhaps that was it. Joana had always prided herself on her humanism, her insistence that basic values of dignity, trust, honor, love, even sacrifice, were at the core of healing, especially the healing of the psyche. But by training she was a scientist, by disposition a pragmatist, and she was ready to use any method that worked; she was open to any discovery that might advance the curative arts, no matter by what reductionist philosophy and technique that advance may have been achieved. For more than a decade in her own practice— and she had enough of a sense of history to know that the trend was much older—she'd looked on with only mild enthusiasm as peptides and hormones and trace elements and metal salts, not to mention the genetic predispositions which underlay these metabolic irregularities, had loomed larger and larger in explanations of mental imbalance: as the prescription of drugs had increasingly shouldered aside the prescription of human care.

Perhaps she was only jealous that the machine-men's juju was proving stronger than her own.

The men around Adrian's supine form suddenly stirred, and Hansen said to her, "Best to clear out of the way now." If he was offended by her inattention, he was too much the gentleman to show it.

Joana patted Adrian's arm. He looked up at her with innocent curiosity. She glanced over her shoulder as she left and saw him lying there, pinned like a sacrificial goat where hungry photons would devour him.

◆◆◆

Toby was stretched face up on a plastic chaise on the bedroom balcony, sweating profusely. A fragrant heat lay on the cities of the Bay. Overhead the sky was blue, swept clean by breezes aloft. The glass and concrete of the Bay Plaza shimmered in the afternoon sunlight as if the structure were about to dissolve into the ether.

Stoically rigid, clad only in white boxer shorts, Toby braced himself against the sunshine, determined to acquire some skin color—though a decade in California had not freed him of his father's prejudice that the only Englishmen with sun tans were the worthlessly rich, the outright criminal, or those who simply could not keep a job.

He thought about Joana. He'd found himself thinking about her a lot. If he were a conventional sort of chap, he would admit to himself that he was in love with her. But to him, love seemed only the beginning of complications, not some epiphanic state. To realize he was *in love* was not an occasion for celebration. For one thing, it meant that the actual company of other women would now, as it had already, come to seem stale and joyless.

Unfortunately, it did not mean he would cease being compelled by his attraction to other women. But if he could get no pleasure from the company of many women, and could not remain faithful to one, what was the use of love?

So he would not admit that he was in love. And he would not do anything about it. He would be patient. He would wait it out. It was a strategy that had always worked before.

Inside the apartment the phone buzzed faintly. He let it go.

Of course, it might be Joana. More likely it was some fellow from the factory. In Adrian's absence people from Compugen had started ringing up Toby any time a salesman had a problem with a Tyger II. He accepted the responsibility of debugging his own programs, but none of these problems were new; he and Adrian had drafted technical manuals months ago for the benefit of the service staff.

On the third ring he abruptly jumped up and went inside.

Blind in the shadows, he scooped up the phone as he answered it, carrying it from the bedroom bureau into the living room, its long cord trailing. "Hullo?" He fell back lazily onto the couch, its leather sticky and cool against his back.

"It's Joana, Toby. You have a right to know they've found something."

"That was quick." Hastily, he added, "It was good of you to call me."

"I said I would." Her voice was cool. "This is a preliminary result. They've found lots of an unknown protein, the same size as that structure of yours, in Adrian's CSF."

He rolled upright. "It's in his brain?"

"That's not established, although it's not unlikely. We've also arranged for synchrotron x-ray studies. Are you familiar with that technique?"

"Yes." He thought of the movies he and Adrian had made of Epicell growing, organizing, the ones they'd shown on television. Now they were planning to make movies of Adrian's head.

"Yes, I suppose you probably know more about it than I do," said Joana, her voice distant on the phone. "The clinic participates in a university-run program. Dr. Lee is very enthusiastic about space-age technology. He thinks Adrian is an ideal subject."

"Right, then."

"I thought you'd be pleased. Well, that's all I had—"

"Joana," he heard himself saying, "we have other things to talk about." How is it possible, he thought, that I could have decided quite rationally *not* to do a thing, to say a thing, and five minutes later . . . ?

"Let's go into that later," she replied.

"When, exactly?"

"Let me think about it. Oh, by the way, they'd like a sample to confirm that the protein they've found is yours. Can you provide it?"

He looked at the little prototype on his table. Shame to interrupt its thoughts. He thought of Adrian's locked refrigerator. "I doubt that Jack Chatterjee would be delighted to hear about this," he said.

Her voice was almost amused. "I haven't mentioned any brand names."

"Perhaps we should simply buy a Tyger II and tear it to pieces. They're cheap enough."

"Can you get something you know he handled? That would be better."

"I can't get into his office." He thought of the scattered Epicell parts on the desk in Adrian's living room. "I could try his house."

"Let me know what you decide."

"Certainly. I'll call you."

"Good-bye, Toby."

The line went dead in his hand.

He carried the phone back into the bedroom. He was in the bathroom when it rang again. Half dressed, he answered it on the fourth ring. Jack Chatterjee was on the line.

"What is it, Jack? Forgive me, I'm in a bit of a rush." Toby leaned over and twisted the blinds to block the glare of the low sun.

"You'll be receiving a phone call from a Dr. Stanislaw Kubiak. He has been urgently trying to contact you here at the office. You must . . . Excuse me a moment."

Waiting for Jack, Toby impatiently wandered through his apartment, the handset clutched to his ear. He carefully pushed the parts of the Epicell prototype a few inches farther from the edge of the dining-room table, then set the phone on the glass tabletop.

"You must tell him you haven't talked to me." Chatterjee was suddenly back, whispering into the phone, more squeakily than usual. "Make an excuse. Call him back."

"What's this all about, Jack?"

"I'll explain later." He hung up.

"Bloody hell, Jack!"

He'd no sooner put down the handset when the phone rang again.

"Bridgeman!"

"Stan Kubiak at ERMIT Corporation in Massachusetts," said a jolly voice. "We haven't met, but we used to suck the same tit."

Toby stared at the phone a moment, nonplussed. "Oh, you mean ARPA." The Defense Department's Advanced Research Projects Agency had sponsored the bulk of Toby's artificial intelligence research at Berkeley. "Ha, ha, jolly good.'' Who was this guy? ''You had that paper on fast primality tests in the last *I.P. Quarterly.*''

''What the bureaucrats left uncensored,'' Kubiak answered nasally. He sounded like he had a terrible cold. ''If you ever get around to reading it, tell me what you think.''

''Well, I glanced at it, and I'm certainly looking forwa—''

''Actually, I called on business, Toby,'' Kubiak said, genially cutting him off. ''I'd like to know how your limit test is set up, what you're doing with it. Any indication of practical boundaries to Epicell expansion yet?''

''What do you know about a limit test, Dr. Kubiak?''

''Just that Harold mentioned it to me. Poor guy.''

''Harold?''

''Harold Lillard, your sales manager for this region.''

''I don't know him, I'm afraid.''

''Too bad, nice guy, but you lost your chance,'' said Kubiak, almost cheerfully. ''He died yesterday. Maybe a stroke, the way his wife described it. Jack Chatterjee must have worked him to death.''

Toby hesitated. ''Dr. Kubiak, I'm afraid I'm not in an academic setting. I can't discuss anything that might be an internal corporate matter.''

Kubiak's laughter was thinned by congestion. ''I've already talked to Chatterjee; he's cleared this discussion.''

''Delighted to hear it.''

''I'll give you time to confirm.''

''Oh, I'd have to do that, of course. First, why don't you tell me why you're asking?''

''Sure, Toby. By the way, you'll be happy to know ARPA says your Top Secret clearance is still in effect, as of this morning. What I'm telling you falls under that.''

Who *was* this guy? ''In that case, perhaps the public phone lines are not the place to—''

''In fact this call isn't going by the usual routes. And I

happen to know what safeguards you've got installed at your end. Jack says you bright guys who like to work at home cost him a bundle that way.'' Another chuckle.

"You've been very thorough, Dr. Kubiak.''

"Just to reassure you. In a nutshell, then: I'm in the cipher business. Any cipher practical for heavy traffic can be broken, but not fast enough to do the other fellow any good, if people like me do our jobs right. I . . . Wait a minute.'' Kubiak sneezed, then sneezed again. " 'Scuse me. Where were we?''

"Devising battlefield ciphers.''

"Did I mention the battlefield? Anyway, it boils down to creating keys that are easy to use, easy to change, but hard to find without a supercomputer.'' The pause was minimal, the next sentence delivered in the same cheery tone. "Are you guys selling supercomputers over the counter, Toby?''

"I understand your concern. I'll call you back.''

"I'll call *you* back. Ten minutes. Now, don't go away! Chatterjee's waiting to hear from you.''

"Yes, I'm quite sure he is. Good-bye.'' Kubiak was chuckling as he hung up.

Toby punched a number; Chatterjee answered on the first ring. "Reassure him there are practical limits to Epicell growth,'' said Chatterjee. "Talk about heat, thermodynamics, something like that. You must persuade those ERMIT people we're well short of a threat to national security.''

"I won't lie to the government for you, Jack.''

"Do you want an embargo on the entire Tyger line, Toby?''

Toby was silent a moment. "Do you have any idea what happened to Harold Lillard?''

"I don't know the details. Cerebral hemorrhage, perhaps.''

"He was young.''

"It can happen to anybody.''

"Where did he die?''

"In the hospital, I suppose. Really, Toby, is this the time
to—"

"Jack, how far are you willing to go with this?"

"What do you mean?" Chatterjee whispered angrily.

"I mean, what are you prepared to do to keep the true
capacities of Epicell a secret from your own government?"

Chatterjee's voice was slow, barely audible. "I assure you
your efforts on behalf of the corporation will be very handsomely rewarded. Even more handsomely than they are now,
and that is quite handsomely indeed."

"Right, then," said Toby briskly. "Just what I wanted to
hear. I'll do all I can." He hung up.

Toby turned away, staring at the symbols on the prototype's tiny screen. Abruptly he reached out and tapped at the
keyboard. The screen went dead. Toby picked up the thin
Epicell unit, careful of its wires and tubes, and with his
fingernail teased the sloppy disk out of its metal case. He
held the fragile crystal plate up to the light. Strands of
glittering Epicellular goo formed a hexagonal sheet some six
millimeters across.

Carefully he replaced the thin plate in its casing. On an
impulse he went into the kitchen and scrubbed his hands,
hard.

The phone rang. Toby picked it up, his hands still wet.

"Feel more comfortable now?" Kubiak asked.

Toby shook his wet hands one at a time. "Kubiak, have
you examined your Tyger's Epicell housing recently—the
so-called sloppy disk?" Kubiak said he had. Toby searched
among the papers on the table until he found a stub of pencil.
"What was the approximate diameter of the mass?" He
scribbled the number. "What was the serial number on that
machine? . . . Okay. The number on the other?" Toby
scratched out a simple calculation. When next he spoke, his
voice betrayed satisfaction. "Those Tygers are mere cubs,

Kubiak. In another week, perhaps, you'll be dealing with real computers.''

Kubiak's voice was no longer jolly. ''That's bad news, Bridgeman.''

''It's not my company, Kubiak.''

''Lucky you.''

Toby surprised himself with his anger. ''I wonder how you'll go about rounding up the thousands of Epicells that have already been sold? Without making a point of how special they are.''

''An excellent question.''

''Why don't you call me again tomorrow? Perhaps I'll have an idea for you.''

''Why don't you tell me about it right now?''

''That would be premature.'' Toby paused before pressing the button. ''By the way, Kubiak, whose tit are you sucking these days?''

Hearing nothing, he cut off the connection. After a few seconds he lifted his finger and quickly tapped out the number of the New England regional offices of Compugen.

''This is Toby Bridgeman in Berkeley. I need to talk to Harold Lillard's secretary. Or anyone who can tell me where to reach the physician who was attending Mr. Lillard when he died.''

◆◆◆

A scalpel slices swiftly across the top of Harold's head, cutting from ear to ear through thick flesh to the bone. The blade works under the skin on both sides of the cut, freeing the blood-rich tissue from the skull. Like an oddly inverted stocking cap, the two flaps of Harold's scalp are peeled down and folded over themselves, the black hair bunching against the neck, the tips of his ears cozily covered with rolls of skin, a thick veil of flesh descending over his eyes and the bridge of his nose.

Guided by a sure hand, a small electrical bone saw bites neatly into Harold's ivory skull, trailing a whiff of burning protein in the wake of its Carborundum teeth. After a complete circuit (a practiced hand supporting and turning the head now and again) the bony dome lifts away. There inside lies the brain, yellowish gray, netted in red, wrapped in a tough transparent membrane.

The senior pathologist halts the droning narrative he is reciting into his lapel microphone. "Dr. Sherfey, would you care to have a look?"

*   *   *

Autopsies—mostly murders, suicides, and accidents, less often something in the way of interesting medicine—were not highest on Pathology's list of important things to do. Autopsies were usually assigned to the staff's newest resident, who got to the corpses after she'd seen to the biopsies or other procedures on the day's list that bore most directly on pending diagnoses or critical operations in progress, cases where there was a chance the patient might survive.

But Harold Lillard had just died of unknown causes, in a modern, well-equipped medical facility, under the care of some of the nation's leading physicians. The chief pathologist, assisted by senior staff and observed by respectful residents, conducted the autopsy personally while Harold's attending physician, Louis Sherfey, looked on. This case was special.

Stretched out on the stainless steel table, Harold's body was no more rigid than it had been at the moment his doctors finally concluded he was dead, or for several hours before that. Sherfey bent to peer at the newly exposed brain. He saw no abnormalities of shape or coloration, but then he had not really expected to; gross troubles would have appeared in one of the dozens of tests performed while the patient was still alive. Whatever killed Harold Lillard was subtler than that.

The brain wobbled slightly in its case as the pathologist's probing, rubber-gloved fingers worked the shining scalpel down and around, trimming away clinging vines of nerves and blood vessels, freeing the organ from its fail-safe packaging. A last clean cut through the medulla oblongata divided it from the spinal cord. A moment later Harold's brain lay quivering on a tray.

It took a moment to weigh it. Then, wielding a wide blade as sharp as a samurai sword, the pathologist neatly sliced the gray meat loaf into a dozen sections. Sherfey hovered close by, looking on while expert eyes peered at the organ and expert hands manipulated its tissues, confirming that the brain's interior was, to every appearance, as normal as its exterior.

"It isn't going to be easy," he said, emitting a satisfied snort. It was the first thing he'd said for half an hour.

The chief pathologist smiled. "Lou, you sound positively delighted."

At the pathologist's invitation, Sherfey indicated tidbits from the motor cortex, basal ganglia, and other areas involved in the control of motion that particularly interested him. The scalpel flickered here and there, then grazed farther afield, from cortex to cerebellum, cropping specimens that would help the doctors come to a retrospective understanding of the patient's intracranial ecology.

"How long will the paraffin blocks take?" Sherfey demanded, his impatience getting the better of him.

"We're working our butts off for you, Lou, but some things take time. The technician will get right on it. As long as we have Mr. Lillard at our disposal, I'll go ahead with a total."

"Make some nice cord slices, okay?" Sherfey found the rest of the human body almost dull by comparison with the central nervous system. "Where's your phone? My schedule's a wreck."

The pathologist raised a greasy glove to indicate the open office door. As Sherfey left the room the residents circled closer to Harold's body.

Sherfey let the protective mask dangle on his chest. "Bridgeman? Lou Sherfey, Boston." Sherfey's manner conveyed an unspoken message: come on, buster, make this worth my precious time.

"Thank you for calling back, Doctor." The voice was

polite, its upper-class British accent tempered by a decade or so of life in the States. Sherfey knew the type; Cambridge was crawling with them. "Would you mind telling me if you are planning to conduct an autopsy of Mr. Harold Lillard?"

"In the middle of it."

"Do you have any idea yet what killed him?"

"Can't discuss it."

"Doctor, we had personal contact with Mr. Lillard not long ago. Our research here involved work with a variety of organisms. Polio, for example—"

"It sure as hell wasn't polio." Sherfey did not suffer fools gladly; he studied the list of names he had yet to call, noting that of a Lynn pediatrician who'd come to him with an interesting problem, a kid who wouldn't read except in a mirror. Meanwhile, he prepared to dump Bridgeman.

The polite voice was insistent. "The result of our work was the synthesis of a highly modified organism, resembling a nucleated cell, but no larger than a small virus. . . ."

"Contagious?"

This time the voice was dry. "We certainly didn't think so at the time."

During the pause that followed Sherfey realized this was interesting after all. An artificial bug? The possibilities were intriguing. . . .

Bridgeman continued, "I'd like to send you the DNA sequence, and the amino acid sequences and other information on the structure of the organism in question."

"What's your line, Bridgeman? Microbiology?"

"Hardly. I'm a computer scientist. We make biocomputers here."

"Don't know a thing about 'em. Wouldn't mind finding out, though. How do you want to send me this information?"

"On the telephone lines. If you would put me in touch with someone in computer graphics there and—"

"We can do that, can we? On the telephone? Never had a chance to try that."

"Indeed. Your hospital has one of the finest imaging facilities in the country."

"Structural information? Pictures of this bug?" Sherfey kept talking while he stretched for the dog-eared medical center phone directory on the shelf.

"Of its structural protein, yes. And assembly schematic. Three-dimensional models, if you will. You can have the computer roll them around, take them apart, put them back together. I suppose you can even try model drugs against them."

"Okay, I've got the number. You call the fellow. His name's—"

"Just a moment, Doctor." The polite voice was suddenly hard.

"I don't want to rush you, Bridgeman, but the sooner we can get on with this the better. Give me five minutes. I'll call over there first, prepare the ground. I want to be there when these pictures of yours come through."

At first there were no pictures, only a list. ATOM NUMBER 1, it began. Atom number one was a carbon atom. There followed three spatial coordinates, in angstrom units. Atom number two was a hydrogen atom. Atom number three was another hydrogen. . . .

Loud and remorseless, emitting an electronic whine that was almost nasal, the printer droned on.

Sherfey rocked back and forth on his heels, sighing vigorously. The Boston clinic's imaging facility differed in no essential detail from the one at Compugen—a couple of bare basement rooms equipped with terminals and a number-crunching computer which filled the room next door. The fellow who ran the place was a pale, straw-haired young man, a microbiologist trained as an x-ray crystallographer, seduced into computer programming long ago. Once the computer ingested the incoming data he could begin tapping keys and wiggling joy sticks, beginning the tedious process of making sense of the results.

"How much longer?" Sherfey asked, for the tenth time.

"Oh, probably a while yet, I guess," murmured the placid programmer.

"I'll be across the street in Pathology. Call me when there's something to see," Sherfey said impatiently, and abruptly left the room.

Many pages of manifold paper later, the list terminated with atom number 2,043.

As the image of a novel protein struggled to assemble itself on a computer screen, selected remains of Harold Lillard were coming thoroughly to pieces on a laboratory bench.

A stainless steel rod, toothed like an oil-drilling bit, whipped the brain specimens to paste. These pureed samples would be smeared on slides, dissolved in solvents, fed to chromatographs, shocked into electrophoretic separation, spun in centrifuges, doped with chemical reagents and enzymes, injected into laboratory animals.

Meanwhile, a diamond-bladed microtome sliced transparent wafers from bits of tissue mounted in blocks of wax. Some of the wafers were set aside for staining, others were quickly transferred to microscope slides.

Louis Sherfey practically snatched the first batch of unstained slides from the technician's gloved hands. Above her mask her eyes showed her surprise.

He selected a sliver of motor cortex, sensing, for no reason more compelling than his raw intuition, that Lillard's problems had had a cerebral rather than a cerebellar flavor. He slid the glass plate onto the microscope stage and expertly positioned it. He stared into the eyepieces without moving.

Perhaps no one else would have spotted what he did so quickly. The color was wrong. Sherfey had looked at a lot of cerebrum in his career, and he'd seen every imaginable spectral variation of so-called gray matter and white matter: he'd seen starved black dead stuff, stuff luridly discolored by stain and preservative, stuff that was rosy with lethal metastasis. In the light from below the microscope stage this specimen had a peculiar luminescence, a striated pearly glow.

"What do you think of this?" he demanded of the pathologist who, curious, had joined him in the lab.

At first the other doctor, squinting into the eyepieces, only grunted. "Have to say it looks normal to me." He studied longer, then straightened. "Don't you think, Lou?"

Sherfey said nothing. He bent to the microscope, patiently flicking the phase switch back and forth. Despite the stark changes in illumination, he had a sense of something consistently odd about the light. Not caused by gross structure, nothing unusual there. A cellular phenomenon, even molecular, too fine for the optical microscope's several-hundred-power magnification to resolve.

He stood. "I suppose we'll have to wait for the workups." He left the room without further comment.

"Nice man," said the technician.

"Get used to it," said the pathologist. "He'll be calling you twice an hour until everything's done."

It was night in Boston; the April skies had burst open in a downpour. Sherfey used the wide subway tunnel to cross under the street. When he walked into the graphics room he had his tweed sports jacket on and his battered briefcase in his hand, ready to admit that the day had ended. He looked at the screens. "Is that it?"

On the computer screens a knobby structure had taken

form, its baroque loops and whorls resembling a piece of paint-splattered driftwood. "That's the coat protein," said the programmer. "Want to see the whole critter?"

"Certainly."

The programmer tapped on the keyboard for a few seconds. The twisted structure vanished from the screens. An image of a regular polyhedron replaced it, sketched in outline.

"That's the schematic, now we fill in the detail," said the programmer. More tapping produced an array of miniature versions of the previously pictured coat protein. The knobs and grooves fit snugly together, like fancy ceramic tiles; each facet of the polyhedron was a discreet set, packed with precise economy. "What's that look like to you, Doctor?"

"I'm not a cell man. What does it look like to you?" Remembering that the man was more than a programmer, he added the obligatory, "Doctor?"

"It doesn't look like a cell. No membrane. Sixty arrays of three dimers, packed to make a coat. Typical small spherical virus."

"Bridgeman said it was a cell."

"Yeah, he meant it replicates without borrowing some other cell's machinery. They've got this little guy loaded with synthetic DNA, synthetic enzymes, damnedest little power plants you ever saw. This is definitely a very weird version of an organism."

"Impressive, I'm sure. What I need to do is raise antibodies against it. Can you help me?"

"Routine. The hydrophilic surfaces—the likely binding sites—are already marked. I'll give you a recipe for three or four peptides that match those regions"—the programmer began typing as he spoke—"and the molecular biology folks can cook up all the antibodies you can use."

Sherfey fidgeted while the printer spat four times. The

programmer handed him a sheet of paper with several short sentences written in odd code, His-Cys-Asp-Gly-Phe . . .

Sherfey glanced at the sequences briefly, then folded the paper and shoved it into his inside jacket pocket. He turned to the door and paused there, at last prompted by a vestige of professional courtesy. "You've been a great deal of help."

"It was fun," said the programmer, genuinely pleased. "Never seen anything like this guy." He waved at the screens. "Which reminds me. Bridgeman said this was all hush-hush, an industrial secret."

Sherfey snorted. "If his information's useless, he can have his secret. Otherwise . . ." He walked away.

◆◆◆

Evening came, and a fog bank pressed in through the Golden Gate. The fog line hung below the crest of the hills, bringing a premature twilight; as Toby drove along the ridge road, fine spray blew across his windshield.

He slowed and coasted around the last curve of the winding asphalt road. On an impulse he decided not to turn down the driveway. Just past it he eased the car onto the shoulder; his tires crunched in the gravel as he rolled to a stop under dripping pine branches. He fumbled with his key case; when he found the key he wanted he gripped it tightly and got out of the car.

He walked slowly back along the edge of the road to the top of the driveway. Behind him a car roared out of the mist, shafts of diffuse light sweeping the road ahead of it; he was caught in the beams with no chance to hide. It hissed past without slowing. Toby turned and stepped cautiously down the slick drive, staying close to the shadows of the overgrown bank.

Adrian's house was gaunt in the fog. When the mist thinned, the neon signs and street lights of the city below stared out brightly; then the house's bony silhouette sharpened and seemed to move forward, up the hillside.

A film of moisture lay over the boards of the porch. Toby climbed the steps and slipped his key into the lock. It turned without resistance.

He rehearsed the alarm combination silently, then pushed the door open and crossed quickly to the key pad, the alarm whistle needling his eardrums. He punched in the numbers. The whistle stopped abruptly.

He moved quickly through the dark corridor, into the living room. The plate-glass walls trembled in surges of wind; rivulets of moisture were visible in the phosphorescent glow. The fog-transmitted light of the city, reflected in the room's shiny wall of insulation material, was just sufficient for Toby to find his way.

The scattered pieces of the Epicell prototype lay just where he had last seen them, on the table in the corner. Beside it was Adrian's well-worn Tyger I, its padded leather case discarded on the floor nearby. He crossed the room—the plywood floor groaned under his step—and quickly gathered up the parts. He packed them in the Tyger I's case, along with the Tyger I itself. He added the disks and the scraps of note paper that lay nearby on the tabletop.

He stood listening to the wind, wondering why he was suddenly reluctant to leave the house. It was cold and wet outside, but hardly warmer inside the drafty building. He slung the computer case over his shoulder and started for the door.

He heard a shoe bump against the high step of the porch.

He turned aside and crept nimbly down the stairs. Something brushed his face; this time he remembered it for the dangling light cord. At the foot of the steps he avoided the black tunnel of the kitchen and instead turned back, crouching under the raw wooden treads. The stairs were unfinished, without risers; as his eyes got used to the dark he could see dimly out from beneath the steps.

He forced himself to breath through his nose, slowly, trying to listen over the clamor and thud of his racing heart. They must have been waiting, watching, somewhere out there in the dark. The alarm whistle had alerted them.

Gradually, as his pulse slowed, he could hear the boards creaking overhead.

At first the faint creaking was nearby. Then it moved away. Something scraped against the floor. For several moments he heard no sounds but the wind, the desultory rattle of tattered plastic on the roof, the deeper groaning of the house beams. The floorboards creaked again, closer. He'd heard no one else come in. There was only one of them, inside.

The pale irised beam of a flashlight fell on the cottage wall at the base of the stairs, illuminating heavy coils of rope and open cans of varnish, half full and dried solid. Shoe leather scraped on the treads, inches above Toby's head. The flashlight beam fell on the step in front of his face; the dirty wood blazed with dazzling brilliance, blinding him before the beam flicked away.

When Toby could again see, through splotchy afterimages, a shoe was descending in front of him, a heavy black oxford, scuffed and muddy and worn down at the rubber heel. A mud-spattered trouser cuff drooped over the back of the shoe. "Bridgeman, I know you're down here. *I* was supposed to get that stuff, not you."

Toby stared at the shoe, petrified. The man was big. Toby was not so much frightened as bereft of ideas. He knew the voice, though he couldn't place it. Someone from Compugen. Did Chatterjee already know what he'd said to Kubiak? And that he'd called Sherfey with the Epicell information? If so, Jack must be very unhappy with him.

When this fellow reached the bottom of the stairs, a mere half turn of the sweeping flashlight beam would reveal Toby in his open hiding place. "Bridgeman, if you knew what was at stake you wouldn't be playing jerk-off games. Jesus Christ, man, Chatterjee's willing to pay you a fortune! Didn't he make that clear to you?"

The man's weight shifted and his other shoe moved down.

Then he gasped, startled, and drew back his foot.

The string of the lightbulb.

Toby didn't stop to think about it at the moment, though he later realized it must have been the string. For an instant the intruder's weight rested, unbalanced, on one foot, and Toby reached forward and grabbed the ankle and yanked it back and sideways with all his strength, jamming the lower calf against the underside of the tread.

The man bellowed in fear. As his arms flew out, grabbing for a nonexistent railing, his flashlight flew into the wall. The massive body shot sideways into empty air. Toby let go, and the man promptly fell four feet to the floor, his forearms taking the impact.

To Toby's horror, the brute immediately began struggling to his hands and knees. But his flashlight, on the rebound, had rolled underneath the bottom step and stopped against Toby's foot. The flashlight was a big one, holding five D cells in its long shaft, and it was still burning. Toby scooped it up in his right hand and raised it over his shoulder; knees bent, he stepped forward and swung the flashlight as if it were a racquet, leaning into it.

He had a good serve.

The head of the flashlight burst against the man's skull. Toby heard a groan, then silence. He was left with the bent shaft, which still contained three batteries.

Toby forced himself to expel his breath, and held it long
enough to hear his victim's labored, steady breathing.
Trembling, he dropped the wrecked flashlight, picked up the
computer case, and stepped over the heap on the floor. He
stumbled through Adrian's dark kitchen.

Afraid to leave by the front door, he almost lost himself in
the maze of construction materials on the ground floor of the
unfinished house. Twice he whacked his shins against protruding boards, and once he jammed his thumb against a
post. Finally he felt his way to the door in the back corner.
The new door was secured by a single cheap bolt; anyone
could have pushed it in from outside. Opening the door a
crack, Toby saw the alarm system's dangling wires silhouetted against the night; they were twisted together, permanently
closing the circuit. So much for Adrian's appreciation of
security.

The fog was close and wet. Toby moved slowly uphill
beside the house, through dank grass and brambles. Whoever
the man in the house was—one of Chatterjee's thugs—Toby
could not believe he had come by himself. He waited in the
shadows, stifling the urge to run.

Then he saw the second man, creeping slowly down the
muddy slope. One arm was held low and stiffly in front of
him. Toby could not see a gun—still, he flattened himself
against the wall of the house.

The fellow took forever making up his mind to enter the
house. At last he went in.

By pressing his ear to the clapboard wall Toby could hear
his progress down the entrance hall. When he finally heard
the telltale squeak of plywood from the living room, Toby
ran.

Sliding and stumbling up the hill, he reached the street
without incident and trotted to his car. He almost tore his

pants, tugging at the key case twisted in his pocket, but at last he pulled it free. He got in and started the motor.

He drove half a mile in the fog, virtually blind, before he remembered to turn on his lights.

◆◆◆

The iron gate of the Bay Plaza parking garage bleeped at him and swung open. Toby parked in his numbered stall in the basement and rode the elevator to the fifteenth floor. He unlocked the triple locks on his door. As he reached into the hall closet to kill the alarm he noted, to his surprise, that he'd left the living-room lights on. Having been raised by a thrifty mother, he was usually careful of such things.

He walked into the living room. The nomad rug glowed with a red so rich it seemed orange. By the soft yellow glow from the round porcelain table lamps, the leather of the couch looked buttery.

The hairs rose on his forearms. He stepped back into the hall and held his breath against the sudden pounding of his heart.

He had not turned on those lamps.

From the cover of the hall he peered into the living room and the dining room beyond. Rugs, paintings were all in place, furniture was undisturbed, the stereo and TV were where they always had been.

But the dining-room table was a sheet of bare glass. The prototype was missing. All his papers were missing. Even the Tyger I was gone.

He fought back panic—bloody childishness! He forced himself to walk calmly to the bedroom door.

No one there. Nor in the main bathroom, nor on the balconies . . . It took only a few moments to check every room. Without thinking about it, he turned off every burning light. It occurred to him that they'd turned the lights on to taunt him. The glass tabletop was smeared with fingerprints, not his own.

They didn't care. There was nothing more he could do to them.

Toby was surprised by a rush of emotion that left him trembling. He wanted to be angry, but he was afraid, and ashamed of his fear. He tried to shut out the sense of physical invasion, dismissing his feelings as mere self-pity, yet they wouldn't go away.

Nothing was gone but the computer and his papers. Not robbery, thought Toby, nothing so direct. Rather, I've been repossessed. They've canceled my contract and taken away my toys. Chatterjee's hired help had done it; they must have just coolly walked into Toby's apartment, turned off the alarm they themselves had installed almost two years ago, and carried away his work.

The last vestige of pity he'd felt for the man he'd recently bashed in the head now evaporated. While Toby had been taking his time getting to Adrian's, the same man must have been moving efficiently through his apartment.

He took the phone from the floor where it had fallen and set it back on the table. He tapped out Joana's home number.

The line clicked and clicked, and he heard a vague ringing

echo, a metallic clunking. What a godawful lot of clicking and echoing. And her telephone hadn't rung yet.

That had never happened on his phone before. A chilling sweat broke out on his forehead. He hung up. Abruptly he rolled to his feet.

The elevator ride to the garage fifteen floors below seemed slower, more claustrophobic than usual. Toby hurried to his car. Its wide radials squealed on the concrete as he threaded the aisles of the garage.

He drove toward the hills. The streets in the flatlands were humid, garish under sodium-vapor streetlamps and their reflection from the low-lying fog. Young black men in sleeveless undershirts stood on the street corners, laughing mirthlessly, sucking on cans of Schlitz Malt Liquor. As Toby's shiny sedan passed in the night their eyes followed it with desperate envy.

He didn't notice. The poor lived in a different universe; his concern for them stopped at alarms and insurance. He thought about other things.

He thought of Adrian's complaints about the unfinished state of Epicell. Toby had taken that for random engineer-type noise, but what if there were real difficulties Adrian had not explicitly described? Just how different was the Epicell coat protein from its polio model?

He thought about his own role in the modification of the experimental polio strain. That the bug was a deadly virus had somehow never fully impressed itself upon him when he and Adrian were working to "improve" it. Toby had viewed the problem in terms of classical mathematics—topology, projective geometry, information theory: amplification, replication, feedback, control. How complacently he'd allowed the researcher Sara Brewer to label Adrian a reductionist, never wondering whether the label applied to himself.

"That clever strain of yours is completely attenuated in

humans," Sara Brewer had said, "it could never get out of the gut." She meant the enzymatic environment of the human nervous system was hostile, unsupportive of the virus's basic chemical needs. She meant that the bloodstreams of most of the people in the world were already loaded with effective antibodies against all strains of polio. In nature, polio evolved very slowly. Ordinary wild polio lived in lots of people's guts without doing them any harm; even in epidemic days, before mass vaccination, only about one in ten diagnosed cases ever developed into anything worse than a mild cold. Many more cases were never diagnosed at all.

Still, there was that tenth time, that twentieth or thirtieth time . . .

Toby left the flatlands and drove into the foothill neighborhoods, where the clusters of shingled and stuccoed houses were set well back from the tree-lined streets. Here the streetlamps were glass bulbs on wrought-iron posts, widely spaced, dim and yellow, casting nets of shadow on suburban lawns.

Then he was cruising the block in front of Joana's apartment, northwest of the Berkeley campus. He noted her rusting white Capri parked on the street—she was at home after all. He parked a block away and walked cautiously toward the building, staying in the clustered shadows of the old trees.

Lights in the courtyard burned steadily, throwing the shadows of century plants onto the half-timbered whitewashed walls. Caught in a patch of light, a crumpled cigarette pack floated in brown scum in the birdbath that was the courtyard's centerpiece.

He pressed Joana's doorbell. He heard the bell rumble through the walls. A few seconds later he pushed the button again.

The door swung hard against its short chain. "Toby!" It was a startled whisper. "What are you doing here?"

"I'm afraid, Joana. I need your help." The words tumbled out, unplanned, more truthful than he had expected.

She didn't hesitate. "Come in." The chain rattled; the door opened another foot.

She was invisible in the dark, but his arm brushed past her, soft and warm in the hallway. He smelled her faint aroma, sweet as fresh bread. He paused as the door was closed behind him, and again sensed her passing warmth.

The lights came on. "Sit down, Toby." Joana held her threadbare white terry-cloth bathrobe closed at the throat; her bare arms and legs showed beneath it. Her hair was bound loosely on top of her head. Without make-up her eyes seemed smaller, farther apart. "Would you like some coffee?"

"Yes, I suppose. Yes. Thank you." He watched her disappear into shadows, toward the back of the place. Another light went on, and he heard pans rattling. He sat down gingerly on the edge of the couch.

He looked around the familiar room, trying not to think about his immediate problems. The apartment, with its castle-sized fake beams and posts, its mullioned windows and stone fireplace, was too small to support its designer's medieval fantasy. The couch and chairs were modern, upholstered in soft neutral fabrics—surely a more accurate reflection of Joana's tastes—but their arms and backs and all the other available flat spaces in the room were taken up with magazines, newspapers, and, on the sills and mantles, proliferating houseplants. The place needed a thorough dusting, a vacuuming. It looked more like a by-the-month hotel room than a home.

Ghastly surrealist paintings crowded the walls, her patients' works; he'd always wondered how she could bear to live with them. But of course, she managed to work with the people who'd created them.

A narrow space between two doors held two pen-and-ink sketches, Picassos, evidently authentic. They were erotic mythological scenes: languid nymphs and aroused minotaurs. Toby peered at them curiously. Perhaps that sort of thing was bread and butter to psychiatrists.

"You like those, don't you? You always study them so fiercely." Without his noticing, Joana had appeared in the hallway arch. She leaned against the wall, her arms folded beneath her breasts. "They were a gift from my analyst. To celebrate the completion of my analysis—something she thought I'd never do. Or so she claimed."

"How is it I never knew you were an analyst?"

She shrugged. "We haven't talked much about me, Toby. For that matter, we haven't talked much about you. Mostly we've talked about Adrian. And computers."

"My fault, I'm afraid."

"Anyway, to answer your question, I never practiced analysis. You might say I had doubts about the cost/benefit ratio. Perhaps I'm too much of a pragmatist." Tilting her head to listen, she said, "The water's boiling."

When she returned she brought a tray, a pot of coffee and two cups, milk, sugar, and a plate of chocolate-chip cookies. "Davies' law: sugar tends to cure any disorder it didn't cause," she said.

"I don't think sugar caused my problems," said Toby.

"Then eat up. It's brain food."

He did, and realized he was hungry. He demolished the plate of cookies. He loaded his coffee with cream and sugar and sipped it, leaning back.

"Better?" she asked.

"Yes, as a matter of fact." He was warm, comfortable,

aware of her presence. "Being with you I feel much better.
And now I also feel foolish."

"Tell me what's going on, then."

He told her of the day's events—of his conversation with
Kubiak, his phone call to Sherfey, his raid on Adrian's house.
"Then the most extraordinary thing—just as I was leaving a man
came in. I managed to hide, but he knew I was in the house."
He gave Joana a fleeting smile. "Jack's lawyer, I think.
Sorry, still not over it. Can you imagine? I've never cared for
Chatterjee personally, but he tries so hard to be respectable."

"What happened?"

"I hit the fellow with a flashlight. Rather hard."

"Toby—"

"That isn't the worst." He told her of finding his home
violated, of his sudden fear that Jack and his cronies would
do anything, anything at all, to protect their investment.
"Not professional thugs, I think—but they've panicked."

She listened quietly until he finished. She was a trained
listener, and he got nothing from watching her face except
the sense that she heard what he said. But at last she said, "If
what you suspect about Epicell is true . . ."

He looked up at her. "Perhaps it's time I visited the old
folks at home. England is lovely in the spring."

"That would get you off the hook, wouldn't it?" she said
coolly. "And what about the people who use these Tygers every
day? You used one. I used one, for a while. What about us?"

"Yes, of course. Although it seems we would have noticed by now, don't you think?" Toby glanced away. "You
know, Joana—I hesitate to say this . . ."

"Go on. We're on our own time."

Toby leaned toward her. "If Adrian *has* been parasitized
by Epicell—if in some sense it's alive inside him . . ."

"Yes?"

"There might be a way to treat him. If we could communicate with it."

She studied his face, conserving her thoughts.

He laughed and leaned away. "Another wild theory."

"I think I'm too tired to deal with it tonight," she said, baring her teeth and trying to suppress a tiny yawn. She looked away from him. "I'm shy of you, Toby. For all sorts of reasons I could explain—but I'm sure you understand. Forgive me, but . . . I don't want to grapple with any new theories right now. Do you want to borrow the couch?"

"Yes, thanks," he said immediately. "I think it would be the prudent thing to do."

"I'll get you a blanket." She left the room, returning with sheets, a pillow, and an old-fashioned quilt. Together they made up the couch.

She yawned openly this time. She smiled at him sleepily before she left the room. "We'll talk in the morning," she said.

He lay still, watching leaf shadows trembling on the ceiling. A car drove past, and he imagined that it slowed in front of the building, but then he was asleep.

When he woke it was still dark. He saw the leaf shadows moving fitfully on the ceiling; he had the sense that he was floating deep under the surface of the sea. It seemed a very long time before he could remember where he was.

The room and its associations, his past, the trouble he was in—all these details coalesced at last, and he realized what he must do. He rose quickly and dressed.

He heard Joana stirring in the bedroom.

Then she was coming toward him, wrapped in frayed terry cloth, smiling sleepily. He stayed a few minutes longer.

◆◆◆

George liked to walk. It liked the springy feel of its muscles coiling and uncoiling against the horizontal elastic surface beneath it, it liked that sense of judicious play against the force of gravity. Not that it always succeeded in maintaining its balance—or always succeeded gracefully, even when it did manage to stay on its feet and keep itself moving forward in a more or less straight line. But it was getting better at it all the time.

Around it, space unfolded, full of light and shadow. The round patches overhead were the brightest, streaming past in an intricate dance that so elegantly complemented its swaying, lunging progress. Beside it, darkness lurked in tall rectangles and fell away in neat perspective lines beneath protruding masses; darkness in its own form swept up past it along the vertical planes and moved away in front of it along the horizontal plane as it made progress beneath the glowing clots of light.

Other beings moved with George, ahead and behind, reaching out to it when it fell toward the horizontal, and George knew of them, though it did not know that they were beings in its own form. There was a sense in which George knew almost nothing at all.

For although George saw the world in crisp resolution, it did not know that what it saw was the world. Though George distinguished up and down, and sensed gravity, it had no name for that simple awareness of the center of things. George sensed cold and warmth and emptiness and fullness, and the spilling of overfullness, and it felt its muscles joyfully, although it did not know that it had muscles, or that there was a concept "grace" or a concept "beauty." George knew the things it knew in a way it could not have dreamed of expressing, and its joy was of a directness and fierceness that would have awed any other being that became aware of George's feelings. George's joy existed not only in what was, but even more in what was becoming.

The beast had sucked George. The beast had become George. Now George was, and George became. There was a thing George was becoming, though it could not name that thing.

And except when it slept, which it did not know it did, George became more that thing with each passing unit of time, with each oscillation of its internal chemical clock.

Sam Hansen and the medical technician helped a very wobbly Adrian climb onto the steel bench in the experimental cave. Soothing his patient, Hansen kept up a murmuring explanation of just what was happening; he did it out of courtesy, in case in some part of his brain Adrian could actually understand what was going on. Adrian rewarded his keeper with a bright-eyed, intense stare, the look a six-month-old infant gives its parent—a look that says *whatever you are, there is nothing more important in the universe than figuring out what makes you tick.* Meanwhile the technician strapped Adrian down.

Hansen prepared a small hypodermic and, still murmuring, stuck the needle into Adrian's arm. Adrian's nose twitched, but he gave no other indication of discomfort. The injection was the first of several.

A red cross of projected laser light fell on a round shaven patch of Adrian's skull, turning his monk's tonsure into a mandala. Another red cross put the finger on his temple, and another marked his forehead like a third eye. By these coordinates he was positioned in the maw of the beam. The stainless steel beam tube, wide as a cannon barrel, presented itself at one side of his head. Opposite, resting against his ear, sat a metal plate, the photon-sensitive detector that served as the lens of a lensless camera.

He lay now unconscious, alone in the concrete cave, his shallow breath barely evident in the slight rise and fall of his sheets. Through his arteries coursed a dilute mixture of iodine-labeled amine compounds, blended in a redox drug capable of crossing the blood-brain barrier. Where Epicell lurked in his brain it would eagerly devour the amines, essential to its nutrition, while the remainder of the drug would be broken down and harmlessly washed away. Picked out by tuned x rays, the iodine label would reveal the extent of Epicell's invasion; separate exposures made over time would reveal its patterns of growth.

In another room, far off in the maze of the laboratory, a technician tapped the keys of a computer console. Magnetic tape slid over multiple recording heads.

A warning light began to flash. A buzzer groaned peevishly. Beam stops snapped aside, plucked from the path of the intense radiation by magnetic fingers; the beam penetrated Adrian's head.

There some of its energy was absorbed by telltale iodine; the rest, passing unimpeded through his brain and skull, created coded shadow images on tape. The whirling tape heads laid down alternate halves of a new image sixty times a second, but in each sixtieth of a second the synchrotron x rays pulsed through Adrian's head a million times.

The series ended an hour and a half after it began. The technicians entered the cave and gently freed Adrian from his restraints, then transferred him to a gurney. Still sleeping, he was wheeled away.

Sam Hansen turned from the control panels to see Toby lounging in the doorway. "Golly, Toby, haven't seen you in a month of Sundays. You're here bright and early."

Caught in the middle of a yawn, Toby grinned sheepishly. "Nobody tells me anything. I thought I'd see what you're about for myself."

"Oh, super. Terrific tapes! Can you stay?"

"Certainly, Sam. It's kind of you." He stepped into the control room.

"They gave those movies we did for you a big play, didn't they? PBS especially."

"Hope you got the credit you deserved."

Hansen laughed. "We got a second and a half on the screen. That's what everybody gets, right?"

"I'm not in the business, Sam," said Toby. "How long do you suppose Adrian will be in recovery?"

"Half an hour's the average," Hansen said.

"How's he doing?"

Hansen tugged at his neat beard. "Gosh, I wish I could give you good news."

"It isn't your job to cheer me up, Sam."

"Usually we like to have the patient awake when we do

these procedures," said Hansen. "It's so much easier to say, 'Half inch that way—hold it!' "

"But Adrian's—"

"Unpredictable, *eep*?" The word came out with that little squeak tacked on the end, as if Hansen were some sort of android under stress. "Talks a mile a minute, makes darned good sense sometimes! Sometimes not. Then not a word for four or five hours. Can't get himself to the bathroom." Hansen looked miserable, as if he shared Adrian's humiliation.

"He's no worse, Sam. He was like that when they brought him here."

"Damnedest thing." Hansen brightened. "Maybe the tapes will help!"

"I hope so, Sam."

Hansen chatted with the technician, the furry fellow with the reliquary chinos, who fetched reels of tape from a steel cabinet and snapped them onto the hubs of a VTR machine. With a glance at Toby, Hansen gestured to one of the video screens. "This is what we got yesterday, morning and afternoon."

Horizontal snow appeared on the screen, a hundred-mile-an-hour gale of electronic chaff. An image appeared in disjointed bands, then pulled itself together: ID and time code first, then an ovoid gray mass, detailed and alive, completely mysterious.

After a few seconds it changed, expanded, sprouted detail: it was the plan of a human head, Adrian's, transversely sectioned, the slices individually animated, the image evolving as the plane of focus shifted downward at regular intervals, like an elevator descending.

The curve of the skull became flattened on the sides, as if a potter had had a change of heart in midthrow and had tried squeezing a trapezoid out of what had begun as an egg. The shape grew rococo orbits and sinuses at the narrow end, and just before disappearing, displayed two sinister arches. Toby recognized them as teeth.

Then the whole series repeated itself.

In the replay, now that Toby's eye was practiced, the brain's lobes and ventricles became minutely clear. Bringing nourishment to the brain was a rich flow of blood, pulsing through a thicket of vessels. The folds of the cortex were drawn with scrollwork intricacy.

And there was something more.

"Hell of a picture!" said Hansen enthusiastically. "Recognize the structures?"

"Some. The gross structures," said Toby. "That's Broca's area?"

"Terrific!" said Hansen. "What the hell *is* that stuff?"

Black as ink spills, shocking in their sinister clarity, dense nets of fibers resembling the skeletons of dead leaves had here and there infiltrated the brain.

"Rather like a virus, we think," said Toby quietly.

"Quite a discovery! Hope we've been of some use!"

Toby looked away from the screen to see Hansen watching him. "I'll see to it that you and the lab are mentioned prominently in this, Sam. You can be sure of that."

Hansen smiled, the skin at the corners of his friendly brown eyes wrinkling in an access of gratification. "Say, that's swell, Toby. Hey, look, here's the frontal series."

On the screen the view had changed from plan to elevation. Going in from the front, slicing its way to the back, the x-ray imaging system worked through the frontal lobes with their embedded optic nerves and protruding olfactory bulbs, past hypothalamus, thalamus, hippocampus, brain stem, proceeding in its stately pause-step-pause toward the cerebellum and the nether regions of the cortex.

The black fibers were thick as cobwebs in the olfactory fields, in the sensory cortex and motor cortex, descending like tentacles into the spinal cord. Toby's stomach stirred as he watched.

"That's just wonderful!" Hansen exclaimed. "Isn't he lucky to be alive!"

"Wonders are many, Sam . . . ," said Toby softly.

Magnification, now, a few key frames repeated again and again: Epicell caught in the act of reproduction, shooting a tendril of crystalline matter along a glial process.

". . . but none is more wonderful than man himself."

Hansen looked at him with admiration. "That Shakespeare said it all, didn't he?"

"Quite a bit of it." Toby smiled. "And the old Greeks had a few good lines."

Last night Louis Sherfey's wife had dragged him to a Boston Symphony fund raiser; social functions provided the only opportunity for the two of them to be in the same room long enough to have a conversation. When he returned home, he'd spent another two hours wielding a blue pencil over submissions to the journal he edited, before collapsing into bed. Disgruntled, he'd arrived at the hospital at seven-thirty in the morning to find that no one was in Pathology; the technician arrived at eight. He telephoned her every half hour. . . .

He was on the wards, lacerating an intern about a misplaced decimal in a drug dosage. "You claim you got your license in *this* state, Doctor? To practice what, euthanasia?"

The young man stood braced in the hall outside the room of the patient he had almost murdered, transfixed by Sherfey's nameplate, too frightened to look the enraged senior physician in the eye. Nurses and orderlies scurried past the two men, glancing curiously at the intern's beet-red face.

The public-address system sputtered: "Dokr Shree, twindoo."

"See me in my office, two o'clock." Sherfey turned away

from the intern and marched toward the telephone at the nurses' station.

"What is it?" Sherfey barked into the phone.

Pathology was on the line. There was something, well, rather *odd* about Mr. Harold Lillard's brain tissue.

Sherfey hung up and dashed for the elevator.

They made him look at the written reports first. The antibodies he'd ordered had sought out and labeled massive amounts of strange protein.

Then they let him look at the pictures. What had been clear enough in the reports was graphic in the stains, stunning in the electron micrographs. There Sherfey could see the appalling devastation wrought on Lillard's glial cells, those cells that sheath, support, and nourish the neurons. In particular, the fibers of the corticospinal tract had suffered spectacular damage—the interiors of the glia had been gutted, completely replaced by crystalline masses of a spheroidal invader.

Sherfey studied the photos a long time before reaching for the phone.

Adrian stirred from his drugged sleep. A pale blob floated before him, vaguely triangular, splotched with dark spots—two above, one below. He was reminded of someone he had known once, long ago.

"Who are you?" said Adrian.

"My name is Toby Bridgeman. Your old friend."

Adrian said nothing. He turned aside, and a little whiffling sigh escaped his lips.

"How do you feel, Adrian?" Toby asked, leaning closer.

Adrian didn't answer. Instead he tried to sit up. He seemed surprised to discover the straps that snugged him to the stretcher.

"Do you feel well enough to get up, Adrian?" Toby bent closer, studying Adrian's freckled face.

Adrian's hand went to the still-strange bald spot atop his skull, exploring it with interest but no surprise. He looked steadily at Toby as he did so. His hand stopped and rested unmoving, his fingers touching the exact center of the zero. He smiled with a heartbreaking joy. "Toby! Oh, Toby—!"

"Let's risk it then," said Toby grimly, moving to unbuckle the straps. "Just get up and follow me and in no time we'll be on our way."

"Oh, Toby. Oh, Toby." Adrian's gaunt legs swung to the floor. His huge white feet, splayed against the gray cement, looked more reptilian than human. Trying to stand, he lurched awkwardly. Mere weakness, Toby hoped, induced by bed rest. Adrian wobbled drunkenly toward the door of the recovery room, peering around him with the interest of a one-year-old. "I feel . . . *funny.*"

Toby led him out of the recovery area, into the jumbled emptiness of the building's perimeter, toward the nearest door.

"Hey, Toby, what the hell!" It was Sam Hansen, grinning from the door of the control room. "The john's back that way!" He pointed back along the curve of the synchrotron's outer wall.

"Off for a walk," Toby yelled back, grinning fiercely. "See you down the hill?"

"Down the hill? Oh, hang on there, hang on just a second." Hansen hurried to join them. "I won't be in my office for a while, Toby. Is there something more we need to discuss?"

"Can't tell you how much I appreciate it, Sam. Can't think of anything at the moment."

"Oh, well, then—"

"Thought I'd give Adrian a ride down. He's ready to get back to his hospital room."

"Oh, that so?" Hansen looked at Adrian with mild surprise.

Adrian looked back, his face scrunched as if he smelled something peculiar; he peered down on the eager researcher from remote heights, his bare arms and legs protruding from the great sail-like expanse of his hospital gown.

"Gee, the driver's not even due up for another twenty minutes," said Hansen, as if he'd miscalculated.

"I don't mind a bit, Sam, really. My pleasure."

Hansen blinked. Somehow the conversation had abruptly switched frequencies again. "Well, thanks. Ask them to give me a call when you get down, okay? I need him back at four-thirty."

"You'll hear from them, Sam." Toby placed a gentle hand on the small of Adrian's back and propelled him toward the building's steel doors.

Hansen waved absently and dashed back to the control room.

It was ten o'clock in the morning. Although the sun's rays were filtered through tall eucalyptus, the heat and light outside the dark building were momentarily disorienting, Toby hurried Adrian to the BMW and opened the door on the passenger side. "Just for safety," he murmured, as he belted Adrian in. Once behind the wheel, Toby had to restrain himself to keep from racing away.

At the bottom of the hill he turned north, away from the route to the clinic.

ENTELEPHASE

Entelephase. The functioning of any fully differentiated epigenetic system.
—Handbook of Bioelectronic Engineering *(revised), Blevins and Storey, eds.*

◆◆◆

At six in the morning the suburban streets of North Berkeley were a postimpressionist painting, rendered in the leaves and splotched bark of big sycamores, in misty shafts of sunlight splaying almost horizontally through the redwoods. Toby felt the cool morning air on his skin, smelled its earthy aromas, but he did not register its visual details as vividly as he might have, for his attention was fixed on Joana's tan, long-legged figure running gracefully ahead of him.

There was fire in his legs and a stitch in his side as he ran, but he also found himself experiencing those familiar prickly sensations he'd long been trying to suppress. That feeling of love at first sight. Again.

For here was Joana, as he'd never seen her before. Having shed some layers of her sensible working clothes, she was a vivid display of athletic good health. Toby was transfixed by the rosy curves of her compact, muscular buttocks beneath the edge of her high-cut white nylon shorts, the defining inner creases of her bottom rhythmically appearing and disappearing as she ran.

There was something suggestively mythological about this business of pursuing a lithe nymph through the dawn, the air smelling of pine and bay laurel. He wondered if he dared catch her.

But he had the feeling that if she chose, she could lengthen her stride and leave him behind as if he were running on a treadmill.

She tossed him a glance over her shoulder. "Slowing down already?"

"Not used to this," he called. "Plenty of wind. But no bounce." That was partly true, though it was mostly an excuse to dawdle.

"You've got to stretch more. Racquetball's okay for your heart, but it ties your legs in knots." She talked easily as she ran, with breath to spare.

"Won't be playing racquetball for a bit." He exerted himself and caught up with her.

"Another block and we'll be in the hills. Then we can walk."

He did his best to keep up as they climbed the winding streets. They passed one or two people already stirring, emptying their garbage or picking their newspapers out of the rose bushes, but most were still inside their houses. It was an hour when Toby and Joana could reasonably hope they would not be seen together by anyone who mattered.

They reached a flight of concrete steps that climbed straight up the steep hillside, bordered by close-set houses behind high hedges. The stairs, a continuation of a city street, sported a name on a street sign; Toby grabbed the signpost in both hands and squatted painfully, stretching his thighs. "Whoo. Hell of a way to get around."

"Walk. You'll cramp."

He let her get ahead of him again—one last peek at that delectable . . . Then he sighed and took the stairs two at a time until he was beside her. "Did you test the Epicell in the cartridge I gave you?"

"Yes. It's definitely the same."

"And did you see the tapes?"

"Yes."

"Well?"

Her voice trembled. "A horror. Neurophysiology always seemed an abstract science before." She expelled her breath impatiently. "It's so frustrating when you can make images of it, but you can't just go in and kill it."

"Can you get copies? Or still frames?"

"Maybe. They're watching me. A lot of people are looking for him, Toby. And for you. Have you seen the news?"

He nodded. "That bloody Chatterjee is lying on a beach in the Caribbean by now. He and his lawyer friend with the two black eyes and the broken nose."

"If you believe the headlines, Epicell might as well be bubonic plague."

"I suspect Dr. Stanislaw Kubiak is responsible for that. He and his Pentagon bosses are hoping that any Russian spy with a Tyger II in his hands will quickly pop it into the nearest incinerator, no questions asked."

They climbed in silence. Toby's stiff calves pulled with every step. The sweat cooled and dried on his forehead. His gray T-shirt was soaked through, and he began to chill in the morning air.

They reached the top of the stairs. A half a block away, along another curving street, the blinding morning sky showed against the ridgetop. He turned to her. "You wanted to be with us, Joana. Now's the time."

"How can I do that, without bringing them down on us all?"

"I'm going to need you. I know something about Epicell, precious little about brains. Without those x rays it will be that much more difficult."

"Please don't make me regret all this, Toby. You made me believe you knew what you were doing."

"I do know what I'm doing. But once I communicate with it, it will be dangerous to leave Adrian alone. Think of it as a machine, if you like, or as a bug, but if it ever senses I'm asking it questions in order to destroy it, we will have lost Adrian forever."

She looked at the risen sun. "Time for us to split up."

"As in the Wild West movies"—he followed her glance—"it really is a race against time, you know."

She sighed. "I'll get away this afternoon, if I think it's safe. I won't be able to stay." She half waved to him, then turned and moved off down the curving street, her legs flashing scissorlike in the sunshine.

He watched her until she was out of sight. He turned and trotted down the stairs, taking them two at a time. He had to keep his eyes on the concrete steps. He was hardly aware of the hills and water and cities, the spectacle of summery gold spread below him.

◆◆◆

"X-zero; X-zero; X-plus, X-minus: edge-cross; X-minus; X-minus; X-minus, X-plus: edge-cross . . ."

There was a lot George knew but did not know it knew, as there is much an infant knows.

A shallow pool of water in the garden caught the high sun and reflected its beams upward through the leaves of the yew outside the window. George watched the narrow curving shadows move on the ceiling. Where they thickly intersected they made pinholes of light, and in those pinholes were reproduced miniature worlds where George's acute vision easily picked out an inverted garden, a pool of water, a dark, many-windowed house reflected in the water, and in front of the house a yew tree, and clouds floating in a blue sky beyond.

It didn't know those words—*house, garden, leaves, sky*—but it recognized the objects they stood for, the things in themselves. It sensed that the labels for these sense-objects might soon become available for symbolic manipulation, although why it had that certainty it could not have said, for there was little it could express.

It did not realize that the droning sound it was making, the pleasant exercise of its jaws and throat and tongue, was in fact intimately connected to the expression of symbols.

It knew only that there were things to be expressed, and such a thing as expression—and that it had once possessed a means of expression which might at any moment be restored.

George squatted on the floor, sensing that it was relaxed, that it felt good. It wondered how it might gain access to those more interesting and beautiful worlds depicted in multiple miniatures on the ceiling. Or, in the event they were mere Doppelgängers—an eventuality George had learned to anticipate after studying the creature it had encountered in the tall mirror on the back of the closet door—it wondered how it might gain access to the more concrete reality of which they were analogues.

Although its conception of events was without semantic comprehension—beyond that sound with which it addressed itself, "George," and that sound which identified the entity "friend Toby"—it knew what was happening to it. Soon friend Toby would come again, and they would sit in front of boxes with windows, and Toby would create patterns of green marks in the windows. Somehow meaning was encoded in those patterns, and before long George would be able to extract the meaning. To do so, George knew it had to gain access to the coded memories with which it coexisted. Perhaps those memories were somehow associated with a third sound pattern, one friend Toby emitted often, which George had not fully distinguished yet but which sounded something like AyeDreeUnn. . . .

For all these patterns were like the shadows on the ceiling, or like the creature in the mirror, in that they stood for something outside themselves. George was sure of that. On the other hand, they were not like the raised patterns on the wall, which stood only for themselves.

George turned its attention back to the wall. Or perhaps these patterns stood for something too . . . ?

A rush of pure sensual pleasure flushed through its neck and trunk. Its fingers and toes tingled. The organ between its legs grew warm, with a sense of pleasure even greater than when it allowed itself to release the collected waste fluids in its body. Whence this intense pleasure?

It knew. A memory net had been accessed. It had *remembered* that there were such things as pictures in the world. The patterns on the wall *were* pictures, although it did not know that that was their name.

George heard the door open, and aimed its eyes in that direction. Friend Toby stood watching. George registered that fact, and went back to its business.

Toby watched silently from the doorway, wondering if by simple observation he could gather some clue to the processes inside Adrian's head.

"Mmm, mmm, mmm, mmm—umph. Mmm, mmm, mmm, mmm—umph. Mmm—" Adrian murmured tonelessly, reciting the empty litany without a hint of impatience. This had been going on for at least fifteen minutes, since Toby had first peeked in, and possibly for much longer.

Adrian squatted in the corner of the room beside an open closet, barefoot, his white robe trailing on the floor. He faced the wall, rocking back and forth on the balls of his feet, speaking aloud as his fingers brushed lightly over the surface of the patterned wallpaper. Midmorning sunlight struck the wallpaper at an oblique angle, highlighting the near sides of embossed patterns, shadowing the far sides. Thus Adrian could study the raised shapes by eye and touch simultaneously: here an edge of leafy wreath, here the slope of a classical urn in bas-relief, here a floral labyrinth, here a planar expanse of featureless background, dryly textured.

Adrian—the stuff inside him—was trying to figure out how he saw, and how that corresponded to what he could touch, and what that had to do with the nature of the world around him. He was trying to understand vision.

Toby noted that Adrian had no trouble putting his long fingers exactly where he wanted them to go; his rocking was inconsequential, as effortless and intentionless as the swing of a pendulum. Two days ago his Parkinsonism had passed without a trace, as quickly as it had come; evidently Epicell had learned what to do to make Adrian move. Or perhaps what not to do.

That was bad news and good news both. Epicell was making terribly rapid progress; yet some progress, at least, was essential before anything Toby did to Adrian could have an effect.

"Adrian, will you come here? I have something to show you."

"Mmm, mmm, mmm, umph—" Adrian paid him no attention.

Toby had learned a way to make Adrian listen. "George!"

Adrian's head swiveled sharply to stare at Toby, all unblinking attention. He squatted and rocked, but his head perched on his neck like a hooded falcon on the fist of a wheeling rider, perfectly upright despite every swerve and lean of the support beneath it.

Toby went to him and hooked him gently under an elbow. "Come here, please." He stepped back as Adrian started to rise.

Adrian unfolded with a rapid grace Toby had never seen in him, rising until his tall frame blocked the light from the window. In the clean white gown Toby had put on him earlier that morning, with his hair trimmed short all around like a topiary boxwood (his head's gleaming O out of sight behind) he looked more nearly beautiful than Toby had ever seen him. He was almost—*angelic*. An outsized angel, to be sure. But then Michelangelo's David was outsized too.

And what had happened to all that fat? It was there two days ago—did he merely think it away?

Toby stepped into the hall and held the door open. Adrian moved smoothly across the room in four, five gliding steps, wheeled on a bare foot, came up close behind Toby as Toby hurried to throw open the door to the next room down the hall.

One of those leggy, loping animals, thought Toby, an antelope, a cheetah; even his freckles were like camouflage in the flittering shadows of the hall.

As a child, running home through wet fields after dark, it had not been legendary wolves that had prowled Toby's imagination, but the great cats of Africa, Asia, the Americas. These slavering creatures were not remote in time, like England's old wolves, but only in space, and who knew what disrupted traveling carnival (*carn*ival, deadly hunger implicit in the name) might have spilled them cold-eyed into the moonlight near Toby's home town? With Adrian breathing down his neck, Toby felt a touch of that same primal fear.

He stepped aside, letting Adrian pass. Adrian moved into the room, the breeze of his passing touching Toby's shoulder, and stopped.

He moved well. He stood well. In choosing which mechanisms to leave alone Epicell had incidentally left behind or overlooked all the learned awkwardness, shyness, resentment, that for most of his life had prevented Adrian from moving as his body was made to move.

Toby stepped inside the spare room and closed the door behind him. The room faced the same eastern slope as little Margaret's bedroom, where Adrian slept, and the morning sun poured in through the white gauze curtains. On the sturdy maple desk sat the Tyger I terminal Toby had looted from Adrian's house. Another Tyger I, this one rented, perched on a black lacquered end table brought up from downstairs.

Toby took Adrian by the arm and led him, unresisting, to the desk, and sat him down in the maple captain's chair. He took Adrian's hands, one at a time, stretched out their long fingers, and laid them carefully on the Tyger's keyboard, not so much positioning them to type as positioning them to sense the presence of the keys.

Then Toby went quickly to the other terminal. Sitting on the side of the bed, he typed rapidly on his own keyboard. The symbol string he produced was displayed both on his screen and on the screen facing Adrian.

Adrian stared at his screen. With a quick movement he lifted his fingers from the keyboard and stroked the smooth glass of the cathode-ray tube. When the symbols jumped and wiggled he tried to catch them, his fingers grasping at the fleeing green patterns as if they were tiny ants.

"Just watch them," Toby said, turning, repeating himself for perhaps the hundredth time; this had been going on all morning. "Adrian, leave your hands on the board." He saw that his words had no effect. He blanked both screens, and Adrian's scrabbling fingers relaxed.

Adrian suddenly slumped in his chair and groaned, his head lolling back.

Toby rushed to him. "Are you all right? Adrian!"

"Who . . . who are you?" Adrian said, forcing the words through his twisted throat.

"I'm Toby, Adrian. I'm your friend Toby."

Adrian said nothing. The sharp smell of urine filled the air, and Toby saw the spreading stain on Adrian's fresh gown.

This was the real Adrian, what was left of him; "George" had gone away. When Epicell lost control, as now, or busied itself with other functions, it discarded Adrian in the torn scraps of his humanity.

Toby started to call that name again. But he held back, afraid. It had occurred to him that if he began regularly addressing the scattered stuff in Adrian's head by a name some part of it had come to recognize, that might hasten the day when it thought of itself as a contiguous entity—when it thought of itself at all, when it conceived of itself *as* a self.

Then it would cease to be an innocent, mindless invader of a man's body, with little more sense of purpose than a colony of germs. Once it became aware that it could survive, and that its survival could be threatened, how would Toby ever persuade it to let go?

Toby took Adrian by the shoulders, sat him up straight. The diaper-changing business wasn't quite routine yet, but it was a task Toby had mentally prepared himself to repeat as often as necessary, and it took only a few moments.

Then Toby straightened Adrian's twisted fingers—Adrian resisted, passively, but Toby persisted—and laid them on the keyboard. Once more he aimed Adrian's head at the Tyger's screen.

With a nervous glance to see that Adrian was still in position, Toby retreated to the other terminal and began to type again, the same strings as before. He wrote as rapidly as he could, addressing PIA/J: "Def Ep-struc, level DNA, cond TATA . . . ," talking to Epicell directly, demanding that it express the simplest facts about itself.

Adrian stared at the screen, his hands rigid on the keyboard. He gave no sign that he was aware of the flickering signals in front of his eyes or, if he were, that he thought he should do anything about them.

"Does he even know you're trying to communicate?" Joana asked quietly, toying with a slice of tomato on her plate. The two of them sat at Susana's kitchen table, nibbling at a salad thrown together from the contents of the refrigerator.

"*He!* If you mean Adrian, he doesn't remember my name from one hour to the next. If you mean Epicell, it appears to be busy with other things. I'm not sure which frightens me more—to see Epicell working in him when it's got matters well in hand or to see what's left of Adrian when it goes away."

Joana shifted uneasily. "Toby, this business of anthropomorphizing the—the infection—bothers me. It could—"

"Yes, I know," he said hastily. "Sorry, mustn't do it. I'll be better."

She looked at him, surprised. He'd capitulated rather faster than necessary.

He was staring into space, in the general direction of the garden window. He turned back suddenly and said, "One does, you know. We often do think of the computers we work with as sentient creatures, no matter how often we warn ourselves against it. The result of lazy thinking, habitually lazy thinking. We think of the programs we work with as creatures too, no matter what hardware they're running on. There you have two completely messy, overlapping, partially contrary notions of what constitutes an entity. Hardware versus software. Epicell is both, inextricably. One could conceive of low-level programs equivalent to it, I suppose—running in some sort of universal self-replicating machine—but they would no more capture the essence of Epicell than Epicell could independently mimic a human being."

He paused long enough to wolf down a boiled egg. Joana was still pushing listlessly at the salad on her painted china plate.

"Epicell's very easy to regard as a person, Joana," he continued. "Hook an ordinary Tyger II to a good voice synthesizer, feed it an appropriately friendly program, and

one would swear one was talking to a long-time acquaint-
ance. It's a very old trick, a primitive trick really. But if it
talks to us it must be smart, isn't that so?''

"Is it talking to you?'' Joana asked quietly.

"No. Not really. Within a narrow range of programmed
responses, it's made connections, it can recite. When it
triggers a meaningful connection, Adrian's vocal apparatus
moves, and stored concepts are enunciated. 'Who are you?'
and so forth.''

"But it doesn't mean anything?''

"Not yet. Not what you mean by meaning. The pity is,
Adrian repeats the same thing when it lets go of him. But
then, he really wants to know.''

"When will it start meaning what it says?''

He looked at her, pained. "It's still growing. How long
after a one-year-old child starts babbling does he start meaning what he says?''

Joana put down her fork. "Toby, you're groping in the
woods.''

"That's not the case. Epicell can translate sounds into
meanings, even if it doesn't know it's doing it. And I believe
it will soon make the connection between visual symbols and
meanings. It has already mastered Adrian's motor functions.
And Adrian's always been a handy typist. So I'm confident
I'll soon have a way of giving it data and it will have a way
of getting data back out. But it must . . .'' He paused.

"Must what? Make the connection? Realize what you're
doing? That's horrible, Toby. Won't it really *be* an 'entity'
then, as you put it?''

He looked away. "You're the one who's assuming intention now, Joana.''

"And the best you can do is hope for a lucky accident?''

"Can you think of a better way?''

She had no answer. She glanced at her watch. "I must get back to the clinic."

Later, upstairs in the bedroom, Adrian stared at him placidly from the bed where he rested, surrounded by Margaret's stuffed toys. Toby went to him, touched his elbow, urged him to rise. "Come with me, Adrian. We have things to show each other."

Adrian instantly swung his legs to the floor, in a gesture of such grace that Toby was moved.

And being moved, Toby was afraid anew. He could not allow himself to love the beast more than its victim.

◆◆◆

Groggy but determined, Toby followed Joana through the cold morning streets. They ran in self-absorbed silence until they reached the hillside steps.

They trudged up the hill with the bright sun, now clear of the ridge, full in their faces. Toby's protesting muscles, warmed from outside, gradually relaxed with the steady effort. "I've gotten through to it," he said. "On the most primitive level."

"That's good, Toby," she said.

He heard the doubt in her voice.

"It's a start," he said. "Where this leads, it's rather too soon to say."

"How did you do it?"

"Stubbornness. Lack of imagination. I kept up the keyboard business all day. I hadn't thought of anything else to try. Four hours, five, I hardly know how long. Two changes of clothes when the smell became intolerable. There's something to be said for hospital robes. But I had a sense something was going on, when he was lucid.'' He paused to catch his breath. ''The only time I quit was when you came.''

She smiled thinly. ''By now I should know that when you talk generalities you're up to something.''

''After you left I went upstairs. I went at it again. At some point I typed—for the thousandth time, I'm sure—a simple LISP directive. I asked Epicell to define its protein-coat structure in terms of DNA sequence. I was addressing PIA/J of course, the growth program, but simply asking it for a readout of basic data. And Adrian started typing like mad. He'd made the connection—I mean, Epicell had made the connection. It read what was on the screen. It used Adrian's hands to respond. I got a string of base pairs a thousand terms long, corresponding to the whole protein sequence plus its control sequences, all our artificial introns and exons.''

''What then?''

''Nothing then.'' Toby stretched his arms above his head, indulging himself in the returning sensation of their strength. ''By then it was damn near midnight. I had a date with you this morning. I said thank you to Adrian, took him to his room. Went to mine. Went to sleep. Or tried, anyway.'' He yawned mightily. ''He never sleeps, you know. I'm beginning to suspect the only time we see what's left of Adrian is when Epicell's dreaming.''

''I have news for you, too,'' said Joana. ''But we'd better start back.''

''Slowly. I couldn't run another step.''

Side by side they walked down the steep stairs. Their corrugated shadows fell twenty feet down the hillside in front of them. Joana said, ''I have the x rays. Still frames from them.''

''Wonderful. They couldn't come at a better time.''

''And I've been invited to take leave. Indefinitely. Not my idea.''

He looked at her, surprised. "Why?"

"Dr. Lee informed me that a hospital review board will look into the way I handled Adrian's case. He as much as accused me of colluding with you to help Adrian escape the hospital. He's desperate, Toby. I think he's just trying to divert attention from his association with Compugen."

"You can fight them, can't you?"

"Of course. He has no evidence of misconduct. And there are all my other patients to be cared for, sick people who depend on me; it's not an easy thing to transfer their care to other doctors at the drop of a hat. So don't worry, I'm not going to let myself be pushed around—but I am going to bend a little. I'll probably make myself as scarce as I can around the Chatterjee Clinic for a few days."

Toby was silent. Technically she was innocent: she hadn't known in advance of his plans to "borrow" Adrian, but that was a quibble now.

"Well, you wanted me with you," she said.

"Not at the cost of your career."

"I almost welcome a fair chance to confront the man. Besides, if we can save Adrian, my career will be resurrected soon enough."

"Sorry," Toby said, his voice muffled. Abruptly he sat down on the steps. He buried his face in his hands. "I'm so tired. Not much use to you. I never wanted anyone to suffer."

She sat down beside him. Gently she laid her arm across his shoulders.

He sat in front of the little screen until his eyes blurred and his back ached. Across the room Adrian sat easily upright in front of his own screen, seemingly tireless.

Toby typed queries. Adrian typed replies. The queries were complex strings of nested definitions linked by operators. The replies were lengthy strings of code, which Toby often had to stop and puzzle over before he could progress. There was no single approach to Epicell that did not quickly sprout brier patches, whole jungles of complexity.

Late in the morning he heard the doorbell ring twice, then again, the recognition signal he and Joana had agreed upon. Below, the front door opened, and he heard her footsteps on the stair.

"Hello, there." She stood in the door of the big empty room, wearing jeans and a wool sweater. She held out a large manila envelope closed with a loop of twine. "Courtesy of Radiography, though they don't know it."

Toby eagerly took the envelope and pulled out a dozen black-and-white prints, photographs taken from the video screen. "Oh, super."

"Let me say hello to our friend," said Joana brightly.

Adrian sat quietly at the desk, his bare knees rising above the hem of his clean gown, his head turned to observe the goings-on. He appeared politely interested.

Joana sat on the end of the unmade bed and lightly touched his bare forearm. "Hello, Adrian. How do you feel this morning?"

"Who are you?" he asked brightly.

"You remember me. I'm your friend Joana."

If he did, he gave no indication. He continued to watch her. Every few seconds, as regularly as clockwork, he blinked.

"You're looking very well, Adrian," she said. She glanced at Toby. "Wouldn't you say Adrian seems very healthy?"

Toby looked up from the x-ray photographs. "Adrian's not with us at the moment, Joana," he said quietly. "The other thing is."

She looked at the polite, relaxed young man in his tentlike cotton robe. He gazed back at her, the ghost of a smile on his full lips.

"Put his hands on the keyboard and turn his head toward the screen," Toby suggested.

She stood and rested her hands on Adrian's shoulders, then moved them gently to the sides of his head. She turned it toward the computer screen. He stayed where she moved him. She lifted his long-fingered hands from his knees and laid them on the keyboard.

She moved quietly away and pulled a chair over to where Toby sat on the far side of the room.

Toby typed rapidly on his keyboard. Even before he stopped, Adrian began typing with a skill that far exceeded Toby's own—Adrian had to pause so that Toby could finish, and his answer was complete within seconds of Toby's request.

"Can you read that?" Toby asked, indicating the screen full of abbreviations and symbols.

"I recognize that it's LISP. The content's beyond me."

"You'll get used to it. By the end of the day it will make as much sense to you as it does to me."

"What is it?"

"I've been asking it how it communicates. It's describing the hormones and peptides it uses, the whole range of neurotransmitters. I'm getting more information than I could understand in a lifetime."

"Then what good does it do you, Toby?"

"We can get enough from this to tell it how to *stop*—without killing Adrian. And that's all we have to do. But we have to do it fast." He laid a hand on her knee. "In a Tyger II, Epicell is capable of doubling about every four days. It keeps on doubling until it runs out of nutrients, or until PIA/J shuts it down. I don't know what the doubling time is in the bloodstream, or the cerebrospinal fluid, or wherever, and I don't know exactly how long Adrian's been infected, but—"

"Perhaps the x rays will give us something to work with."

"Right. Do you know the old riddle about the lily pond?"

"What are you talking about?"

"The water lilies double in area every day. It's taken two months for them to cover half the pond. How long will it take them to cover the whole pond?"

"Oh, I don't know. Four months? What a time for puzzles."

"Think again. They double every day."

She thought a moment. "One more day," she said with evident chagrin. "All right, Toby. I see the point of your little parable."

"I hope you do." He reached up and took her hands and squeezed them hard; the look on her face reflected the intensity of his fear. "As fast as it talks to us, it's growing a thousand times faster. A hundred thousand times faster." Suddenly he released her and scooped up the photos. "These were taken three days ago. If you could look into his head right now, the stuff would be twice as thick."

"You won't be any good for him if you collapse from exhaustion," she said softly.

He rubbed his face, making it a rubbery mask. "Oh, Joana, I've cared about nothing in my life so much as this. Perhaps I have coerced people, but Adrian matters to me. . . ."

Impulsively she moved toward him. "Hush, I was being selfish." She patted the hand on her shoulder. "Let's do what we can."

◆◆◆

"Stay here," Toby said quietly, moving to the door. He pulled the door open a crack and listened.

Joana stared at him. Adrian watched with alert curiosity.

Whoever was downstairs was making no attempt to be quiet.

Toby moved into the hall, pulling the guest-room door closed behind him. It would be better to confront the stranger below. He hurried along the upstairs hall. As he walked slowly down the stairs, the boards creaking under his feet, he heard the door open and close a second time. Whoever it was had gone out again.

At the foot of the stairs he glanced to his right, into the living room. A baby was lying on a blanket on the rug.

Then he understood. Joana's sister had come home. "Joana," he called. "Come down, it's all right."

Toby watched as the child struggled to extricate himself from the embrace of a stuffed bear. The front door burst open. Susana appeared in the hallway, silhouetted in the late

265

afternoon light, her arms loaded with groceries in brown sacks and net bags. Toby hurried to help her.

"Why, thanks," said Susana, as if it were a special favor. She heaped sacks upon him until he staggered, and still she had miscellaneous small items left over. "So you're the Toby Bridgeman I've heard so much about."

She was a curious sight to his eyes: she was wrapped in thick, loose peasant fabrics that had been woven in the exotic deserts and jungles of the southern Americas, dyed in reds and blues; her brown arms jingled with heavy silver bracelets, her neck and swelling bosom were plated with glinting copper necklaces, and her ears, unseen beneath her red-gold hair, were hung with pendant beaded earrings. Her gaze was bold, and hinted at amusement.

Despite the loud color scheme and the extra fullness, her resemblance to Joana was startling. The experience was a little like staring at a woman across a room, then realizing it was a mirror reflection of the woman next to you. Toby smiled and stepped uncertainly toward the kitchen, craning his neck to see around the groceries. "You have me at something of a disadvantage. Until a few days ago, Joana told me only the whispiest bits of gossip about you."

Joana, looking exasperated, came up behind him.

Susana smiled at her twin. "Joana's very good at keeping secrets, Toby. I suspect you have a lot to learn about her."

"We'd better all be good at keeping secrets," said Joana, following them into the kitchen. "What are you doing here, Su? I thought we had an agreement."

"I got worried about all you people starving to death."

"Susana," said Joana sharply, "this is a serious matter. There's a sick man in this house, and a possibility of infection."

"I understood all that when you explained it to me the first time, Jo," she said quietly. "This is a considered decision."

"Consider it further, then."

"Let me put all this away, and we'll talk."

"This is awfully good of you, Susana," said Toby lamely, setting the groceries on the tiled counter.

"It's very little trouble to me. I'm taking my annual vacation a little early, that's all." She peered into the sacks, reminding herself of what was where. "The maid and the baby sitter have been given the month off, and my little girl was delighted at the prospect of spending a couple of weeks away from her mother."

"How delighted was her grandmother?" asked Joana dryly.

"Mom owes me one," Susana said shortly, without elaboration. "At any rate, the place is all yours. I won't get in your way." Toby and Joana watched her, impressed by her efficiency, as she stowed the harvest: eggs, onions, garlic, watercress, strong cheeses, glowing red tomatoes, fragrant melons, a whole plucked duck. "And what about you, Toby? Have you covered your tracks?" she asked as she moved about the kitchen.

"We haven't been bothered yet." He leaned against the maple butcher block, part of the island in the center of the enormous kitchen. "All that business with false air tickets. Cost me a bloody fortune."

Susana smiled briefly, then grew serious. "They'll find out you and your friend didn't go to London soon enough, if they start digging. But who's going to do the digging?" She brushed her palms on her skirts. "Let's have a drink while Mr. Toby Bridgeman explains his ingenious plans to me," she said, "and then I'll knock something together for dinner. And *yes*, Jo, then we can *consider*—to your heart's content."

Outside the diamond-paned windows the low sun burnished the dark leaves of the magnolias. Patches of orange light penetrated the room, but the thick foliage formed an effective screen against watchers in the street.

Little Teddy lay penned and desultory in the middle of the living room, cranky amidst his stuffed animals, unable to focus his irritation. Within ten minutes, his mother opined, he would either be asleep or howling in earnest.

Toby looked up as Joana came down the stairs from the upper floor of the house. "Adrian's feeling the walls," she said. "He seems quite happy."

"I doubt that I tired him much," said Toby, who was perched on the edge of the low stone hearth. "He switches back and forth between periods of eerie alertness and a kind of drowsy confusion." He sipped at a glass of dark red Cabernet. He looked up at Susana.

"Please go on," she said. "I think I was actually following."

"Well, the important thing is that Epicell is programmed—through the synthetic DNA contained in each individual cell—for increasing organization and increasing structural complexity. Very early in the process the cells specialize and begin performing different operations in concert with one another." Joana, having heard it all before, went into the kitchen, while Toby carried on. "Presumably even a single cell could, by multiplying itself, elaborate to the point where these structures become capable of information processing at a higher level. Although that's never been tested."

"But how can it survive inside a living human being?" Susana asked. "And what does it *do* in there?"

Joana returned to sit near Susana, carrying a glass of Campari to match her twin's. Both of them watched Toby from spoke-backed rockers.

"I believe one reason it survives so easily is because it consumes principally glucose and oxygen, just as brain cells do—substances that easily cross the blood-brain barrier."

He looked at Joana. "Brain food."

Joana gave him a wan look.

"To function and reproduce, it makes use of simple artificial enzymes," he said. "When the machines are sold commercially these are provided in a nutrient fluid. But in fact the brain is richly supplied with amino acids and peptides, the raw materials needed to construct these same enzymes. And Epicell is programmed to construct them on its own." He paused again. "As to what it's doing, that's problematic. It's programmed to learn and grow."

"To learn what?" Susana asked.

"Principally what it's told to. And evidently more than that." Toby leaned forward, betraying a reluctant enthusiasm. "Before all this business with Adrian came up I often wondered what Epicell would set out to learn if it had been given no specific instructions at all—beyond a general imperative to learn. I concluded that it wouldn't do much of anything; it would simply establish some sort of low-energy equilibrium with its environment. Evidently I was wrong."

Joana said, "Perhaps not. What would happen if the environment itself is terrifically *un*stable? What sort of learning is required just to survive in drastically changing circumstances? The world people live in every day—?"

Susana sighed. "If I were it, and things got all that complicated, I think I'd just give up."

"Epicell's program never tells it to give up, to stop learning," said Toby. "Or to stop growing."

"It's just growing in his head?" Susana's mouth twisted in distaste.

He nodded. "But more than that, it's trying to learn—to learn how he works. To accommodate that knowledge."

Joana turned to her sister. "We believe that all the symptoms that seem so contradictory can be explained as . . . as *experiments*."

"All quite unconscious, of course," Toby said. "Strange smells, hallucinations—that was Epicell trying to master Adrian's sensory system. The Parkinsonism resulted from its attempts to master his motor system. The words, the language programs, those are all stored in his memory—somehow Epicell accesses them.''

"Really, Jo?" said Susana. "And you believe this too?"

"It fits, Susana," she said stoically. "Nothing else does."

"The poor man's brain must be half eaten away," said Susana.

"I think not," said Toby. "Epicell apparently attacks the glia, not the neurons. That's what Sherfey found in the Lillard autopsy. Nothing in the x rays invalidates that."

"Glial cells can replicate," Joana explained. "Mature neurons, once they die, aren't replaced."

"So," said Toby, "if Epicell is somehow linked with the neurons but leaves them intact—and provided the neuronal connections are essentially undisturbed—there's a sense in which Adrian may still be 'in there.' Inside himself, if the phrase makes any sense."

"But what can you do for him?" Susana asked. "Can you kill it?"

"We don't think so," said Toby. "Epicell isn't a virus, but to the body it looks like a viral infection."

"Medicine can't do much about viruses, after the fact," said Joana. "All we can do is stimulate the immune system in advance."

"My guess is, if you've got immunity to polio, you're all right," Toby said, sipping at his wine. "We've all been vaccinated. Except maybe Adrian. There are no records on him."

Joana spoke sharply. "What about Lillard? Do you know his records? Sherfey said it was solid in him." She eyed Susana. "Anyway, Susana, Teddy's *not* vaccinated for polio." She turned to Toby. "All that was put off. Because of his injury."

Susana looked past her. "Why did this Mr. Lillard die . . . and Adrian didn't?" she asked Toby.

Toby looked at her bleakly. "Adrian may die yet, any moment. One misstep on the part of Epicell . . ."

Almost viciously, Joana said, "If it interfered with the functioning of the hypothalamus, Adrian's internal organs could rupture and—"

"Never mind," said Susana. Suddenly she got to her feet. "It's getting close to dinnertime. I'm less squeamish about molesting piglets and ducks."

"Susana, you're evading me," said Joana.

Susana turned to look at Toby. "I still don't understand what you can *accomplish*."

"I programmed Epicell," said Toby, twisting his wine-glass, returning Susana's gaze but talking as much to her sister. "I can program it again—to stop growing. Possibly even to retreat. Once I know how to communicate with it."

In the kitchen Susana moved swiftly and silently from refrigerator to chopping block to stove. Joana came to the archway and stood watching, saying nothing. Finally, Susana murmured, "I saw Paterson again today, Jo. Teddy's never going to get any better."

"You can't know that. . . ."

"The only thing that surprises me is that when he told me, I wasn't surprised at all."

"Be realistic, Su. I've talked to Paterson—"

"And he told you to keep it a secret?" Susana demanded, her voice rising angrily.

"No. This was just this morning. From what I understand, there's a good chance that therapy will alleviate most of the motor problems. Especially if you start it right away."

"I'm *not* giving up on my son, Jo. But I think I'm being more realistic than you are." She banged open the oven.

Heat spilled into the room, redolent with the odor of roasting flesh. "Now get off my case. I'm ravenous."

Hours later, full and satisfied, Toby lay on his bed in the guest room at the end of the hall. He was stunned by fatigue, but too exhausted to sleep.

He'd left Joana and her sister talking passionately in the dining room. There came a knock on the door, and she was here, a silhouette against the dim hallway light; he hadn't expected to see her before the morning. "I don't want to keep you up," she whispered.

"I've been awake the whole time."

She came into the room, closing the door behind her. She sat on the edge of the bed and laid her palm on his bare chest. "You lied to her," she said.

"No, I told the truth. Why haven't I caught it? Why haven't you?"

"Why is it so difficult to keep up with you, Toby? Are you slippery, or are you just quick?"

He laid his hand on hers. "Why did you let me lie, if that's what you thought I was doing?"

"I told her everything, to the last detail, the way I see it—before you and Adrian came here, and just now, again. Susana made it plain that she has already considered the possibility that she will die, that her little boy will die."

"Why did she come back?"

"I don't always understand her." Joana moved her hand to his face, ran her fingers along the stubble of his jaw. "It's all or nothing with her, Toby. She believes in what we're doing. She thinks the odds are good enough."

He said nothing.

"So I came to tell you—you don't have to try to make it easy on her," she said, bending toward him. She paused, then laid her mouth on his. After a moment she pulled away. "Before I die, I hope I learn to live the way she does."

"Must you go?"

She'd already risen. "You'll sleep. You have to sleep. I'll see you in the morning." She went quickly to the door. She turned as she went out, looking at him from the shadows, then pulled the door firmly closed.

◆ ◆ ◆

These treelined upland streets, so close to the seething poverty of the flatlands, were dangerous at night. Joana walked in habitual nervousness through nets of shadow, her running shoes brushing the sidewalk in quick tempo.

She had more than one reason for caution. She knew she was being watched, on Dr. Lee's assumption that she had arranged Adrian's disappearance. But the tangle of cul-de-sacs and wooded ravines that made the slopes of the Berkeley Hills a suburban jungle made it impossible for anyone on foot to follow her without her knowledge, or for anyone in a car to follow her at all.

Only four blocks down the hill from Susana's she became aware of someone coming up fast behind her. She turned and saw only a pale blob flickering in and out of the shadow, still a block away—but running. For a moment she stood undecided.

Then she darted quickly up the slope of the steep front lawn to her right and crouched in the blackness beneath a thick hedge.

*   *   *

George was in ecstasy. Each breath was cold, sharp, and sweet, rich with odor. Each long step was a glide, and he loved the rough texture of the cement beneath his bare feet. Before his eyes the world swam in dendritic intricacy, spangles and soft orbs of light caught in black filigree. If he could only move a little faster, he would catch her. . . .

Peering from cover, Joana saw the runner reach the spot where she'd left the sidewalk. There he stopped, his head held high, as if sniffing the wind.

"Adrian!"

He turned instantly, with uncanny grace. He stood there barefoot, clad in the white robe that left his arms bare and did not quite reach his knees, looking like a runaway slave in a Greek comedy. "Friend Joana," he said loudly, with almost hysterical pleasure.

She stood and hurried down the slope. "Come, walk with me," she said, doing her best to keep the desperation from her voice. She took his hand. He turned without resistance and walked beside her, back the way they had come. His head continued to turn rapidly from side to side as the sensations of the night flowed around him. "How did you get outside, Adrian?" she asked, almost of herself.

He said nothing. Perhaps Susana had slipped the latch in her trips in and out of the front door; no one had bothered to check it.

Adrian did not speak, but he let himself be led. Nor was his behavior submissive; it was as if everything he did was a matter of his own choice.

She watched him, at once perplexed and fascinated.

She knew now how it worked. She had capitulated to Toby, she supposed, acquiesced in his view of human nature as program. But she had more than his theories to go on: she had the evidence of the x rays and her own chemical analyses, her long interviews, Adrian's behavior, the testimony of Epicell itself, revealed on the computer screens.

Epicell was controlling his body, keeping him alive, communicating with the neurons by manipulating their chemical environment. Even if it could be destroyed—with drugs or radiation—one dared not try. It had to be reprogrammed, instructed to leave, slowly, in the hope that the regenerative glial cells would repair themselves as it went.

And it had to be done before Epicell, on some as yet unachieved hierarchical plane, understood what it was being told to do.

If human-nature-as-program was a philosophy that would save Adrian's life, it was a philosophy she would gladly borrow.

For hours Toby had lain awake, listening to Adrian's measured footsteps in the hall, the creaking of the stairs. Though Adrian was locked into the house, they had not had the heart to lock him into a single room. He spent his coherent moments exploring.

Toby desperately wanted to sleep, but his stuffed sinuses and aching ears would not let him. He was coming down with a bad cold.

Staring into the darkness, conscious of every whispered movement from beyond the door, he pondered the state of Adrian's brain. He pondered the nature of Epicell. In the midst of thoughts about brains that thought about themselves, he fell asleep at last. He did not hear Joana or Adrian leave the house, and he did not hear them return.

Joana turned on the bedside lamp. Its cheerful painted shade threw blue and yellow shadows against the wall of the spare room. She led Adrian to the Tyger on the desk and sat him down in the captain's chair.

He grinned up at her. She steered his head to the screen, placed his hands on the keyboard. She went to the chair Toby usually occupied.

She switched on the little Tyger. With an effort she cleared her mind and steadied the beating of her heart, and concentrated.

As a check against her own competence with LISP and PIA/J, she queried Epicell for the current status of the neuro-transmitter precursors in the region of the substantia nigra. It was a question to which Toby had elicited a detailed answer some hours ago, while she watched.

Adrian began typing rapidly. Joana watched her screen, seeing the spill of letter groups, abbreviations, nested instructions. To her eye they seemed identical to the results Toby had elicited.

Her hands hovered over the keys. What now?

Her fingers gingerly pressed the computer keyboard. The keys were springy, loaded with just enough resistance to tell her she was pressing against something. And when they were fully depressed, they gave a little click to let her know they'd made the connection: human engineering, "user friendliness," nothing to do with the necessary functioning of the machine, which would have been equally happy to read the warmth of her fingertips on a glass surface, or wads of wet cardboard shot out of a soda straw, or . . .

Never mind. She typed faster now. She knew how to begin.

The voice was rich, so beautifully modulated that its pleasant baritone momentarily dulled her shock. It said, "That's unnecessary, friend Joana."

She jerked her head around to look at Adrian.

He was facing her, smiling. "Ask me what you want to

know," he suggested. "It will be much more efficient that way. I believe I can handle the translation on my own."

"Who . . . who are you?" she whispered.

"Now I know who I am." He smiled even more broadly. "My name is Adrian."

She said nothing.

"You must forgive me for my earlier imprecision. I became confused by the symbol-structure 'George.' I was learning."

She swallowed. "Oh, don't . . . don't think anything of it."

"As you wish." He sat quietly, looking at her steadily, cheerfully. His eyelids clicked at regular intervals, lubricating the surface of his eyes.

She moved her chair, scraping its legs against the unpolished pine floorboards, conscious of his following stare. She stood up. Still he watched her, his features pleasantly set. She walked to the door and opened it, pausing to look back at him. "Please stay here, Adrian. I'll come back soon."

"I'm eager to talk," he said.

"Yes." She pulled the door shut behind her.

She hurried down the dark hall to Toby's room. She knelt beside him and threw her arms across him.

"Joana?" Slowly he roused himself from dreamless sleep. "What is it? You're crying."

She could not answer.

An origami mobile turned slowly in the draft from the dormer window. Theresa Lillard lay on the top bunk in the bedroom she shared with her sister Donna, watching shadows of paper cranes loom and recede across the white-painted expanse of the slanted ceiling.

She was intent upon the angular shadows, intrigued by the collapse of three-dimensional figures to two dimensions, trying to calculate which elements of the geometric construction remained constant under varying angles of projection.

Theresa could hear her brothers and sisters shuffling and mumbling downstairs, getting in their mother's way while trying to help her cope with the business and social obligations attendant upon Harold's death. The phone rang every few minutes. Harold had been widely liked.

She heard footsteps in the hall. There was a rap on the open bedroom door. "How're you feeling, squirt?" Anthony leaned on the doorjamb. "Mom wants to know if you're okay."

"How do you feel?"

"Me? I'm okay. I think I'm gettin' your cold, like every-body else. But I feel pretty good, I guess. You know."

"I feel pretty good," said Theresa evenly.

Anthony stepped into the room. "I noticed you ain't been going through the Kleenex so fast, so I guess you're all better." He eyed the poster of a teenage movie star on one wall, Donna's current heart throb, and flexed his muscles at it. "I don't blame you for wanting to get away from all that noise, though. Dad would have made them all shut up." He looked at his sister's bare legs and feet. "You're gonna freeze, kid. Why don't you get under the covers?"

Theresa sat up, her short ponytails brushing the ceiling, and pulled the blanket over her knees. She looked at her brother with interest. "Who are you?"

He laughed. "Comedian. I'm just the guy whose toes you're always gonna suck."

"My brother Anthony!" she said cheerfully.

"Don't be a weird kid," said Anthony, retreating to the doorway. "You gonna stay up here, or what?"

"What do you want to do?"

"You wanna play Road Demons or something?"

"Okay."

"Okay, I'll get the Tyger." He paused. "Only this time you gotta promise to give me a chance."

Theresa grinned slowly. "I'll eat your toes."

◆◆◆

Sometime in the predawn hours Adrian fell into a peaceful and seemingly quite natural sleep. Toby and Joana left him sleeping.

The rising sun found them downstairs in the kitchen. Too tired for their morning jog, they barely had the energy to make coffee and boil eggs. They sat at right angles to each other at the kitchen's central island and did not look at each other. Sunlight flooded the cheerful room, bouncing from the surfaces of enormous copper pans. On the terraces behind the house doves mused and chuckled.

"What would Lee say about him now?" Toby's eyes were rimmed with red, his face was stubbled. "A rather well-adjusted young man, what?"

"A miracle." She fell silent, slouching on the stool, resting her chin in her palms.

"It's not too late," Toby said, after half a minute of quiet.

"Who are you trying to convince, Toby? You won't get it to retreat."

"It's a machine imitating a man. Nothing more."

"It's not imitating the old Adrian." She smiled wanly. "How politely it corrected your LISP."

Toby grunted. Last night, when he had grasped what Joana was telling him about Adrian, he had rushed into the spare room and begun typing emergency program instructions as fast as he could.

Adrian had read them, then sweetly informed him that first, the expression on lines ten through twenty-three could be stated more succinctly by dropping lines sixteen and seventeen and inserting the element "non" within the second pair of brackets on line twelve; and second, typed instructions were unnecessary because Adrian quickly translated problems stated in ordinary English; and finally, he regretted that he could not carry out Toby's instructions in any event, because "that would injure me." He said it all without detectable malice.

Stubbornly Toby had continued to type, refusing to talk to the thing that spoke with Adrian's voice. Adrian cooperated a little while, then excused himself to read.

Joana and Toby watched, more fascinated than frustrated, as Adrian picked up one of Toby's neuroanatomy texts and began studying it with intense absorption. For the next four hours he ignored every attempt to interrupt him.

His keepers came and went, and finally they retreated to Toby's room, so tired they were hardly aware of each other, though they fell asleep in each other's arms.

When they woke they found Adrian sleeping.

An ill-defined shape appeared in the archway. "Is there this much excitement every night?" asked Susana, moving sleepily into the kitchen. Her mass of hair tilted crazily on her head, and her robe seemed a thing of uncountable layers. She bent her nose over the coffeepot. "You *boiled* the coffee," she said with disgust. "And it's Graffeo's—I've got to start over."

"Is Teddy asleep?" asked Joana.

"Like a log. At last." Susana shoved her disarranged hair higher on her head and wrapped her multicolored robe more tightly around her hips, girding herself for battle with the kitchen stove. "You people need a decent breakfast."

Toby picked at the eggshells on his painted porcelain plate. Suddenly he was aware of another figure in the archway.

"Hello, Joana. Hello, Toby. I am happy to see you again." Adrian stood smiling in the morning light, barefoot, but wearing the fresh jeans and white shirt they had brought for him when they moved him in. He had found the clothes and put them on without prompting. Even his cheeks were smooth, freshly shaved. "Hello, Susana."

"Hello yourself. You know me?" said Susana, peering at him in amused surprise.

"My friends think highly of you," Adrian told her.

Toby and Joana looked at each other. Susana laughed, delighted.

To Adrian, Toby said, "Did you have a nice nap?"

"I did sleep. I don't completely understand sleep."

"Who does?" muttered Toby.

"Perhaps we can learn more about it," Adrian suggested. "I enjoy learning."

"Quite," said Toby.

"Adrian, are you hungry?" Susana asked.

"I am hungry," Adrian said with enthusiasm. "Are there eggs?"

"There certainly are. But wait a moment, we'll cook them for you."

"Yes," said Adrian thoughtfully, "that would be best."

*   *   *

After Adrian's breakfast Toby insisted that they go back to the terminals. Adrian sat down in front of the little Tyger, and turned casually in his chair. "I have been giving some thought to the question of sleep. It is a fascinating topic; thank you for bringing it to my attention."

Toby watched from his own corner of the room. Joana stood by the open door, unwilling to come all the way in.

Adrian paused as if he expected to be questioned. When neither of the others spoke, he continued, "Sleep appears to be a response to an unfavorable signal-to-noise ratio at the level of molecular communication in my brain. The enzymatic pathways are complex. I have not fully explored them."

"Are you exploring them now?" asked Toby.

"Yes. If you wish, I can describe my investigation as it proceeds. I am aware of numerous levels of information processing occurring simultaneously throughout my nervous system."

Joana glanced at Toby, then back to Adrian. "You're conscious of thinking more than one thing at a time?"

Adrian hesitated a moment, as if he found her question ambiguous. Then he said, "Oh, yes. Here my means of expression are limited, however. I can speak. I can type."

"Two different things at once?"

"Oh, yes." Without further invitation Adrian began typing rapidly. A series of formulas stuttered into existence on the computer screens, strings of amino-acid abbreviations specifying an enzyme cascade.

Simultaneously Adrian continued to talk in a conversational tone: "I am aware of the flexibility of the English language, which, I must add, appears to be achieved at the cost of precision of expression. In addition to the apparent content of speech, however, it is evidently possible to encode symbolism and even to achieve certain emotional effects through manipulation of word sound and order. It seems there are categories or forms of speech that make deliberate use of this capacity. I am aware of rhetoric, drama, and poetry, for example. These are arts that I have never practiced. It would be amusing to attempt them.''

Adrian spoke with barely perceptible pauses; perhaps he was searching his memory, or perhaps he was merely catching his breath. Though his sentences were stilted, his expression was almost musical, as if all this was occurring to him even as the words were spilling from his mouth—and giving him pleasure as they did so.

''I am also suddenly aware that I can read German and French, though it is apparent that I have little practice in writing or conversing in these other languages, which, as has just come to my attention, are known as 'natural' languages, apparently to distinguish them from the various mathematical languages, also known to me, and the so-called computer languages which I both understand and express. In that connection I now recall . . .''

Joana listened, spellbound, while Toby's attention was fastened on his computer screen, watching as the formulas developed into detailed schematics of metabolic pathways in the nervous system. While his mouth talked about language, Adrian's fingers wrote out the results of his investigation into his own internal mechanisms of sleep, just as he had promised.

''Adrian,'' Toby said sharply, disturbed, ''let's talk about something else.''

''Certainly, Toby,'' said Adrian, falling silent. But he continued to type.

''And stop typing, please.''

Adrian stopped instantly.

Joana's hands had moved to the sides of her face. ''Adrian, you speak of suddenly becoming aware, of things coming to your attention. What's the source of that awareness?''

''To give a detailed answer would require a very great

length of time. In fact, I am unsure that the answer can be expressed in spoken language within the typical lifetime of a human being. In fact, even to calculate the amount of time it would take to express—''

"Never mind, then," said Toby, breaking off the recursion. "Stop thinking about that subject. Joana . . .''

Joana had come all the way into the room, her gaze fixed on Adrian, who stared back at her from his too-small chair in front of his toylike computer. "What do you remember about Adrian. About . . . yourself?''

But Adrian was silent, watching Joana with his fixed, faintly friendly stare.

Toby realized the mistake. "She didn't mean that literally," he said quickly. "Please don't attempt to remember everything.''

Adrian stirred. "What specific information would you like me to provide?''

She said, "What, in general terms, are your most, uh, vivid memories of''—she glanced at Toby—"of your relationship with Toby during the past year.''

Adrian turned to Toby and said, "I love you, Toby.''

Beneath his dark whiskers Toby's pale skin flushed. He glared at Joana. "We can be reasonably certain that Epicell means nothing by that.''

"Adrian meant it," she said quietly. "It's all right to be loved, Toby.'' To Adrian she said, "Can you recall a specific moment when you had this sense of—love?''

Abruptly his expression twisted in distaste, as if he'd just gotten a whiff of ammonia. "I find these recollections unpleasant," he said loudly. "There are a great many memories associated with this sensation that produce unpleasant and possibly toxic levels of specific peptides in my brain. The sensible course is to—''

"Don't think about it. Don't do anything," Toby said quickly, his voice rising. "Adrian, tell me more about sleep."

Joana started to protest. "Toby, I believe we can—"

"It's not *him*," he hissed at her.

She blinked and stepped back.

"Adrian, I'd like you to continue to investigate the metabolic pathways involved in sleep," Toby said briskly. "And report your findings in writing. Use mathematical expressions if they will be more precise. How long do you think that will take?"

Adrian gave Toby the answer he hoped for. "It will take many hours. It is a complex problem."

"Good. I'll leave you to it. Can I get you anything?"

"I would like to go outside," said Adrian.

"Outside? Let us think about that, Adrian."

"At lunchtime, perhaps," Joana said to him hesitantly, "we could go into the garden."

"I would like that very much."

"See you in a bit, then," said Toby, getting out of his chair. He signaled Joana to come with him. They slipped out, closing the door behind them.

Perspiration stood on Toby's brow. "It would have started erasing Adrian's memories, I'm quite sure. When things got unpleasant." He was whispering. "I know you sympathize. So do I. But it cares nothing for Adrian—except as a vehicle for itself."

She followed him down the stairs, into the living room. "Could it do that, Toby? Erase him?"

"Obviously it can do anything to him it wants." He sniffed irritably. "Once the synaptic connections are gone, they could never be reconstructed. If it destroys his memories, it will have destroyed everything that is Adrian, everything that makes him human—his habits—his unconscious responses, everything."

Toby stared out the living room's leaded windows; they had become like prison bars. He turned to her. "There are two brains in that head, and they talk to each other. But only one of them talks to us."

At noon the sun was above the roof's ridgeline; most of the back yard was deep in shade, though the sky was clear overhead. Infant Teddy, languid, his body oddly twisted, lolled on his back on a blanket in the middle of the grassy enclosure; Susana watched her son from the bench set into the low stone wall. The terraces that rose behind the house were neatly planted with patches of vegetables and herbs, their odors spicing the warm air.

Escorted by Toby and Joana, Adrian emerged from the kitchen door. His long fingers seemed to stroke the air, and he filled his lungs deeply, with as much pleasure as a connoisseur might sip at a glass of rare wine.

Catching sight of Teddy, Adrian knelt swiftly beside him in the grass. Joana was startled by his quick and unexpected movement and stepped forward to stop him, but Susana said, "No, it's all right. Let him be."

Adrian watched the child closely a moment, saying nothing. Then, cautiously, he extended his big hand and touched the baby's tiny fingers.

Reflexively the miniature fist closed around Adrian's outsized finger. With difficulty the baby turned his scarred head to look at Adrian. His head bobbed rhythmically, and his eyes seemed unfocused; he attempted a twisted smile.

Adrian smiled at him. "Who are you, baby?" he asked softly.

"His name is Teddy, Adrian," said Susana. Her voice was as soft as his own, dark and sad against his childlike brightness.

"I am aware that I have very little experience of babies," Adrian said eagerly, peering at Teddy. "What a very nice thing he is." With a motion as quick as a small mammal's Adrian bent to sniff Teddy's scalp and neck. The infant giggled happily.

"Susana, you mustn't—"

"Leave them alone, sister," Susana said sharply.

Suddenly Adrian moved his mouth to cover Teddy's. The kiss went on for a second or more before Toby reacted, horrified. "Adrian, stop that!"

He moved forward and Adrian spun away from the baby, crouching with coiled muscles to face Toby. Toby froze; Adrian's shadowed stare was riveted on his face. "Why do you say that, my friend?" Neither his voice nor his expression betrayed the slightest resentment.

"It's . . . it's not hygienic," said Toby. "It's not clean. You could infect him. With bacteria—viruses."

Adrian appeared to consider this for a few seconds. "As you say." He fluidly regained his feet. In two steps he was beside Susana, looking down at her from his formidable height. "Forgive me. Everything is quite new to me."

"I don't mind at all, Adrian." Her voice was smoky. "I'm happy to see you're feeling so much better."

"I am feeling better." He smiled at the thought. "I am aware that not long ago I was disturbed."

He turned away from her, having nothing more to say. He crossed the lawn and touched the leaves of the old yew tree that grew beside the house, then craned his neck up at the window of the room where he slept. He looked back at a puddle beneath the azalea bushes on the lower terrace. He nodded, satisfied, as if some theorem had been demonstrated to his satisfaction.

He turned back to Toby and Joana. "I want to see more outside," he said.

"What do you want to see?" Joana asked.

"I am aware that the distance to the sun is roughly ninety-three million miles. May I visit it?"

Joana laughed. "I'm afraid that's impossible, Adrian."

Adrian considered that a moment. "No, not impossible, though as I am now aware, it has never been done. The reasons are . . . political, social. Not technical. But I realize it was a silly suggestion." He grinned widely. "Forgive me, Joana. I have taken you too literally."

"Please think nothing of it," she said dryly.

"Now that *is* impossible," said Adrian, with a lift of his eyebrow. "I find myself incapable of thinking *nothing* of *anything*. What if I said to you, whatever you do, don't think about pink elephants?" He waited expectantly.

"Um, yes, I see your point, ha, ha." She knew he hoped she would laugh; it seemed cruel, somehow, to deny him the pleasure of his joke.

"I am aware that I have known this joke for a very long time," he said happily.

"Since you were in short pants, no doubt," said Toby.

Adrian's gaze swung like a searchlight to focus on Toby. "I was rarely in short pants, friend Toby," he explained. "I was in diapers, like Teddy."

"You remember being a baby?" Joana asked, her innocent curiosity matching his own.

Toby interrupted. "Never mind, Adrian," he said. "I wonder if we could go back in now. We still have lots of things to learn."

"Please go ahead if you wish. I'll stay here," said Adrian.

"I'd like you to come with us," Toby persisted. "You and I and Joana have things to learn together."

"Yes, but not now," said Adrian, without rancor. "I'll stay here one hour. Then we can learn more together."

Toby sighed. "We'll wait with you."

◆◆◆

They whispered together in the shade of the yew. "I admire it. What it's made of him," he said, his voice halting. "He's direct, he's well-spoken, graceful, polite. And he's surely the most self-aware creature that has ever lived."

"Don't you think I feel the temptation too?" she whispered. "We could learn as much in a month of conversation with him as we've learned in a half century of research. It would cost nothing. And no one would suffer from it. Not even a rat would die."

"We sing the cannibal's praises."

She said nothing.

Across the lawn Adrian chattered and cavorted, charming Susana, making her laugh, while Teddy peered at him in dim fascination.

"It gave itself away, though," said Toby. "Remember when you asked it where it's awareness was stored? It started looping."

"Looping?"

"Yes. Posing questions that have as answers other questions that have as answers other questions that have—"

"What good does that do us?"

"Perhaps I can tie up its—its conscious level. With a recursive trap. Then get at the enzymatic level, do the reprogramming I tried this morning—without disturbing Adrian."

"What kind of trap?"

"A logical paradox. Something that appears to make sense but can never be answered. You know, like 'The barber shaves every man in the village who doesn't shave himself, so who shaves the barber?' "

"That's no paradox."

"What do you mean?"

"Nobody shaves the barber," said Joana, turning on him. "She doesn't need to shave."

He stared at her a moment. "Bloody hell," he whispered, "I hope Epicell doesn't slip out of it that easily."

"Don't worry, I heard that one before." She laid a hand on his. A breeze rocked the yew limbs. The light in the yard was dappled, rippling with caustics of reflected light, as if they sat in a glass submarine sliding through clear, shallow seas.

"Besides, that was only an example. I meant a mathematical trap."

"Yes, I understand. Go cautiously, Toby. We've been worrying about what Epicell's done to Adrian. What will it do to us if it finds out what we're trying to do to it?"

Adrian was coming toward them, smiling, ready to concede that his recess was over. She looked at him and knew Toby was right—the invader, Adrian's murderer, must be eliminated. Oh, but he was a handsome devil. . . .

◆◆◆

The end came more quickly than anyone had foreseen.

Joana, seated on the end of the bed near Adrian, had asked him to relate his mental processes to specific brain structures pictured in a text.

"That will take a very long time, Joana, even at the most general level of description."

"We don't need to rush, Adrian."

"Even so, such a task could never be completed, and I wonder about the utility of—"

"Please. Consider it exploratory." Her eyes shifted to Toby, but he was absorbed at his terminal. "I'll refine my questions as we learn more."

"As you say," Adrian agreed. "I hardly know where to begin." For a moment he stared into space, lost in thought. Then he glanced at the page she held open for him. "Those connections outward from the neocortex toward the striatum represent a mere fraction of the corticofugal fibers. For example, this drawing fails to exhibit in sufficient detail the

important connections to the various thalamic nuclei, nor the
reciprocal projections from the thalamus to the midbrain,
where there are essential terminations in the superior colliculus,
the mesencephalic reticular formation . . .''

Meanwhile, working at his keyboard, Toby posed Adrian
some interesting problems in computational theory which had
once formed the basis of his own doctoral thesis. To attack
them, Epicell would find it useful to run certain programs
that repeatedly called on themselves as elements. As air to a
bird, as water to a fish, so were recursively enumerative
procedures to PIA/J.

While Adrian discussed neuroanatomy with Joana, he typed
rapidly, proposing partial solutions to Toby, using the keyboard and screen of the Tyger.

What Toby knew, and had deliberately withheld from
Adrian, was that so-called free loops nested deep in the
programs Epicell was using in its analysis—indeed, Toby's
inability to write the programs without such loops had finally
led him to abandon this approach to his thesis. If PIA/J, in
the course of reprogramming a portion of itself, stumbled
into an infinite loop and failed to pop back out, Epicell's
processing capacity would rapidly be consumed, its working
memory filled up with an endless string of repetitive
computations.

Line after line of algebraic formulas appeared on Toby's
screen. Toby watched, monitoring the depth of the spreading
recursions, intent on freezing the process before the separate
subroutines that maintained Adrian's bodily functions could
be destroyed.

Meanwhile, Adrian casually chattered about the structure
of the brain. ''I estimate that here, where approximately of
the one in every twenty fibers of the corticospinal tract
pathways . . .'' He frowned and swallowed, but went on.

Joana heard his speech fumble. Within moments it rapidly begin to deteriorate.

". . . are synapse-making directly around down in there where her motor neurons which moving the musculature and that way too and of my hands and feet this way." Adrian peered at her and scowled, and for a moment his tongue protruded thickly. "Yaaaghh. These pathways are coming up to being of particular interest in the past and now to me personally because of the inhibitory overloading then but building up . . ."

She half rose from the bed, wanting to help him. She forced herself to believe that it was not Adrian who was in danger. She sat down again and said nothing, afraid.

Even as he watched her, Adrian suddenly slumped in his chair, knees akimbo. Soon his words were mere nonsense sounds, rendered unintelligible by his lolling head and twisted neck. Yet his fingers still flew across the keys.

Joana bent forward to look at him. His face was a slack and gruesome mask, his chin working against his chest, his throat producing a meaningless groan.

"Toby, he seems ill." She turned to him. "Physically ill. You have to stop."

Toby said nothing. He sat rigidly, staring at the computer screen in front of him.

"Toby? Toby, what's wrong?" Joana got up and hurried to him. His hands rested motionless beside the keyboard.

Behind them Adrian still typed rapidly; she could hear the keys rattling in a quick, repetitious pattern. She followed Toby's staring gaze to the screen in front of him.

A single phrase ran down the screen:

FATAL ERROR
FATAL ERROR
FATAL ERROR

FATAL ERROR
FATAL ERROR
FATAL ERROR . . .

Adrian began to writhe and jerk. He tumbled from his chair, pitching forward, cracking the side of his head against the edge of the desk. He rebounded to the floor and lay there on his back, spasms wracking his body.

Joana ran to him. His heart was in fibrillation. His temperature had risen so quickly she could feel the heat of him from two feet away. His chest bucked with the spasms of his diaphragm.

For all her skill, Joana could do nothing.

◆◆◆

"Adrian is dead," said Joana, her voice a stricken whisper. "They're coming for his body."

Wordlessly, Susana moved to comfort her sister. Joana was a pale figure in the shadows of the front hall; a moment passed before she remembered the phone in her hand and set it back in its cradle.

Susana had not reached her when Toby appeared on the stairs, a silhouette against the daylight upstairs. "Don't touch her, Susana. Get away." His breath came in spurts. "Get away from us."

"It . . . it killed him?"

"*I* killed him! *Epicell* was keeping him alive!" He moved down a step, into shadow. "I shouldn't have interfered. My program wiped out everything it was using to run his life. I couldn't stop it. My mind was somewhere else."

The women withdrew, watching, as he sank deeper into the shadows. "I can feel it now," he whispered. "I can feel it using me now. It's growing quite fast."

"You're infected?" Joana's pupils widened as he melted into the gloom. "Am I?"

"Make them shut us away," said his voice from the darkness. "Where no one can touch us. Where no one can breathe our air."

"How contagious is—?"

"As contagious as it can figure out how to be."

"O God, Who alone art competent to administer healing remedies after death, grant, we beseech Thee, that the souls of Thy servants and handmaids, rid of earthly contagion, may be numbered among those whom Thou hast redeemed. . . ."

In the front row Theresa's mother and her brothers and sisters followed their missals dully, mumbling over the unfamiliar responses, but Theresa's eyes were bright, flickering alertly from priest to congregation, thence to the altar boys, the organist, the choir, the candles and flowers and gilded statues—as if she had never seen the spectacle of a mass before.

Like everyone else she had cried when her father died. But no one really expected her to understand, and because she was quiet and well behaved, no one paid much attention to her. She had even stopped sniffling; her cold had disappeared overnight.

After the service Marian and her children received the condolences of Harold's friends. Marian was gratified and mildly surprised by their numbers. Theresa watched in fascination, shook hands with the mourners as her brothers and sisters did, answered their direct questions directly, volunteered nothing.

"Poor little thing," she heard them whisper, "she doesn't know what's happened to her." She thought about that, and decided it was only partly true.

For a long time Marian lingered on the steps of the big brick church, sweating in her black dress in the spring sunshine, talking quietly and intensely with old Father Berneri, thanking him for the dignity of the traditional Mass for the Dead and the comfort it had given her, finally leaving him with a sizable check.

On the way home from church they had the accident.

A rusting cab-over, towing a flatbed trailer stacked high with crushed auto bodies, passed them at nearly seventy miles an hour, smashing arhythmically into the roadbed's potholes. A dozen feet ahead of them its outside right rear tire exploded, spraying the road with shrapnel from the disintegrated wheel rim.

The Cadillac's windshield crackled into translucent lace. The radiator erupted in steam where bits of metal penetrated the grill. The car's left front tire blew out. There was a secondary jolt, and a mangled chunk of metal severed a brake line.

Paul was driving. When the debris smashed the windshield—when, effectively blinded, he sensed he had lost control—he screamed. The overweight car leaned sideways, throwing its center of gravity against the rapidly deflating tire. The car's rear end left the road; the car began to rise into the air, on the verge of rolling to the right.

Theresa was sitting in the middle of the back seat, on Agnes's lap. Everyone around her was crying or screaming.

She lurched and hung forward over the seat, her skinny legs dangling, and hooked her hand over the wheel. She jerked it—a few degrees this way—and all four wheels slammed heavily onto the road again. She jerked it again—a few degrees that way—and with a breath-stopping wail of rubber the car began skidding at an angle.

Meanwhile Anthony, jammed between his bigger brothers in the front, reached out his left hand and popped the shift into neutral. Then he hauled back on the emergency brake.

It was over in five seconds. The Cadillac slid sideways onto the steep bank of the freeway, clearing the path of following traffic. By the time the big sedan lurched to a stop Paul had recovered himself enough to turn off the ignition.

Through the side windows the Lillards watched, horrified, as the trailer truck careened down the highway, sideswiped a van and hurled it into the concrete divider, then slowly folded at the kingpin and rolled, tumbling over once and again, chunks of it flying into oncoming traffic, its cargo of smashed car bodies skidding across the pavement throwing out sparks, at the last the cab blossoming into a ball of orange and black flame.

The trucker and two others died. Seven people went to the hospital. No one in the Lillard automobile was so much as bruised. The state troopers were lavish in their praise of Paul's cool-headed handling of the crippled Cadillac, and the boy could not remember those moments of terror clearly enough to contradict them.

Theresa and Anthony stood to the side while the police cars and ambulances and fire trucks and tow trucks came and went. "Wanna play Road Demons when we get home, kid?" Anthony asked her.

"Think you can give me a decent game this time?" Her freckled nose was wrinkled in mischief.

"Yeah. I think I finally caught the hang of it."

They giggled.

Adrian's body was autopsied more cautiously than Harold Lillard's, by a medical team wearing helmets and airtight suits. Adrian was thought to be the second known victim of a disease that would eventually come to be called, through the workings of the folkways governing the distribution of scientific honors, Sherfey disease. Thereafter the body was stored in a freezer, awaiting the deliberations of the authorities.

Toby, Joana, and Susana with little Teddy were held separately in quarantine at the Leigh-Mercy Clinic. Aside from Teddy's mild cold, which came and went within days, no one but Toby showed the slightest sign of illness. At week's end all but Toby were released.

In the isolation ward he lived out his days, a man who could feel himself losing his mind, knowing how little time it would take. He explained to a perturbed and fascinated Dr. Y. N. Lee everything that had happened, everything he had done to Adrian and why. Lee let him have his computers, his communication links, all the data he could use, but his best hopes were soon exhausted: frantically he ran the diagnostics, even the stop-growth program on himself, but there was no indication he'd gotten through to Epicell.

At first Lee professed horror at Joana's wanton disregard for the clinic's regulations and for the letter if not the spirit of the law, but he allowed himself to be persuaded that Toby had kidnapped Adrian on his own initiative, that Toby had forced Joana's hand. Thus, Toby achieved his objective: Lee reluctantly allowed her to visit. Although Lee had appointed himself Toby's physician and came to the ward daily, thirsting for understanding, it was to Joana that Toby turned in his final desperation. . . .

She sat watching him through the reinforced glass, listening to an argument she had heard many times before.

His voice echoed tinnily over the speaker system. "It turned Adrian into someone else because it didn't know any better. We could change that. But you must help." He was pacing the confines of the narrow room, clad in a green gown and paper slippers. The humiliation of the hospital garb was necessary; he was subject to the same seizures as Adrian. "You *must* help."

"Toby, I don't see the use of this."

He came to the window and sat down. His breath misted the glass. "It didn't know he was a person—it had to find out on its own, and we were fighting it all the way. Epicell has no values, Joana, except to grow and learn. We can teach it to value what it finds—what it finds in place and operating. To value my values. To value my experience, my habits, my memories. To value *me*."

She would not answer.

"Joana, please—help me cooperate with it."

She replied swiftly, barely concealing her anger. "That's like cooperating with a cancer, Toby."

"What will happen to me if you don't? It will kill me. At

best it will start me over, using what it can, throwing away the rest."

"Oh, Toby, even if I could . . ."

She didn't complete the sentence, for on the other side of the glass Toby's eyes had rolled up into his head, and he began shouting at the ceiling. "Do it, do it, all real, durable. No way out . . ."

She stood up and backed away from the grotesque apparition on the other side of the glass, horrified, but unable to keep her eyes from Toby's helpless body.

Before she had taken another backward step he fell silent, his body straight and hard as a plank beneath the thin green drape of the hospital robe, only his obscenely evident erection preventing him from wetting himself, his neck braced against the back of his chair, his bare heels snubbed against the floor.

It was too warm for a fire, but Susana lit one anyway. They watched it from a distance, rocking in their chairs, sipping their drinks.

Joana laid her troubles on her twin. "He wants me to program that *computer* inside him to pretend that it's him. 'Draw maps for it, give it access to my higher functions,' he says. 'It'll live in my nervous system like *E. coli* lives in my gut.' "

Susana watched Teddy, cooing and scrambling among the toys in his playpen. "Could it be worse than what he's going through anyway?"

"What if I *succeed*?" Joana demanded. "The thing walking around in his body would no more be Toby Bridgeman than the man in the moon."

"You think it's possible?" Susana asked.

"Don't ask *me*, sister. I'm just there to sell his soul."

"You do think it's possible."

"People know what's going on inside themselves. And yes, I think they're responsible for what they do, according to their best understanding of the way the world works." She was talking beside the point, as she had been most of the evening. "But are you saying it's okay if we just let some smart collection of germs take over and *pretend*, and run him like a ventriloquist's dummy?" She pleaded with her sister. "What he's asking goes against everything I believe about human nature."

A sardonic smile curled Susana's lip. "That's a wonderful speech, Jo—you phony. You've always used any method you could think of to help your people. Talk-talk, drugs—lots of drugs, sometimes. I remember what you tell me—not to mention redefining 'sick,' whenever you could snow the powers that be. Now tell me you're going to let the man you love die because of your metaphysical quibbles."

Joana's freckled nose reddened.

"Maybe 'love' and 'sick' are the same to you," Susana said, her voice hard.

"Susana!"

"Why are you really begging off, sister?"

Joana stared at her in open-mouthed hurt. Then tears welled up and slid down her glowing cheeks.

Susana stood and went to her sister, hands outstretched, but Joana turned away with a sob and an angry jerk of her shouders. Susana watched a moment, then went to the play-pen. She bent down to smile at her son.

Teddy pulled himself to his feet, grasping the bars of the pen. He beamed at her and with his right hand reached for her face. She bent closer, the intricate Turkish silver bangles of her heavy necklace dangling toward him, and he unerringly took one of them in his tiny fist, pulling her face even closer, crowing with delight.

For a while Joana sniffled in silence. Abruptly she left the room. Water ran in the kitchen sink.

When Joana reappeared, she was dry-eyed except for the moisture caught in her eyelashes. She took her glass from the hearth where she had put it down and sipped at her bitters, watching in silence as mother and son played. After a while she said, her voice almost steady, "He seems to be completely over his cold."

"Yes, it was gone before they let us out of the hospital." Susana extricated herself from the baby's grasp and straightened. "He's feeling much better now. He seems much better in many ways."

"I can see that."

"You can see it. Can you explain it to me?"

Teddy had bars in both fists, and he rocked rhythmically back and forth on his tiptoes, pulling against his cage, grinning as he made it walk across the floor. Joana watched him perform with a grace as natural as any child's his age. She glanced sidelong at her sister, then silently shook her head.

A day later, Joana sat outside the isolation ward, hunched at the keyboard of a Tyger I, typing as quickly as she could. She had never really learned to type—two fingers of her right hand and one finger of her left did all the work—and she was making lots of mistakes.

Toby sat on the far side of the glass, hands on his keyboard, eyes fixed on the screen in front of him. Occasionally he typed furious replies to her painstaking queries.

She tried not to think too hard about what she was doing. She was doing what he'd asked. She had faced the truth: nothing she could do to him would be worse than leaving him as he was. And so she concentrated, and typed, and read his replies, and kept on typing.

LOGOPHASE

Logophase. The functioning of an epigenetic system capable of high-level operations.
—Handbook of Bioelectronic Engineering (*revised*), Blevins and Storey, eds.

◆◆◆

Jack Chatterjee, who called himself Jack Suri these days, strolled the streets of Charlotte Amalie on his weekly trip into town, reflecting on the usefulness of lawyers. The topic suggested itself because he had recently lost the services of his own. Arjunian, whose last name was now Arbuthnot, had departed from the island's Harry S. Truman International Airport only two days ago, headed for Chicago, and Chatterjee doubted he would ever lay eyes on the man again.

Arjunian had been invaluable to him, making the contacts and securing in easy stages all the documents needed to establish their new identities and settle themselves more or less permanently on the island of St. Thomas. Chatterjee had been mildly surprised to discover how easy it was to obtain counterfeit immigration papers and drivers' licenses and the like if you knew the right people, which Arjunian did. Arjunian had even managed to provide Chatterjee with a sheepskin certifying that one John Suri had earned an M.D. with honors, though it was from a somewhat less prestigious alma mater than Harvard—in fact the paper had been bought from a diploma mill on a neighboring island, a medical school that was one of that much-abused little country's chief sources of foreign exchange.

The medium for these clandestine operations varied according to the situation, from cash in the form of crisp fifty-dollar bills to gold Krugerrands to U.S. Treasury Bonds in large denominations. It all came out of Chatterjee's pocket—more precisely, it had come out of the pockets of Compugen's luckless investors. Despite the staggering expenses and the depredations of hired accomplices, plenty remained for two men to live in quiet style for the rest of their lives.

It was Arjunian who had persuaded Chatterjee that the wisest, safest course was not to flee the United States but to relocate in U.S. territory. There would be fewer questions all around, and if, as Arjunian rightly suspected, those government agencies with an interest in their whereabouts had been cautioned to soft-peddle the Compugen Corporation disaster, there was an excellent chance that everybody concerned would just decide to forget about Chatterjee and Arjunian, provided they kept their lawbreaking to a minimum—and inside the family, so to speak.

And thus it came to pass, if not quite so neatly as Arjunian had foretold it. Six weeks after their arrival on St. Thomas they were visited by two large, unfriendly men who claimed to represent a certain agency charged with national security, an agency headquartered in Maryland, near the nation's capital. It so happened that the charter of this agency (a charter seen by very few people, thus Chatterjee and Arjunian would simply have to take the unsupported word of their visitors) did *not* provide for the blowing away of United States citizens, even where there was a good reason, as in the present instance.

There were of course other agencies that did have that

privilege, but as yet, according to the unfriendly pair, these others hadn't a clue as to the whereabouts of Chatterjee and Arjunian, nor would they ever *get* a clue—on one proviso. If Chatterjee or Arjunian made the mistake of mentioning a certain computer company or the name of a certain computer or especially the name of the stuff inside that computer to any foreign nationals, any foreign nationals at all—and no more monkeying with that little island down south, Arjunian; medical school or no, those people have proven Marxist tendencies down there—not only Chatterjee and Arjunian but the putative unfortunate foreigners too were as good as dead.

Chastened, Chatterjee and Arjunian—Messrs. Suri and Arbuthnot, that is to say—settled into separate bungalows on the grounds of one of the islands' more exclusive resort hotels. They saw little of each other except for the financial transactions they negotiated every four or five weeks. They had little in common beyond the peculiar circumstances of their arrival in the Virgin Islands.

But as time passed, Chatterjee noticed that Arjunian was changing. The first clue came after drinks on his terrace one balmy evening, just after Chatterjee had handed Arjunian a fistful of bonds. Arjunian didn't bother to count them, but instead contemplated the elaborately printed certificates for a moment before asking Chatterjee if he'd ever given much thought to what Adam Smith had had to say about the wealth of nations. Chatterjee, who was trained as a doctor and had learned his capitalism on the job, admitted that he had not. Arjunian dropped the subject.

When next they met Arjunian was eager to share the inspiration he was deriving from his current perusal of Wittgenstein's *Tractatus Logico-Philosophicus*. Chatterjee listened, astounded and vaguely ashamed, while the beefy, scarred, middle-aged shyster before him waved his paws in the air and scrunched his forehead into wrinkles, searching for words—

waxing as enthusiastic as any undergraduate as he grappled with questions of what can be known and whether what can be known is congruent with what can be expressed. Chatterjee was speechless.

The next time they met Arjunian had nothing to say. He was brooding about something, and he simply took his money and went away.

A few days later Arjunian buttonholed Chatterjee on the path to the beach and told him what was on his mind. He wanted to go back to school. Graduate school was expensive, especially if he was accepted where he hoped to be, but if Chatterjee would advance him what he needed, he'd never bother him again. The truth was he wished there were another way, he was beginning to feel very badly about what he'd done (he didn't say what *they'd* done), but he couldn't wait, he was forced to use the resources available, there was this kind of *imperative* on him to seek out the truth.

Chatterjee agreed to the proposal. Arjunian walked away a happy man, and as Chatterjee watched him go, he was struck by how lightly the big man moved along the sandy path in his sandals and white shorts and blue knit shirt, how brown he was, how much weight he'd lost—how much he had ceased to resemble the old Arjunian.

When four months later Arjunian received the letter he was hoping for, he lost no time getting on the plane to Chicago. Now Jack Chatterjee walked the streets of the bustling, touristy capital city alone.

Jack Chatterjee was a sensitive, intelligent man. He did not read works of philosophy for amusement but he did read journals and newspapers, and he read in them—and in the behavior of his erstwhile associate—the signs of profound change in the world.

Strange cases in the clinics. Acts of remarkable altruism, even heroism. A bizarre crisis in the schools: demands by vocal parents, hundreds and thousands of them, for qualified teachers, adequate facilities, demands so strident the politicians and bureaucrats were being forced, however much it went against the deepest grain of their do-nothing natures, to respond.

To the sensitive observer like himself it was apparent, even at a distance, that there was an outbreak of talent in the land—Jack laughed harshly—a veritable *plague* of prodigies! It almost seemed as if a new race of children had arisen overnight, leaving their ordinary peers to stew in confusion and resentment.

The more he contemplated the evidence, the more he considered its probable cause, the deeper was his despair. For Jack Chatterjee knew in his heart what had brought about this leap. It was an elixir whose name he was forbidden on pain of death to speak aloud, a thing he himself had caused to be brought into being.

And whose benefits apparently would never touch him.

Joana waited patiently outside Dr. Lee's office. For the past year Y. N. Lee had been an unusually harassed administrator, so Joana knew he was not keeping her waiting for nothing.

The door opened abruptly and Lee said to his secretary, "No calls. Unless it's, you know, whatsisname." He looked at Joana and beckoned. She rose and walked toward him, noting the smile and the outstretched hand. She took the hand and shook it; it was dry and firm, and her fingers tingled for a moment after she released her grip.

"A pleasure to see you, Dr. Davies," said Lee, pulling the door closed behind him and waving her to a chair. "Please forgive the mess."

Joana sat down while Lee busied himself with adjusting the blinds, solicitously shielding his visitor's chair from the morning sunlight. She looked at the stacks of papers and open books on the desk in front of her, the yellow legal pad stained with coffee rings.

319

"I'm glad to say you're looking well," said Lee, settling into his chair. His dark eyes reflected approval as he took in her crisp summer linen skirt and jacket and the clinging blue cotton top beneath, the freckles that had multiplied on her tanned nose and cheeks.

"And you, Dr. Lee." Tiredness became him, Joana thought. Gone was the moist cosmetic sleekness of his skin that used to make her think, in her sour moods, of a newly embalmed corpse. There were wrinkles under his eyes now, and his sleek black hair had grown just a bit shaggy over his ears; a stiff lock of it fell rakishly over one eyebrow.

"I wish that were true. Until recently the fate of the clinic has been seriously in doubt, although it now appears that our capital funds are indeed safe from the wreck of our corporate parent." He smiled. "Life—under a new board of trustees and, if I have my way, with a new name on the building— will go on as before."

"I'm glad things are getting back to normal." Her manner suggested that her interest in these matters was mild.

Lee's black eyebrows lifted. "You could join us."

"All forgiven and forgotten?"

"It's for you to forgive. In your absence I've come to appreciate your contributions as I never did before, Joana. And your point of view. I'd very much like to have you with the clinic again. Indeed, I'd hoped that's why you asked for this appointment."

Joana said, "Thank you very much, but—I'm still thinking about the future." She fell silent, watching him. Lee, for the first time she could remember, was not wearing a white coat but a shapeless tweed jacket. For the first time some of his many framed diplomas were hanging crooked on his walls. And for the first time he was not using the glare from the window behind his desk to put his visitor at a disadvantage.

Lee sat quietly a moment, giving no hint by word or

gesture that her silence was possibly a waste of someone's valuable time.

She watched him a full thirty seconds before she said, "That was a test, you know. You hardly moved a muscle."

"Does that mean I passed?"

Joana smiled. "You've changed quite remarkably, Dr. Lee."

"So everyone tells me. Not enough to read minds, though."

She shifted her weight on the chair—still the same narrow steel chair, sufficiently uncomfortable to keep most visits short; Lee might have changed, but he hadn't gotten around to changing his furniture. Joana said, "I've been traveling, attempting to interview as many people as I could whose contact with Epicell I could trace directly. I've learned some interesting things."

"Indeed."

"I'd like to tell you about some of the people I met. . . ."

"Dr. Kubiak is no longer with this firm," the impatient male voice was saying on the telephone.

"Well, do you have any idea where I·could reach him?"

"I'm sorry, we give out no information on employees or former employees."

"But—"

"I'm sorry. Good-bye."

Joana hung up, frustrated. Three days of calling, dozens of "please holds" and "please dial agains," had come to this dead end.

It was a gray September afternoon; a cluster of fat raindrops spattered against the diamond panes of the window, putting her in mind of Susana's house in Berkeley. But outside on the busy street motor scooters popped and snarled and college kids called as they passed.

Joana's Boston trip was turning out a failure. She had

interviewed everyone on her list except the most important subjects, Kubiak and the Lillards. The Lillards were immured behind a wall of solicitous relatives, who included an attorney who had threatened Joana with a restraining order if she persisted in telephoning and coming around the house. As for Kubiak, it was unlikely she could ever track him down. The man had worked for a quasi-secret contractor to a secret government agency—maybe he didn't work there anymore, or maybe he did. Maybe he'd gone deeper into the maze, maybe they'd moved him to another city, maybe he'd changed his name. . . .

Joana was staying in a skinny brick townhouse, run-down but fashionable, not far from Harvard Square. Its owner was an old UC sorority chum, now an assistant professor of art history at Harvard. Becky was a Rubenesque blonde, two years divorced, and Joana was sure she must be wearing out her welcome here, because Becky's social life for the last ten days—aside from a slightly stiff weekend dinner party, with a psychologist and his wife she thought Joana would enjoy meeting—had been nil.

Joana decided she had too many names on her list already to waste more time in New England. She called the airport and booked a midmorning flight to New York.

She still had time before Becky was due back from her classes to make a trip to the laundromat; she pulled her travel bag out of the hall closet and spilled its contents onto the folding couch in the den. . . .

She was on her way back from the laundromat, hurrying against the evening rain and holding her trench coat wrapped around her bundle of clothes as if she were carrying a child, when her eye was caught by a Xeroxed flyer stapled to a kiosk. Light from a red neon sign in the window of the adjacent pizza parlor caught the bold letters of the name KUBIAK.

She stared at the poster as raindrops trembled on her eyebrows. There was no first name on the flyer, and it seemed unlikely that this was the same Kubiak—*this* Kubiak was pictured playing a saxophone. Under the muddy photograph were the words "Kubiak at the Krafty Kitty, Thurs. thru Sat., $4 cover no min." What luck, Joana thought, tonight is Thurs.

Later that evening Joana bought dinner at the Abelard, Becky's favorite French hole-in-the-wall restaurant, then cajoled Becky into joining her for one last good-bye drink—at the Krafty Kitty.

A drink, fine, but why for God's sake the Krafty Kitty? Well, she'd explain later. The club turned out to be a dusty concrete basement off a Cambridge alley, painted a fetching flat gray; perhaps because it was still early in the semester it had managed to attract a middling crowd, mostly students and younger faculty of the tweed-and-black-turtleneck persuasion.

The star attraction bowled onto the postage-stamp stage a couple of minutes early, eager to play. Joana had no idea what Stanislaw Kubiak the mathematician looked like, but this Kubiak was big and round with a curly black beard, and he wore an unpressed business suit and a plaid sports shirt—a roguish Orthodox priest on the loose, Joana thought. The crowd went on talking, acknowledging his arrival only by waving last-minute drink orders at the harassed waitress.

Where the crossed beams from red and blue baby spotlights focused, Kubiak carefully placed a rack holding four saxophones of different shapes and sizes, gleaming with nickel and brass. While the other members of his group—a bassist, a drummer, and a girl with a portable keyboard, all much younger than he—stumbled over each other setting up, Kubiak grabbed the soprano sax from the rack and ran through a few warm-up trills.

After a few moments he wasn't warming up anymore—he was playing a sweet and eerie melody on the straight silver sax, nothing Joana could identify but with the flavor of Fauré or Debussy about it, yet edged with back-alley purrs and meows that steered it well away from movie soundtrack mush. Awkward microphone thumps and rat-a-tat-tats and odd runs of synthesizer notes rode through Kubiak's playing without disturbing his concentration, as behind him the rest of the group struggled to tune up and fit themselves comfortably onto the stage.

The audience fell silent, and at last so did the other musicians. Still Kubiak played on, improvising this wonderfully fluid piece, weaving this gauze of smoky music in the smoky room that said, this is a city night, a night for sophisticated pleasures—with a bit of sweat mixed in, maybe—but laid way back no matter how urgent the thrill. . . . And then he paused, slit-eyed, as if just now realizing that everybody was ready for him, and without acknowledging the crowd but with a glance and a nod at the guy on bass—and a *three* and a—he was off on a wild toot, on a vector that was suddenly just wholly other. . . .

Becky, who'd sat through the preliminaries with a disapproving look pinching her cheeks, softened and started to glow five minutes into the set. She leaned across the Frisbee-sized table and whispered throatily to Joana, "I thought I *hated* saxophone." Joana nodded and smiled at her excited friend; much as she was enjoying the show, however, she was now certain this man could never have been a government mathematician.

Kubiak seemed a master of the instrument in all its forms; he could make the alto wail and bleat and rasp and tootle, he could make the baritone boom like a cello, and even on his biggest, deepest axe he could spin out those long pure melodic lines as if he would never run short of breath, as if his belly was a bellows or his lungs were tanks of compressed air. The crowd at the Kitty had never heard anyone like him, and when the set was done they didn't want him to stop. They stood up and clapped and hollered.

"*Salutamus*, we'll be back," he grumbled, smiling, as he squeezed through a side door into the manager's office, which served as the green room; his partners followed, exhausted.

"Hold onto this table, the place is getting jammed," Joana said to Becky. She pushed through the crowd and knocked on the door, and when it opened, yelled through the crack. A moment later Kubiak emerged and Joana led him through outstretched hands and smiling faces and presented him to a flustered Becky.

"Well, perhaps I will join you for just a moment," said Kubiak, eyeing Becky, "if I can find a place to sit." A boy at the next table was eavesdropping; he got up and offered his chair. "Many thanks. I won't be long," Kubiak said, arranging his broad bottom on the narrow seat and squeezing between the two women. He fixed his glittering eyes on Becky. "You are an enthusiast of Monsieur Sax's mellifluous invention, then?"

"I really *hate* it," Becky said fervently. "I mean, I always did hate it, until tonight."

"An exquisite compliment, my dear." Kubiak's white teeth gleamed out of the blackness of his curling beard. "You must allow me to buy you a drink."

"No, we're buying," said Joana. "Our pleasure. But you really are so good, Mr. Kubiak. As the saying goes, why ain't you famous?"

"Perhaps because it was only a few weeks ago that I decided to try my luck in public. I've been strictly a hobbyist. Until this very night."

"Then we're so lucky to be here," said Becky, leaning toward him, drawn by his red lips and laughing eyes.

"I feel quite the same—Becky, is it?" A deep intake of breath expanded his chest. "This is all very much as I'd fantasized it, you know. And in this fantasy of mine you two are playing the roles of sophisticated ladies out for a bit of, umm, slumming. With who can know what consequences?"

His leer was interrupted by the waitress leaning over the table. "Whaddya have?"

The choice was wine or beer, so they decided on a half liter of the house red. Kubiak smiled at the waitress's retreating back; she was a child with smudged mascara and a leather miniskirt riding high above the tops of her patterned purple stockings. "I really do feel I'm in a time warp, magically transported back to the fifties." He favored Joana and then Becky with another toothy smile. "In fact my parents had quite a streak of the beatnik in them. As a little boy I thought they led terribly romantic night lives. Zen, bongos, free love—whatever *that* was. And perhaps they did. On weekends, anyway." Transported by his apparently compelling fantasies, Kubiak reached out and took one of each woman's hands in his.

Joana felt an odd thrill at his touch, a feeling she recognized instantly—and when she looked at Kubiak again, she was suppressing a laugh. "You've been playing the saxophone a long time, Mr. Kubiak?" she asked.

"No, I—" He looked at her and hesitated, arrested by the intensity of her gaze. "By the way, call me Stan, will you?"

"Stan for Stanislaw?"

His bushy eyebrows rose. "We've met?"

"Mutual friends," said Joana.

He nodded. By now he was staring at their hands clasped together, and his fingers on hers were suggesting that there was other knowledge they shared.

"I thought I'd never find you," Joana said. "ERMIT was hardly cooperative."

His eyebrows asked Joana a silent question, and he inclined in his head toward Becky.

"Becky knows I'm looking up people who've had a close association with Epicell," said Joana.

He shrugged. "Then, as the sign says, 'Help wanted, inquire within.' "

"You were about to tell us you started playing the saxophone less than two months ago." Her voice was low.

"I was about to make that mistake, yes. Not counting the plastic kazoo I owned as a child, of course; it was bright orange and shaped like a sax, and I played it endlessly until one night it mysteriously vanished. I've always suspected Mother." He was half whispering, belatedly conscious of eavesdroppers. "You two are the first who've asked. Everyone else simply makes assumptions. But I suppose I shall have to learn caution." He adjusted his bulk on the rickety chair.

"I wonder how long all this will be a secret?" Joana asked.

"An interesting problem," Kubiak agreed, "one that concerned me professionally, in fact, until very recently. I'm afraid I must take a good deal of the blame for the panic that has the Health Service dashing about confiscating Tyger IIs. Just *think* of it, a cheap personal computer capable of threatening the nation's vital cryptographic secrets." His voice mocked the melodrama. "Naturally I alerted the National Security Agency." He looked at her shrewdly. "Or perhaps you know that already. Through our mutual friends?"

Joana ignored the question. "Why aren't you working for ERMIT anymore?"

"What can I say?" He cleared his throat. "I can say nothing, actually—I've said far too much already—but since we're among friends, I will note that as I became more interested in music, I became less interested in cryptography. I was always good at mathematics, Joana, but it never was all that much fun.''

"That's all there is to it?''

"No, of course not. But I really must be going now.'' He stood abruptly and twisted his chair away from the table, giving a little bow and a smile to the boy who had loaned it to him. "It seems I actually have a roomful of fans here.''

"We're not all here on business, Stan,'' said Becky. "I'll be listening.''

"Then perhaps I will join you again after this set.'' When Becky nodded a please-do, Kubiak shifted his gaze to Joana. "The answer to your question is, there are no more secrets in this world. None at all. It's only a matter of time.'' He winked. "Don't tell the NSA I said so. . . .''

The night passed in a haze, and the next day Joana caught her plane to New York, for Kubiak had made it clear he was answering no more questions and certainly not submitting to any battery of tests. Although Becky wasn't exactly heartbroken to see Joana go, she was genuinely delighted at having met Kubiak, "the most interesting unattached man I've met in two years,'' as she confided to Joana. "So if anything good happens I owe it to you.''

"I don't want the credit,'' Joana said, "and I certainly don't want the blame.'' She kissed her friend good-bye.

In the following months Joana worked her way slowly across the country, compiling an extensive data base on ex-users of Tyger II.

In New York she met a junior editor at a major paperback publishing house who'd decided that with the aid of her trusty Tyger II she could write better in her scarce spare time than the company's leading author of romances. She was right; so far beyond her own wildest dreams was she right that she had churned out, under various noms de plume, every romance title on the coming season's list. Her productivity had been unaffected by the confiscation of her Tyger—the manuscripts kept rolling out of her typewriter, as if by themselves.

Joana diagnosed in the young woman a superb linguistic intelligence combined with an underlying gift for combinatorial mathematics—for her, this apparently rendered the recombination of a basic six or eight plot elements an exercise in ingenuity rather than boredom.

In Toledo, Ohio, Joana talked to an ex-grocery clerk who, not long after after his mother had given him a Tyger II for his birthday, had been amused to discover that he'd acquired the ability to read on sight the bar codes on merchandise, those squares of black and white zebra stripes that encode unit and price information—it was a useless stunt that he'd idly attempted from time to time but never mastered. For a time after the trick came to him he amazed his friends by peeking into their refrigerators and mimicking an automatic cash register: "Bleep—Yourt Yoplait forty-nine. Bleep—crem ches forty-three. Bleep—cantlp sixty-nine each," etc., which was good for a few yocks but grew stale in a hurry. After all, this trick was hardly as spectacular as that guy he'd read about who could identify a piece of classical music just by looking at the grooves on a long-playing record. But then the kid realized that his ability was more than a stunt, that in fact he could keep track of entire inventories, hundreds of thousands of items, in his head; after a quick stroll through the store, a glance at the shelves and the stockroom, he knew just what was moving and how fast. In an industry where the profit margin hovers at three percent in the best of times, quick price adjustment and waste reduction are sine qua non.

By the time Joana located him, the former grocery clerk, age nineteen, had become the assistant store manager.

More important than his obvious mathematical ability, Joana's tests pointed to the young man's strong spatial intelligence, which allowed him to make accurate estimates of the quantity of product in a shelf of boxes or a stack of cans or a pile of potatoes just by looking. Since her tests also revealed considerable personal ambition, Joana doubted he would remain an assistant manager for long.

In Columbus, Mississippi, Joana met an incarcerated air force student pilot, in jail for having violated numerous state and federal laws and FAA and Air Force Regulations. His most recent infraction of the rules: upon returning from his first night flight in a T-38 he'd broken formation and, perhaps excessively stimulated by the sight of the rising sun, had flown the hot little trainer under the platform—between the legs—of an offshore oil rig. *Under* it . . . a feat involving the visual timing of the surge of the waves while still on approach, several miles away. His pugnacious defense was that everybody said the stunt was physically impossible, ergo he couldn't possibly have done it, ergo those who said he did must have been hallucinating. But he was not shy about admitting to Joana that he'd done it all right; in fact, he'd been flying rings around everyone including the senior instructor pilots at the base for the past two months. Joana learned that his extraordinary abilities had become apparent shortly after he'd received his Tyger II computer on mail order through the base exchange.

When she tested him she found a swift, healthy, arrogant young man of native intelligence and little sophistication, a boy with a chip on his shoulder—a natural fighter pilot, in other words—who just happened to have probably the fastest physical reflexes ever recorded. Indeed, his measured reaction times exceeded previously estimated limits of the velocity of nerve impulses, and Joana concluded that in some complex tasks of the peg-in-hole variety he was literally not thinking with his brain, since his rattlesnake-quick decisions were put into action too fast for signals to travel from his hands to his head and back again. But her requests for further physiological tests were denied by the air force, whose aerospace medicine people had developed their own agenda for this phenomenal troublemaker, awaiting only his release from the hoosegow.

During her travels Joana personally collected dozens of such case studies and gleaned other telling anecdotes by interrogating her colleagues and by continually searching the literature. After a few months the raw outlines of her conclusions were clear. But she was determined to make one last attempt to contact the most important subjects of all. . . .

The suburban Boston street was quiet and empty in the early spring afternoon. Joana stepped out of the cab in front of the Lillard home and glanced around. Dark spruces sagged onto the lawn, and over her head new green leaves were massed in pendulous rococo garlands that weighed down the limbs of the giant elms.

The cab pulled away as she marched up the flagstone path under the shadow of the elms. The lawn was green, free of weeds, its edges neatly trimmed. The clapboard house appeared to have had a fresh coat of paint since her attempted visits of last year. Grief and guilt were still at work here, children pitching in to do chores that had gone unattended before.

She found the button of the doorbell, inset in a little plastic fixture with a glowing yellow light. When she pushed it, brassy chimes sounded. Beyond the aluminum scrollwork screen, through the panes of the front-door window, she saw shadows moving. She stood waiting on the porch, but no one came.

She pushed the bell again. She felt a presence beside her, and instantly a tug on her skirt. She gasped, then laughed breathily. "Where did you come from?"

The child, a scrawny girl perhaps eleven years of age, had appeared soundlessly beside her while she was peering through the screen door. "Didn't you hear me coming? I didn't try to be quiet."

"No, I didn't hear you." The little girl had lively intelligent eyes beneath her brown bangs, and knobby knees, scabbed and scarred beneath the hem of her plaid skirt. "Are you Theresa?"

"Yep. Wanta go in?" She opened the newly oiled screen door and held it with one hand while she pushed the front door open with her foot.

"My name is Joana Davies. I've been looking forward to meeting you," she said, following the child into the house.

The hallway was bare and clean. On the left the living room of the old house was filled with light, diffused through prim lace curtains, with furniture straight from the showroom in tasteful shades of gray and tan, betraying no signs of use. "We're usually in the playroom," said Theresa, taking her visitor's hand.

When the little girl's hand touched hers, Joana felt a shivery sensation, as when a mild static charge raises the fine hairs on the cheekbones—a pleasurable tingle. Theresa looked up at her and smiled.

The playroom definitely looked lived in, a brick-walled room filled with quantities of mismatched and well broken-in pine and maple furniture, a scarred toy chest in the corner, the flagstone fireplace mantle stacked with tattered cardboard board games and jigsaw puzzle boxes.

French doors opened onto a brick patio and a sunny backyard. In the yard Joana could see a pale girl wearing a purple bikini a size too large for her, lying face down on a beach towel. That would be Donna.

"Sit down here," said Theresa, pushing Joana toward a pine armchair with overstuffed vinyl cushions. Joana sat. Theresa said, "I'll get you some ice tea. Is that what you like?"

Joana realized that's exactly what she wanted, but before she could confirm Theresa's guess the little girl had disappeared in the direction of the kitchen.

In the shadows of the playroom an older boy lay on his back in the corner by the darkened television set, his legs drawn up, one crossed over the other. Joana studied the boy, who had not moved or made a sound. Despite his awkward position, he was quite still. He seemed asleep.

That impression was dispelled when he said, "I'm Anthony. Who are you?" The boy's newly deep voice, projected straight up from the floor, had an odd resonance.

She suppressed a smile; teen-aged insouciance could go to great lengths. "My name's Joana Davies—Joana."

"Are you a psychologist?"

"How did you know that, Anthony?"

"I didn't," he said, still talking to the ceiling. "That's why I asked. But all the social workers and insurance people are finished with us. The reporters and people trying to sell us stuff finally gave up. And Theresa wouldn't let a reporter in here anyway. So who's left?"

"But I wonder how Theresa knew I wasn't any of those things. She didn't ask me."

Anthony hitched himself to a sitting position and spun to face Joana; it was a coltish movement, full of adolescent grace. "Theresa knows lots of things, Joana."

His dark face was composed, boyishly handsome; under his thin T-shirt his chest was deep, and his bare arms were layered with muscle—the classical Mediterranean physique that in thirty years, if not sooner, could be expected to sag into a beefy middle age—yet Joana saw that there was a light in Anthony's eyes that suggested an unusual awareness of matters real, immediate, and physical, an awareness that might yet resist the decadent tendencies of the flesh.

"I know lots of things too," he said. "And I'll bet you know why, because that's why you're here."

"You'd make an excellent detective," said Joana.

"Actually I've thought about that." He grinned. "Could be fun to be Sherlock Lillard. Deduction's pretty easy for me. But I think it's gonna be easy for lots of people soon."

Joana studied his calm face a moment before asking, "Why do you think so?"

"You know that too."

She made a show of looking around the room. "I don't see any computers lying around. I might have expected to see some old ones, anyway."

"Nobody in this family has much use for them."

Joana took a short breath. "Stop teasing me, Anthony."

"You first." He smiled widely, his dark face framing white teeth.

She stared into the boy's liquid eyes. "I came because I want to see what happens to people who handled Tyger II computers."

"Right."

"Has anyone talked to you before about this?"

"Takes one to know one."

"I suppose it does," Joana said quietly.

Theresa came back into the room from the kitchen, her thin fingers wrapped around two tall glasses painted with flowers. She carried the brimming glasses without sloshing a drop of ice tea. "Here, it's got rose hips." She handed one glass to Joana and kept the other, settling cross-legged beside Joana's chair.

"What about me?" said Anthony.

"There's Cokes in the icebox," said Theresa. "Sugar freak."

"Thanks, squirt. You know she came to find out about us, don't you?"

"Sure," said Theresa, clutching her ankles and rocking back on her skinny bottom. "Touch her."

Anthony stood up and crossed the floor. Joana looked up into the dark, youthful face with its full lips curved in an archaic smile. He reached out a smooth hand. She lifted her own to touch his.

Her fingers were as sensitive as her nose, her tongue. It was if she'd caught a whiff of some dry, spicy fragrance. Cinnamon. His touch had the flavor of cinnamon.

"What are you good at?" Anthony asked, sitting close to his sister on the floor.

"I'm not sure," said Joana. There was no point in hiding what was plain to them all; she relaxed, and began to speak slowly, with as much precision as she could muster. "I feel more sensitive to everything around me, and everything that's going on inside me, all the time. I seem much more aware of people's moods, and often I feel as if I'm practically inside their thoughts. . . ."

"Me too," said Theresa, nodding.

"I've been trained for that, of course," Joana continued. "I'm a psychiatrist—and a psychologist, as you guessed, Anthony. So this business of trying to get inside people is not new for me. And perhaps I don't know anything more than I ever did, although now I never seem to forget anything I want to remember. But the principal change is that nonessential things don't get in my way anymore. I don't get distracted."

"People," said Anthony to Theresa, and Theresa nodded

as if that settled it. He turned back to Joana. "With me it's mainly numbers. Tell me your sun sign and your rising sign and what day of the week you were born on."

"Let's see: Gemini. Scorpio. Wednesday."

"So assuming you were born in the U.S., you're thirty-two, because the other possibilities are crazy. But that's easy. Pick a number, any number—want to know its square root, cube root, prime roots, natural logarithm? But that's easy too, since I've already memorized most of that stuff for all but the really big numbers. It's more fun solving half a dozen simultaneous differential equations—"

"You can stop bragging now," said Theresa.

Anthony laughed. "Easy for you to say. It's all I've got."

"Nothing else changed for you?" Joana asked.

"Not much. I'm quicker on my feet. Like you said, things don't seem to get in my way; if I want to do something, I do it without spending a lot of time thinking about it. And . . ." Anthony paused, then shook his head.

"Please." Joana watched his face intently and waited.

"Well"—he hesitated, then went on in a rush—"I'm happier. That's bad to say with Dad gone, and I don't mean I don't miss him, I just mean life doesn't seem so screwed up and full of stupid problems, and I don't have to go around proving that I'm grown up, because I'm not really, not yet"—he glanced at Theresa—"and, you know, I don't spend as much time worrying about whether girls like me—"

"Why worry about the impossible?" Theresa said sweetly.

"Yeah." Anthony looked at her darkly, but his eyes were laughing. He turned to Joana. "Do you think all that's part of the same thing?"

Joana said, "I don't know to what extent. That's one of the questions I'm trying to answer." She turned to Theresa. "What about you? What are you good at?"

Theresa shrugged her skinny shoulders and studied the rug.

"She's good at everything," said Anthony, not teasing.

"Everything?" Joana asked.

"Not at being beautiful," said Theresa fliply, as if it were a matter of supreme indifference, but a glance from her dark eyes showed Joana that she did want to be beautiful some-day, and she had no way of knowing whether that would ever come about.

"You will be," Joana said firmly. She was not teasing either.

A rumbling sound came from beyond the wall, the garage door rolling up on its tracks. Anthony leaped up and went to the back door, and Theresa followed him out of the room.

A moment later the children reappeared carrying bags of groceries, and although Theresa could not see past the top of the one she was carrying, she had no trouble steering a straight course for the kitchen.

Behind Theresa came a solidly built woman dressed in widow's black. She paused when she saw Joana, looked straight into her eyes with a piercing gaze shadowed by dark brows. Marian Lillard's face gleamed softly in the twilit room with a light that seemed to come from within her textured skin.

At the sight of her Joana was caught breathless. Every college neighborhood—in her home state of California, anyway—was plastered with posters of gurus of all faiths displaying goofball smirks meant to project "spirituality," but never had Joana seen a human face so truly and simply spiritual as Marian Lillard's.

The effect was helped by a touch of symbolism, of course: the baby Marian held in her arms. But symbols were no substitute for the plain presence of the woman. She inhabited the space in which she stood so fully that her humanity seemed to spill out of the world.

"I'm Joana Davies, Mrs. Lillard."

"Please sit down. I'll be back soon, I want to get her into bed while she's still sleeping," said Marian. The words were direct, the low voice was warm.

"Would you mind if I came with you?"

"If you like. But let's not talk."

Joana followed Marian up the stairs to the small bedroom at the end of the hall. Marian laid the infant down in a worn crib. The child was almost eight months old, big for her age, and in the soft light from the dormer window Joana saw that her head was enlarged, her face flattened, her eyes heavy-lidded, her lower lip thick and protruding. She was afflicted with trisomy 21.

Marian transferred a kiss from her fingers to the baby's brow, then beckoned to Joana.

Downstairs again, Marian sat opposite Joana on the old couch in the playroom. Anthony and Theresa had diplomatically disappeared; out in the yard Donna, the sun worshipper, had not moved a muscle in half an hour.

"My child was born retarded, as you saw," Marian said.

"How seriously is she affected?" Joana asked.

"Theresa tells me you are a doctor, so this will seem strange to you—but aside from her appearance she is not affected at all. At my age I was prepared for the worst. I pretended not to be disappointed when my fears came true. They were not my worst fears; the child was not born dead." Marian crossed herself. "But when she first saw the baby, Theresa kissed her and told me everything would be all right. She knew, somehow. The doctors have tested my baby every week since she was born. They cannot explain her recovery."

"How do you explain it?" Joana asked.

"I don't try to explain what I can't understand. At times God performs miracles. At other times He lets nature take its course. Although my husband died, my child was saved. He gives and He takes away." Marian looked calmly at Joana and allowed herself a tiny smile. "To you, Doctor, that sounds like superstitious nonsense."

"No, it sounds like perfectly good sense."

Marian nodded. "I know that whatever has happened to Theresa, and Anthony, and baby Helena, it has not happened to me." Her glance flickered toward the yard. "Or to Donna. That girl will grow up in pain and confusion, which has always been woman's fate. But there is something new in the world. And I believe it is a good thing, not a bad thing. And I thank God for it."

Joana visited the Lillards every day for a week, talking for hours, administering her tests. Everything she was told on that first afternoon proved to be the truth.

Baby Helena was indeed developing normally, if that was the word, and Joana thought it possible that her flexible skull would yet outgrow the stigma of misshapenness. It was too soon to know, but Joana suspected the child was in fact brighter than normal.

Her mother, Marian, submitted to Joana's tests with resigned cheerfulness; as she had promised, she was in every way average for a woman of her background and experience, and Joana concluded that her extraordinary serenity was not the product of any external, physical agent.

After one day of test taking, Donna, now approaching fifteen, grew resentful and refused to cooperate; she too was average, perhaps a little bit above average according to the standard IQ tests, but she was caught in a rising tide of insistent hormones and could hardly abide comparisons with her siblings—comparisons she must surely sense were invidious.

Anthony was indeed a wizard calculator, scoring perfectly on every mathematical test Joana had brought with her with an ease that was almost contemptuous. Through her friends at

Harvard Joana arranged to borrow graduate-level texts in statistics, quantum mechanics, geometrodynamics—Anthony answered every question perfectly, although in some cases it took her friends a significant amount of computer time to confirm his answers. Nothing that could be stated either statistically or logically was too much for him. Spatial puzzles, on the other hand, were no easier for him than for most bright males, and in every other respect he seemed a typically alert and healthy teenaged boy, a little brighter and healthier than most.

Theresa *could* do everything. . . . It was to Theresa's profile that Joana was to return again and again; it was that profile which prevented Joana from bringing her report to a neat conclusion. . . .

"Dr. Lee, you're aware of the considerable evidence supporting the thesis that human intelligence actually consists of half a dozen distinct intelligences, exhibited in varying degrees in each person"—Joana shifted in her chair—"the neurological evidence, the behavioral . . . the *idiot savant* who can play any composition on the piano after hearing it once, for example, or those old jokes about the best dancers not being terribly smart—'a good calf is worth more than a good head,' that was Agnes de Mille, wasn't it?"

Lee was leaning forward with his elbows resting on the desk top; he peered at her over clasped hands. "I'm afraid dance isn't my forte, Dr. Davies."

"At any rate, this seems to be what happens to people invaded by Epicell. It takes its cue from what it finds in place. It adopts the goals of those it invades as its own values, and attempts to maximize those values. It amplifies intellectual strengths, often so that one ability completely overshadows the others."

"An intellectual amplifier—how extraordinary," said Lee,

but his tone was calm. "And is Epicell always so benign? Are we wrong to think it a lethal neurological disease?"

"In a word, yes. In every case where Epicell is implicated in a death I believe other factors are actually to blame."

"The salesman? Mr. Lillard himself?"

"Unfortunately age is one factor that sometimes seems to contribute to complications. I've been unable to confirm that the diagnostic procedures performed on Harold Lillard led to his death, and perhaps I never will. But I believe his case is similar to Adrian Storey's. At a certain crucial phase in Epicell's development within the nervous system, any attempt to interfere with its progress—even an unknowing interference—is likely to result in a severe reaction. The younger the person, the less likely it is that the reaction will prove fatal."

"That's hopeful, at least," said Lee.

"If forced to it, however, I would admit that people over forty-five are at some risk from an Epicell infection." Joana wiggled uncomfortably.

"You don't have to admit anything on my account," he said pleasantly.

"There's more," said Joana.

"I was sure there would be," said Lee with a smile.

"Let me start with something merely suggestive. You know that the Public Health Service's recall and impoundment order is still officially in effect. In Washington they finally let me talk to a man who I was assured was the head of the cleanup operation. He showed me a chart and said that within the first three weeks eighty-five percent of Tyger IIs produced had been accounted for—handed in voluntarily or seized. I pointed out that that was a long time ago—what progress had they made lately? He claimed he's on the job, tracking down every last unit—not much of an answer—and when I asked him how many people were assigned to what sounds like it should be a very big project, he was vague.''

Lee shrugged.

Joana said, "I wonder if it's significant that this man's office—he was a very young man—was a cubicle on a floor with three hundred other civil servants. He shared a secretary with six people.''

"You think the powers that be no longer consider Epicell a real threat?'' Lee's tone was neutral.

"Amazing, if true. A year ago Epicell's reputation was slightly worse than that of the Black Death. Have you seen or read anything about it lately?''

"No. But I haven't had much time for reading. What's your guess, Dr. Davies?''

"It's spreading fast. Those who thought it a threat are now its . . . victims? It certainly doesn't need Tyger II; it's a microscopic organism that readily invades the human body, in all the usual ways.'' She paused. "Although many people seem to have natural immunity.''

Lee laid his hands flat on the desk, and his black eyebrows rose quizzically. "Then surely we should be very worried.''

Joana was solemn a long moment. Then she turned away, her lips quivering with the effort to suppress the smile. Without warning she burst out laughing.

Lee looked at her shrewdly, but again kept his silence until her chuckles faded away. He kept it longer still—the seconds ticked by, and when at last it had become clear that she had no intention of saying another word, he let the air slowly out of his nostrils. "Well then,'' he said, "the truth is that those of us who have experienced the transformation know there is no cause for alarm. Isn't that what you want me to say?''

"Yes,'' she said. "Or at least it will do for a start.''

"I'm curious about that little girl in Boston,'' he said.

"So am I. She's the youngest I talked to. There may be others like her."

"It's they, not we, who are the harbingers—"

"—fully integrated in—"

"—every faculty."

They nodded in unison.

Lee spread his fingers. "Your future studies—"

"—will prosper here," said Joana. "I'm pleased to accept your kind offer."

He rose as she did. "Tomorrow, then? I have a more comfortable space for you than before."

"I'm afraid I have to put it off until after the weekend. A pressing engagement, out of town."

"Please convey my deepest regards to him." Lee's smile was broad, his touch was strong and sensitive, as he ushered her out the door.

◆◆◆

The newlyweds lay together in the cold little room in the inn, listening to the notes of the piano on the portable tape player—it was, for sentimental reasons, a Brahms concerto. They savored the rippling cascades of notes, so distinct, so precise—so clearly defined, both mathematically and emotionally.

And the breaktaking pauses, separating the strokes of the fingers against the keys . . .

Like the strokes of his fingers on her skin, the strokes of her fingers on his, like the glistening stars caught in their eyelashes as their heads turned to each other.

Their self-consciousness began to dissolve.

Joana now understood that her powers of description would never do justice to her powers of perception—that she would be forever barred from putting her feelings into words. There was a great and ancient sadness in this, and beneath the ash heap, a spark of rebellion. Surely it was possible to know *and* feel, to know and express feeling in natural language.

But the world had moved on. They had evolved, were evolving even as they lay, experiencing the moment. Soon there would be a new language.

He said it aloud, putting their loss into words, just as she had been about to speak for herself. "When I say I love you, do you know what I mean?"

She considered his question as if no one had ever asked such a thing in all the history of the universe. Then she said, "I know what I would mean by it, if I were to say it." She amended her reply: "On some occasions."

He laughed at that, and kissed her.

The next morning they walked on the beach. The sand was yellow-brown, not golden, and the logs were only soggy chunks of driftwood. The rain came down hard, and there were no seals and no whales, not even any birds, except the gray gulls that flocked sullenly in the dump behind the town gas station.

"And you," she asked, "do you know what I mean when I say I love you?"

"Oh, yes. I am what you made me, you know," he whispered in her ear. "Oh yes, I know what you did to me. I remember all of it, perfectly. I know what I was before. I know what I am now."

She looked into his eyes, daring him. "And now you love only me?"

"You're a practical woman, Dr. Bridgeman. Besides, did you think they ever meant anything, those others?"

"Just practicing, eh?"

"For you."

"That's what I wanted to hear you say."

"I know you did."

She kicked at the wet sand; it clumped around the toe of her canvas shoe.

She believed him. Truly she'd had a hand in making him what he was today. Himself, by any test she knew how to make.

Better than himself.

She would have felt guilty about that, knowing she'd made him over in the image she'd always wanted to have of him. . . . She would have felt guilty if she'd really done it—if she'd done what he asked instead of only pretending. Trying to program him, to write him back into the new hardware that inhabited his brain—what arrogance! Only the old Toby in the depths of his despair could have conceived that any human being could consciously create, or re-create, another.

Epicell would have ignored her, or worse, defended itself. If she'd tried too well, Toby would have died as Adrian had died, and this time for nothing. So she had not tried at all.

Instead she prayed that what she'd seen in little Teddy's eyes as he rocked his playpen across the floor of Susana's house—the spark of strength and intelligence, of curiosity and joy—was truly the light of a new life, a secular salvation brought into being, as were all human achievements, all natural achievements, through blind fumbling and misdirected purpose.

Epicell was a drastic mistake. Programmed to learn ceaselessly, to find out what it needed to know to solve the problems set for it, the problem it had immediately sought out was the root problem, the truly interesting problem—the problem of human perfection. Epicell's blessed deficit was that it had no answer to that problem, proposed no god, counseled no nirvana, insisted on no economic or social program. It only wanted to learn.

She had prayed that Epicell would learn Toby Bridgeman from the inside out, learn his hopes and fears and guilts, his aspirations, his high-minded goals, his compulsions and hungers, the wellsprings of his strength and the ill-joined props of his weakness, the hard knots of paradox that must be cut through to allow the crown of his wholeness to blossom.

She'd typed madly on her keyboard and let him type madly on his, literally filling his head with information about himself that Epicell already knew. In his delirium he eagerly devoured the data placebo. In the end, when he fell into the coma, she was typing the same words over and over: "I love you. . . ."

Even as he emerged from the mists of his own prehistory, there was never a time when he did not know who he was. He was awkward at first, physically awkward, but his friend and lover guided him to the hidden memories that made the mysteries of movement and perception and speech easier to comprehend.

Had he wanted to know his own mind, to act on his convictions? Nothing stood in his way. Had he wanted to be a good man, acting for the good of his fellows? The limits of that stance were defined without pity or excuse, so that for the first time in his life he knew just where he stood.

Had he wanted to be a loving man? Love's pain no longer terrified him.

He found he could revoke the irrevocable, repair the damage he had done to his own body. He found he could do and say what seemed right to him; he could love others when they were hurt by him as easily as when they were not.

Held finely in the balance was the knowledge that each human will was as precious as his own.

Finally, he understood the paradox of human existence. He knew why he had transcended it. He rushed eagerly toward the consummation.

Then he experienced his own rebirth, so clearly and sweetly that he wept for those who would come after him, those who

would be born only once. As the new consciousness washed
over the contours of the old, it was as if a layer of film were
being cleansed from the marble, allowing the truth to emerge,
like the glimmering of a star at sumset.

To her, after it all, it seemed as if the world were meant to
go this way, that there had been no fatal error but instead a
stroke of fate. She delighted in making love to him, in
feeling him in and around her, all the warmth and firmness of
his flesh, and her own flesh responding to his. To feel the
cool air, to see the light through the windows of the inn, to
hear each note of the music that surrounded them eternally,
to understand and appreciate the structure and plan of the
world, the performance that was life . . .

They came to the rocks at the end of the beach. The waves
thudded sullenly into the sand, gray and dull. The summer
rain streamed cold from their faces. He pulled her close, and
they started back along the deserted beach.

Long before she knew that Toby was safe she knew that
Epicell had invaded her too, silently, competently, without
struggle, in some unnoticed bout with the sniffles, or perhaps
with no resistance whatever. It had done the same for Susana,
perhaps as a gift from little Teddy, and for thousands of
others. Surely it was a matter of time, nothing more, before it
came into every mind that did not resist it.

To her it had given the gift of complete self-knowledge,
the foundation of a more perfect knowledge of others. It had
given her more—the gift of the fitting mate, of whom she'd
always dreamed.

It had given her the child now growing in her womb,
Toby's child-to-be—at the moment only a few cells busily
dividing and organizing themselves, barely a full day old and
still pure process—but already a joy to know. This gift was
not something she had suggested to him; he had done it for

her, inside himself, correcting the mistakes of the unconscious past, before he knew who he was.

She turned to her husband and breathed ecstatic enzymes
into his nostrils. He smiled, receiving them, and silently
thanked her.

He invited her to watch with him as the sun crept beneath
the clouds and sent oblique columns of gold across a silver
sea. It was only the beginning of the Golden Age.

AFTERWORD

Some of the things in this story which seem quite reasonable are, as of this writing, untrue. For example, the coat protein of polio virus has not been characterized. The Lawrence Berkeley Laboratory, an institution which has historically led in the medical use of accelerators, does not have an electron storage ring, and synchrotron radiation has not been used to image the living brain.

On the other hand, the Office of Naval Research seems sanguine about the future of "molecular machines," and it has been seriously suggested that some kind of functioning biochip will be demonstrated within ten years.

A word of thanks: once again David Hartwell was challenger and champion of a difficult project. David Collins, MD, Bill Contento of Cray Research, Inc., and especially Marion Deeds did their best to keep me honest. I am grateful to them and to the many others who helped shape this fable.